THE SQUARE

ENTER AT YOUR OWN RISK

KAREN WOODS

First published in 2015

EMPIRE PUBLICATIONS
1 Newton Street, Manchester M1 1HW
© Karen Woods 2015

ISBN: 978-1-909360-35-8

Printed in Great Britain.

ACKNOWLEDGEMENTS

Thank you to all my readers and my family and friends for all their support. This is my twelfth novel and I'm still pinching myself. I took a chance and it paid off.

Thanks to my children Ashley, Blake, Declan, and Darcy for all their support. Also a big thanks to my mother Margaret and my father Alan. Thanks to James for all his support.

"If you do what you have always done,
you'll get what you have always got."

Follow me on Twitter @karenwoods69 - www.karenwoods.net

I'm working hard on my next novel now and readers won't can have a sneak peek of it on the final few pages of this book.

I'm a real person writing real stories. My last thanks as always goes to my son in heaven.

"Goodnight God Bless Dale."

Love

Karen

xxxxx

CHAPTER ONE

"You lay one more finger on me and I'm ringing the dibble. I'm telling you now, I mean it Darren, look at the state of my face, you bastard." Janice Goodman was reeling as she poked her crooked finger over at him. "Get out of my face you dick-head, just leave me alone. I've done fuck all wrong. How many times do I have to tell you? Are you thick or something?" Janice shielded herself as Darren, her boyfriend, booted her in the stomach, blood splurged from the side of her mouth as she struggled to keep her balance, this was a battlefield. These two were half killing each other; it was going off big time, cups being hurled through the air, glasses smashing.

"You're a slag, a dirty lying cunt. Go on, tell me his name, because I know you've been banging someone else behind my back, just give me a name." Darren stood near her cracking his knuckles ready to beat the living day lights out of her, urging her to reveal her lover's name. Janice pleaded with him and yanked her black leggings up to her waist, begging him to stop. She knew she had to start talking quickly before her life ended. And, he would have you know, he was ready to do her in, stop her breathing, put her in an early grave. Darren was off his head on drugs and booze, he wasn't on this planet. His eyes rolling rapidly, unsteady on his feet, jaw swinging...

Janice was, by her own admission, an easy leg-over. She'd always been like that. She didn't value herself;

she was an out and out slut, easy meat who'd drop her drawers to the highest bidder. Darren punched the wall behind him, counting in a chilling voice, slurring words. "One, two, three… you'd better start confessing bitch!" He snarled as he neared her, circling her, ready to pounce. He was a bad-tempered man and she'd seen him snap before. He was ruthless and held no pity for his victims, especially women. He had a reputation in the local boozer as a head the ball. Nobody messed with him unless they were looking for trouble. Darren shot a look over to her, a menacing psychotic look, his eyes danced with madness. Darren wasn't all there in the head, something was missing.

Janice held her hands out in front of her and sighed. She'd had enough and she was ready to give him what he wanted to hear. She let out a laboured breath and started to confess. "I slept with him once okay, a daft fucking mistake. It meant nothing to me. Look where I am now. I'm with you. Darren," she smiled softly hoping her words would comfort him. What the hell was she thinking? "I love you for crying out loud. Just let's go to bed and forget about this. It's stupid and not worth falling out over." She was lying through her teeth of course and he could see she was hiding something; her eyelids flickered rapidly as she neared him and she couldn't look him in the eye. Darren barged passed her and rolled his sleeves up. There was no way he was getting any blood on his crisp white shirt, it was way too expensive. His biceps were bulging, she was getting it now. He was going to kick ten tons of shit out of her. Who did she think she was taking the piss out of him? He was nobody's fool. There was no way she was mugging him off.

Darren ran at Janice and gripped her by the throat stopping her from breathing; his knuckles were white as he clenched her windpipe tighter restricting her breath. She was struggling but it was no good he had her in a death grip. Darren loved her pain, he loved that he controlled her. No woman would ever get the better of him, ever. They needed keeping in their place; speak when they were spoken to. Janice started turning blue and she wriggled about frantically, her pale white feet dangled above the floor. He was nose to nose with her, spit hanging from the corner of his mouth. "Don't you realise what you've done to us now", he screamed. "You've ruined it all. I can never trust someone like you. You're just a slapper, just like everyone said you were. Why the fuck did I let you get inside my head. I'm doing one from here. And," he spat in her face, "I'm going for good this time. I'm not listening to any more of your bullshit. You're just a lying bitch." He flung her across the room like a rag doll, smashing her into the table. Janice sprang up from the floor and held her hand around her neck. Deep red marks started to appear, she was gagging for breath as she ran back at him with fists of fury.

Her true colours were coming out now. It was do or die time. "Go on, you just walk away like all the others have. I don't need you in my life. I never have. Men like you are ten a penny. Go on, fuck off and leave me to get on with it," she turned her back on him and got ready to deliver the killer blow. This would shut him up. This would hurt him and bring him down a peg or two. "You're not a real man anyway, you never satisfied me in bed. Why the fuck do you think I had to go somewhere else for it," she flicked her honey blonde hair over her shoulder and

7

chuckled. "Did you really think that fucking wet slug of yours really turned me on?" she held her stomach and pretended to laugh. "I'd rather sort myself out than have you and your small cock bouncing about on top of me." His eyes closed slowly as the pain of her words soared through his mind. She was one cheeky cow and she knew how to hurt him. Curling his fists tightly into two small balls he ran at her again, she didn't stand a chance.

Lay upstairs, Alice Goodman rolled about in her bed restless .She was fifteen years old and sick of the life she was living. Day after day she lived in hope that something would change, it never did. This girl should have been in care with proper adult supervision. She was a car crash waiting to happen. Everybody knew about her but yet not one person phoned the social services to report the abuse, spineless the lot of them. They were always there calling her family skanks, but they never did a single thing about it. No child should have ever had to live like this. Alice was lucky to eat most days. If it was left to her mother she would have starved to death months ago. It was a crying shame. Nobody cared about her, she was alone and scared and left to face the world and her pathetic life. Alice had been fending for herself for as long as she could remember. Shoplifting for food and clothes was her only way of surviving .She hated that she was a criminal but what other choice did she have? She was good at it too, quick and snappy. This was her secret though and she told nobody. Alice kept a lot of secrets close to her heart; she was deep, very deep and she never let anyone get inside her head. If Janice had got wind of her talent for having things away she would have had her at the local Nisa shop nicking booze for her. No, she kept schtum. Night after night she listened to her mother arguing with her latest knock off. It was just something she was used to and, this wasn't the first time she'd heard Janice getting beaten either, it was a regular occurrence in her house, especially if she'd been on the lush. Janice was a piss-head and every night she downed a bottle of vodka, the cheapest kind. She would have drunk piss if it would have blanked her mind out, the tormented thoughts that kept her awake most nights. One pale thin leg dangling out from the bed as Alice held her ear to the door; she was debating her next move, biting hard on her fingernails. Surely it would be over soon. It never usually lasted this long. This argument had been going on for over an hour now. Sex usually came next, Janice groaning and screaming as some random guy shoved his cock deep inside her, abusing her for a second time. She could never really understand why her mother had sex with her attacker just after they'd chinned her; it was sick, so sick, disturbing.

It was time to get up, she couldn't stand it anymore. This argument was getting out of control, banging, screaming and shouting, walls shaking. The council had already sent them endless letters threatening to evict them if the noise continued but Janice couldn't have cared less if they were homeless or not. She'd toss the letters aside and wouldn't give them a second thought. "Fuck them," was always her answer to anything she couldn't cope with. "Fuck the lot of them!" Nothing ever got sorted out; it was swept under the carpet and was never mentioned again. Alice decided to save her mother from another punch; it was doing her head in now. She could hear the neighbours banging on the paper-thin walls shouting abuse to her mother to keep the noise down. Alice should have left her really, left her to get a good bleeding hiding. She probably deserved it anyway. Janice was always winding her men up, she wasn't happy unless she was getting a slap. She wasn't right in the head. Pulling her t-shirt down over her cold legs Alice headed towards the bedroom door, floorboards creaking noisily. There was no carpet on the floor in this room. It was cold and dark, depressing. Black mould gripped the corners of the room, climbing the ceiling, spreading every day. There was no pink wallpaper hanging from the walls either, no signs that a young teenage girl slept in this room. It was barren and stank of misery and depression. Janice always said she was going to jazz the bedroom up, buy a new bed and some curtains. But, that was when she was pissed out of her head and chatting shit. Janice always thought she could change the world when she'd necked a bottle of vodka, make things better and solve all her anxiety. But, it never happened, the room was still a shit-tip. Janice pledged she was going to get the house fully carpeted out of the housing grant she got from the social, but that day never came either, she blew the fucking lot on drugs and booze and only got one carpet for the front room. She couldn't be trusted with money. She was a hopeless lying piss-head.

It was cold tonight, bleeding perishing. You could see the goose pimples all over Alice's thin arms as she crept down the stairs with caution. Janice had spent the gas money again, this was nothing new though, she was always doing it. The woman was a complete bitch and she should never have had any children. As soon as her giro came each week she'd go out and blow the lot, every single last penny she spent, there was never anything left. She'd always have some excuse as to where the money had gone. Janice never thought about filling the cupboards with food for Alice, she was a selfish bitch who always put herself first. She didn't care about anyone or anything.

Alice sneaked into the hallway, tiptoeing slowly towards the living room door, shivering, her teeth chattering together. You could see her rib-cage as she pulled her t-shirt tighter around her nervously. This kid was undernourished and looked like she belonged in a concentration camp. The living room door opened slowly. Her slim fingers gripped the edge of the door as she peeped inside. Nobody saw she was there, she stood frozen. Janice was shouting with her hands on her hips, ready for round two. Thick red clotted blood dripped from her nose. Alice covered her eyes; it was all too much for her to take in, deep breaths trying to control her breathing. Darren was ready to knock ten tons of shit out of Janice again. You could see he was getting ready to strike the killer blow that would knock her out for good. Janice could never keep her big mouth shut; she didn't know when enough was enough. She pushed her men right until the end. She wasn't happy until she was leathered within an inch of her life. Alice swallowed hard and played with the edge of her t-shirt dangling just over her knees. It was time to come into the room; she needed to do something and fast. Alice opened the door fully and stood shaking, quivering.

"Mam, are you okay?"

Darren was gobsmacked and ragged his fingers through his hair. He shot his eyes over to her, pleading with her, looking for some kind of forgiveness. He hated that the kid had seen his true colours. "She's a fucking slut Alice. A dirty brass who can't keep her knickers on for two minutes. It's all her fault this. It is, believe me honest. You know I'm a nice man don't you Alice?" He looked over at her mother and growled. "Go on Janice; tell your daughter how much you love cock. Tell her this is your doing. Go on, tell the fucking truth for once in your life."

Alice was aware that at any second now her mother would hurl something through the air, she was watching her like a hawk. Alice dodged the broken glass on the floor, hopping about moving closer to her mother. The silver framed mirror was broken, sharp shards of glass scattered all over the place. This mirror was the prize possession in the house and Alice was always looking into it thinking it held magical powers to transform her life, to whisk her to a faraway land where everything was peaceful, where happy endings really existed. She wanted to be as far away from this shit-hole as she possibly could. Janice carried on winding Darren up with her cocky attitude. She straightened her hair and pulled her shoulders back and walked towards the dining table. Blood was still dripping from her injuries. Popping a cigarette out of the packet she slung one into the corner of her mouth as she flicked her blood-stained hair back over her shoulder.

"Ignore him love. It's just because he can't satisfy a woman like me. He thinks I should stay at home all bleeding day cooking and cleaning for him. I'm not like that. I'll never be the woman he wants me to be, it's just not me," she leaned forward and darted her eyes into him. "I'm a good-time girl. I like to party. You can like it or lump it."

Alice covered her ears with both her hands, she was sick to death of this kind of abusive talk. She just wanted a normal life, just some peace and quiet, just to be normal. Her life was anything but normal though and everyday she had a different drama to deal with. Alice was at breaking point. Drug dealers threatening to boom the front door in for the money Janice owed them, bailiffs posting letters through the door and that was just the half of it. The family was up shit-street. Darren marched about the room and grabbed his coat from the back of the chair, he bent down towards Alice. He liked this kid and he would have taken her on as his own and loved her with all his heart if the relationship would have worked out. But, not now, no way, he had to leave. This relationship was over. Alice cringed as he kissed the top of her head, she hated him touching her and she pulled away from him straightaway, he made her skin crawl. She hated any man touching her; they were all perverts in her eyes.

Darren dipped his eyes low and tried to salvage any respect she had left for him. "Alice, you take care love and promise me now that you won't end up like that spineless twat over there. The sooner you get out of this place the better because she'll only drag you down with her. Trust me, I know. You need to get as far from here as possible, she's evil, pure evil."

Janice banged her flat palm on the table and growled. Who the fuck did he think he was talking to? Alice was her kid not his. "Oh, fuck off if you're going. We don't need any long goodbyes, just do one. Go on, jog on. I'm done with you." She blew large grey smoke hoops out of her mouth and nodded her head slowly. She just couldn't leave it there; she had to have the last word. Even from being a young girl she never knew when to keep her big gob shut. It always got her in trouble, big trouble. Darren watched her as she sat back in her chair; she had something up her sleeve. Her expression said it all. "And, if you think I'm keeping this baby, then you can think again. It's going straight into the spit bucket as soon as I can get in to see the doctor. Do you think I want some prick's kid inside me who treats me like this? Nar, I'm done with you?"

Darren swallowed hard, his nostrils flared and his ears pinned back as he walked back to where she was sat. She was dicing with death and she knew it. Janice's head slammed against the side of the wall as the blow connected with her cheek, blood splurged from her mouth and he was ready to finish her off, you could see it in his eyes. He'd lost the plot. Alice ran at him dragging at his arm in desperation. "Please, just go Darren, she's pissed, she doesn't know what she's saying," she sobbed, tears flooding from her eyes. "Please just leave her alone, do it for me. She's drunk, she's probably lying, just ignore her. You know what she's like when she's twisted."

Janice lifted her head slowly and wiped her mouth with a swift movement. She stared at the bright red blood on her hand and licked the deep gash on her lip slowly. This woman had a death wish; she was still winding him up. Why didn't she just let sleeping dogs lie? Janice stood up and wobbled towards him, she poked her finger into the side of his head. Her stale breath sprayed into his face. "Yeah, I thought that would shut you up now you daft bastard. Get it into your thick head that your baby is going down the shitter."

Alice stood in front of her mother quivering. It was such a crying shame for her, she was helpless, a victim of circumstances. Alice was the complete opposite to her mother she had dark brown hair and hazel brown eyes that looked like big brown conkers, angelic looking she was, or so her nana Pat told her. Pat was Janice's mother and even she'd washed her hands off her own daughter. The devil in disguise she called her and looking at her now she was right, she was a nightmare, pure evil. Darren spat in Janice's eye before marching towards the doorway, thick green mucus dropping onto her cheekbone. He turned his head slowly and spoke in a chilling voice. "I wouldn't want a kid with you anyway. You're off your rocker, fucking twisted in the head you are. It's a wonder Alice is still here. Mark my words slut, she won't stay around here much longer either. As soon as she'd old enough she'll be gone too. And then what, ay?" He held his head back and chuckled sarcastically. "You'll just be left with the pathetic sad old woman that you really are, a sad old bitter bastard with a baggy fanny that everyone's had a go at. You're just a worthless tramp who drops her knickers for anyone who's flashing a bit of cash about. I'm done with you" Darren calmed his voice down and dipped his head low. "Alice, if you ever need anything, you come and find me. I'll help you. I'll make sure you're alright." Alice cowered away from him and raised her arm over her head, he scared her, you could see it in her eyes.

Janice clenched her teeth tightly together, she knew he was right but there was no way she was admitting it to him. She rammed her two fingers in the air behind him. "Whatever, just fuck off loser. And, don't fall over the welcome mat on the way out either". Darren turned and stormed out of the room. The front door slammed behind him and the house shook. Alice stood frozen, had he gone, was he hid away until she'd gone back to bed ready to attack her mother again? Her eyes were all over the place and her heart was racing. This wouldn't be the first time this happened either. No, she was staying put until her mother was safe. Janice stubbed her cigarette out in the ashtray. Silence. Her eyes met her daughter's and she was growling at her. "What are you fucking staring at? Go on, I suppose that was my bleeding fault? The guy's a wanker, don't let him fool you with his soft talk. I had a gut feeling about him from the start. I should have known he was a wrong'un," she held her arms up in front of her. "Look at what he's done to me, the bastard."

Alice placed her hands on her hips and faced her mother. "When are you going to learn, ay? That's the fourth man you've had in here this year. Why don't you just stay single and look after me, you know, like other mothers do?"

Janice chuckled as she dabbed an old tea-towel on her bleeding lip. "Oh, so I'm a shit mother now then, am I? I'll tell you what, Mrs fucking up your own arse, go and find a new mother who will look after you properly. You're an ungrateful bitch. I don't even know why I had you. You should have gone into the spit bucket too then my life would have been stress free. You ruined my life." Janice was out to hurt her daughter and she was striking some low blows. "I could have had so much more if I didn't have you. You're not even worth the child benefit I get for you." Janice was evil with her mouth; she didn't give a flying fuck who she hurt. It was her way or the highway. She had no shame.

Janice Goodman was thirty five years old and you could see in her day that she'd been a real stunner, a beauty. She'd had it all at her feet and she could have had a good life, but she was bad news and nobody ever stayed around her for long, she was fucked up in the head, a couple of butties short of a picnic.

Alice bent down and started to pick the sharp jagged shards of glass up. There was no way Janice would have cleaned this mess up. Holding a jagged shard in her hand she looked at her mother who was sat at the other side of the room. She wanted to dig it deep into her heart, plunge it deep down inside her so she never breathed again. Looking down at her hands, blood trickled down her slim fingers as she gripped the blade of glass tighter. Alice watched carefully as the blood streamed down her fingers, she was in some kind of a weird trance. Standing to her feet she held the weapon in her grip, she'd had enough. Alice ran over to her mother ready to end her life, she'd couldn't take it a second more, she'd flipped. Janice caught her hand just in time before she plunged it deep into her heart. She was white with fear as she wrestled with her to get the sharp object from her hand. Fighting with men was second nature to Janice, but this was her own flesh and blood, her first born baby, she didn't want to hurt her. Alice was flung to the ground and Janice stood over her gasping for breath. "What the fucking hell are you doing, get back to bed now before I fucking shove that glass down your throat. Were you going to stick that in me? Was you, go on, tell me you crazy fucker?"

Alice was in a panic, she didn't know what had come over her, she'd lost the plot and for a split second she had no control over her actions. A red mist had covered her eyes and she wasn't aware of her surroundings. Janice slapped her around the head and she brought her back down to earth with a bang. Janice was marching about the front room in a panic. "You simple bitch, how dare you ever think you can do something like this to me. You need sectioning you daft cow. Go on; fuck off out of my sight before I have you put in a straight jacket, you mental bitch." Alice ran from the living room sobbing, she was in shock. The anger had just taken over her and she was shaking from head to toe. She'd hadn't had this feeling before but now she'd felt it, she was scared of what she was going to do next. Was she losing the plot? Something was happening to her. Running into her bedroom she flung herself onto the bed and dragged the covers over her head. She was just as dangerous as her mother now, she was a nutter.

Janice reached for the bottle of vodka. Her face was badly bruised and she was still bleeding. Slurping on the alcohol she held her head back and chuckled to herself. "Men, who fucking needs them? I don't need anyone. I'll do what I have to do on my own" Folding herself in two, she curled up into a tiny ball. She held the bottle over the arm of the sofa and raised it into the air. "I'll show them. I'll show them all," she mumbled as she stared at the ceiling.

CHAPTER TWO

Tavistock Square was quiet today, but it was only early in the day. Nothing really happened here until night-time - that was when everybody would be out wheeling and dealing, eager to make some money. The usual crowd were still in bed recovering from the night before. They were probably drunk or stoned. As soon as darkness fell this place would be buzzing with people. You name it; you could get it here: sex, drugs, knocked-off clobber the lot, it was like Aladdin's cave. It was all here for the taking. Six shops were situated on the square and each of them had been turned over in the years gone by, raided, ransacked and shopkeepers beaten within an inch of their lives. All the traders knew how quick the takings could be had away and they always made sure they had the latest security equipment set up to keep them from being robbed again. They were never safe though, cunning eyes from all over the square were always watching them, waiting for them to let their guard down.

Terry Marland was the main head in the square; he was eighteen years old and built like a brick shit-house. He was ruthless and feared by all who knew him. He was up and coming in the area and even at this early age he was rattling the cages of the main dealers in the area. Terry was into everything and anything that could earn him a few quid. Most of his youth had been spent in and out of jail and he knew how smart he had to be to make it big on the outside. He had dreams, big dreams. Terry had fended for himself for as long as he could remember; his parents had disowned him years ago. He was a handful and the police were always knocking on his door looking for him, he was well known to them, a local tearaway. Eighteen months he'd been banged up for, in all that time there had been no visits from his family, no money sent, fuck all, he had to soldier on alone. The time he'd spent in the slammer was hard and at one point he looked like he wasn't going to make it. Yet there was sadness in his eyes. All he ever wanted was to be part of something, for somebody to love him.

Terry's dad wasn't having none of his shit though, not now, not ever. He was an ex-military man and he demanded respect from his children, to abide by his rules. Terry was banished from his family home, never to return. He just rode it out and got on with his life without his parents. Since getting his own house he'd kitted it out with all the latest gadgets; flat screen TV, top music system and a large king-sized bed. Hats off to him, he'd made the place look top. He loved that he'd done it all on his own, he loved that he owed nobody. Terry had his head screwed on too; he didn't have stolen gear in his home. He had receipts for everything he owned. There was no way he was getting busted and losing everything. Lying in his bed he looped his hands over his head and snarled at the body lying next to him. She was just a back warmer, a sack emptier, his booty call. "Come on, you need to do one, I've got to go out," he said as he pushed his hand into the small of the female's back.

Tina wasn't Terry's girlfriend, she was just someone who was there when he was feeling horny. She raised her head from under the sheets and rubbed her knuckles into the corner of her eyes. "Fucking hell Terry, what time is it, just let me sleep for a bit longer will you, I'm knackered?" Terry ragged the blankets from her and pushed her out of the bed with his legs, he was getting annoyed. He'd had his way with her the night before and no longer had any use for her, she was a slut in his eyes, a dirty slapper, begging for cock from anyone who would give it her. Terry pushed her again and this time he used more force. "Nar, come on yo-yo knickers, you need to do one. I've got things to do and places to go."

Tina knew he was lying; he was always like this with her, he had no respect. She jumped back on the bed next to him and tried to snuggle up to him, sinking her head deep into his neck. You could see Terry was ready for snapping; this girl was a coke whore and she only wanted free drugs off him. He'd met her type a hundred times before; he'd been on a bender with her for days and knew she only had one thing on her mind. Of course he had a past with her but that was over years ago. She wasn't wife material. "Will you get ready and fuck off home, Tina. I swear I have to go out, get your kit on and do one."

This time his voice was louder and she knew it was time to leave. Flicking her raven black hair over her shoulder she sneered at him. "If I'm just a bang then say it how it is. I'm sick of the way you treat me anyway. You've got a problem with women you have." Terry was never subtle, he was straight talking, he said it how it was and this girl was bugging the life out of him. He bolted up out of bed and searched for his boxer shorts on the floor. His body was ripped up and there wasn't one ounce of fat on him, pure muscle he was. Prison had made him like this, he'd trained every day there during his sentence and he never missed a session, he became a bit obsessed really. Most inmates in the jail trained every day. It helped pass some time. And, if you were lucky you could get a grip of some steroids to help boost your muscle growth. That's if you had the money to pay for them of course. Everything in jail had a price and steroids were one of them. The steroids were bang on at the beginning and Terry loved the way they made him feel inside; strong, invincible like iron - fearless. He thought he was the dog's bollocks every time he jabbed the steroids into his arm. And he was at first I suppose, but then the side effects kicked in. Paranoia, mood swings, no sex drive, a cock like a shrivelled acorn and all the other shit that came along with injecting drugs into his body every day. He was off the juice now and he was doing his best to never touch it again. He worked out the proper way, he didn't cut corners anymore. Terry was a handsome man, there was no denying that fact and he knew it too, full of himself he was. He loved that he could pull almost any girl he wanted. His hair was light brown but it held a hint of red in each strand of hair. Ginger, some people would say but he always denied it saying his hair was brown. This guy was a ginger, who was he trying to kid! During the time he'd spent in jail his nickname was the "Ginger Ferret," he didn't mind his nickname, all the lads had them and he just took it on the chin but the description was apt - he was quick, cunning and fast on his feet, just like a ferret.

Tina pulled her dress over her skinny torso; she was all skin and bone, anorexic looking. "Well, are you going to ring me tonight or what?" she moaned.

Terry sniggered and blew a laboured breath. He

had no intention of phoning her and as he stood tall he popped a cigarette into the corner of his mouth. "I've got a lot on at the moment. You had a good time last night so stop fucking moaning, just chill," he held his hands out in front of him. "What is it with you girls anyway? Fuck me, I shoved my cock up you for a couple of nights and you think I'm on lock-down. You can do one if you think I'm wifeing you off. You're just a bang, nothing else."

Tina had a face like a smacked arse; she slipped her shoes on and tied her hair back. "Get over yourself Terry Marland. You think you're God's gift. I don't want to marry you or anything like that. I just thought we could see each other again that's all, so don't flatter yourself. You think you're fucking Brad Pitt."

Terry blew cigarette smoke into her face and smiled, he was winding her up. "Who are you trying to kid? Girls like you are just after a free ride, you're all gold-digging bitches. Out for what you can get."

He stood flexing his muscles admiring them, stroking them. Tina snarled at him, she wanted to claw his eyes out. Who the hell did he think he was, some kind of Greek god? "I'm going Terry, it's obvious I was just a shag to you and nothing else. I'll see you around," she reached for the door and turned to face him. "Me and you could have had something special, but you've fucked it now. I'm gone. I'm not begging, no way."

Terry watched her leave and chuckled to himself. He didn't bother with girlfriends anymore. Girls were too much hard work, way too much pressure, he was riding it solo. Night after night he'd watched his pad mate sobbing his heart out over some girl he'd been seeing before he was banged up in nick. She was messing with his head, playing mind games with him and she broke his pal in two. He crumbled and never got over it. Terry vowed to himself that he would never let some bird get into his head like that, not now not ever. In those months spent behind bars he'd had a few girls visiting him, but he was never into them, it was just a quick grope on the visit and that was it. Tina had sold him out when he needed her most and he couldn't forgive her. A Dear John she'd sent him, just saying she couldn't wait any longer. He just used girls now to sort out parcels for him, drops of drugs and steroids, spice and anything that would earn him a few quid inside the prison walls. To be honest, love scared Terry, he'd felt it once before and didn't want to feel it again. There was too much pain when love was involved, tears and heartbreak, he never wanted to fall in love again. A car honked its horn outside his house. Terry peeled the curtain back from his window and waved his hand over his head. "Two minutes pal, I'm just getting ready," he shouted with his hands cupped around his mouth. Checking his watch he realised he was late. Running to the bathroom he started to get his clobber on.

Skid sat in the car with the tunes pumping, his head nodded to the beat of the music. He loved dance music and he seemed in a deep trance when the base kicked in. His fingers tapped the dashboard rapidly. Skid was twenty years old and he had chestnut brown hair and a similar build to Terry, he was not as good-looking though, he was a bit of a minger. The car door opened and Terry jumped inside. "Fuck me, you're like a woman getting ready you are. What the fuck have you been doing, you pussy?"

Terry sat in the passenger side and punched Skid in the arm playfully. "Women isn't it. Fuck me, once they get into my bed there's no shifting them. Once they get a taste of my big python they want to stay around as long as they can, the dirty bitches." The lads chuckled as they high-fived each other. They were both players and loved treating women like shit. Skid, whose real name was Aaron, started the engine and eased off onto the main road. The lads had met in jail the year before. Forest Bank was a Category B prison in Manchester and lots of the local scallies went there to serve their sentences. An easy jail they called it, like Pontin's holiday camp. Skid and Terry just clicked from the moment they first met. They were both from the same area and they became pad mates from day one. "Hinge and Bracket" the screws nicknamed them. They knew everything about each other, they were brothers in arms. Skid had no real family, well except for his cousin Janice. She was a piss-head and he often went there to smoke a spliff with her to chill. She was on his wave length and knew the score with life today. She understood him, she got him.

Terry dug deep in his pocket and checked his mobile phone as it started to ring, he giggled to Skid and showed him the screen. "Told you didn't I? These bitches can't get enough of this stud muffin." Terry ignored the call and rammed the phone back into his tracksuit bottoms, chuffed that he was on top of his game.

Skid turned the music down and waited in the traffic. "I've got us some graft lad. A quick earner. A kid I know from Cheetham Hill wants us to give him a lift with some dick-head he's been having a bit of trouble with, nothing too serious. Just a few slaps to the guy if you know what I mean." Skid gave him a cheeky wink and smirked over at him. Terry rubbed his hands together, he loved this kind of job, he loved that men feared him. Terry liked to see his victims crumble in his presence and beg for mercy. All of his life he wanted people to notice him and gain their respect and it looked like his dream was coming true, people did fear him, he was ruthless. Skid moved along in the traffic and headed to meet the man who wanted some help. It was going to cost him though, there were no freebies; not if they were getting their hands dirty anyway.

Terry spat in the man's face as Skid held the victim up against the brick wall by the scruff of his neck. They were behind the shops in the square, well away from prying eyes. He squeezed his cheeks together so his lips touched at each side. "Don't ever think you can fuck with Johnny, do you get me mate?" The man was shitting his pants and he was white with fear as Terry jerked his head back and head-butted him with force. The man dropped to the ground like a sack of spuds – he was dazed, spit hanging from the corner of his mouth. Terry stood back and inhaled; his chest was fully expanded as he stood tall, cracking his knuckles. He was willing the man to get back on his feet so he could open a can of whoop arse on him. He wanted to hurt him bad, mark him for life, make him remember his name.

The fat Asian man started to come around, he opened his eyes slowly and realised that his attackers were still standing by him waiting to finish him off, he pleaded with them, desperately begging. "I won't bother Johnny again. I promise you, it was all a misunderstanding, my mistake." Skid nodded his head at Terry, it was job done. There would be no more trouble from this guy, he was an arse-hole. Terry stood tall and walked over to where his victim lay. There was no way he was leaving him with just a few scratches; he had a reputation to keep. No, he was going to waste him, make sure he never came back at him. Blood surged from the man's mouth as Terry booted him from the side. He belted him at least ten times; ten knock-out blows, each causing injury to his victim's head. Now the job was done, now he felt like he'd earned his money. This man wouldn't trouble him again. That was the thing with men like him, they were all fine shouting the odds but when it was time to back their mouths up they all kept schtum, not a word muttered, shit-bags the lot of them.

Skid pulled Terry away by his arm as the man howled out in pain. "Come on, we've done what we said we would, let's go and get some money now from Johnny. Five hundred quid he owes us. The prick better have it waiting for us too. We're not a fucking charity case." Terry licked the blood dripping from his knuckles and turned his head back to look at the man crawling away from the alley-way. They'd have no more trouble from him, not now, not ever. They'd put the fear of God in him.

Johnny Vickers shook Terry's hand as he walked into the room. He could tell his orders had been fulfilled by the dried blood on Terry's knuckles Skid was the talker with this man, he'd organised the graft. Terry didn't know him that well, it was Skid's acquaintance. Skid bounced about the room, proud as punch he was. "We fucking leathered him mate, on the floor he was begging for us to stop. You won't get any more shit from him Johnny and if any of your mates need anything sorting out, we're your men for it. Me and Terry here are like fucking ninjas. We're straight in and out, no fucking about." Johnny smiled at them; he'd known Skid for a couple of years and often put work his way. Looking at Terry he looked uneasy, he didn't know this kid or anything about him. He dug his hand inside his pocket and pulled out a wad of cash. He passed it over to Skid with his eyes still on his partner in crime. "There's three ton there lads. I'll have to go to the bank later for the rest of it."

Terry growled at him and walked over to where he stood. Did this cock think they were born yesterday or what? It was pay up time or get kicked to fuck time. The man was treading on thin ice. "Listen mate, you know how much it is so don't fuck us about. Get to the fucking bank and pay us what you owe us. Fuck me, you'll be asking to pay us by direct debit next." Terry smirked and shot a look at Skid who was on edge. Johnny chuckled but his fear was there for all to see, he was lost for words. Terry held a look in his eyes that scared him, unnerved him. If Skid had been there on his own he would have stalled him and paid him on another day but looking at Terry he wasn't taking any chances. He was going straight to the bank. Johnny grabbed his jacket from the side of the chair. He gripped his car keys and made his way to the door. "Yeah, no worries. Just follow me in the car then lads. I'll sort it out for you." Terry gave Skid a cheeky wink, nobody was taking the piss out of them anymore, Nobody.

CHAPTER THREE

Alice watched her mother waking up at the side of her. She was licking her dry cracked lips slowly before she opened her eyes, she looked in pain as she moved about. "Pass me a drink Alice. My mouth is like bleeding sandpaper." Alice reached for the glass of water nearby and passed it her. She watched her swig it and sat back down in her chair watching her from the corner of her eye. The empty bottles of vodka scattered around the front room told her this was going to be a long day. There was no money, no food or no alcohol left in the house, they were potless and up shit-street. Janice dug her grubby fingers in the ashtray and found an old cigarette butt; she straightened it out and popped it into her mouth, gasping for a few blasts of nicotine. Janice choked on the cigarette and banged her clenched fist onto her ribcage hoping to calm down her coughing. "You'll have to go to your nanas and see if she will give you a borrow until my giro comes next week. I'm skint and we don't have any other options."

Alice folded her arms tightly in front of her and shook her head. This was a regular occurrence and she hated begging money from her nana. She sighed and shook her head. "No mam, I'm not doing it. You said you would pay her back the last time I borrowed some money from her and you never did. I'm not doing it again. We'll have to do without."

Janice blew the smoke from her mouth and licked

her lips slowly. "You'll do what I bleeding well tell you to do lady. I don't know where this cocky attitude has come from but you can stop it right now before I knock it out of you, cheeky twat you are." Alice rolled her eyes and looked up towards the ceiling. She couldn't be arsed with all the drama. Janice would just peck her head all day until she got what she wanted anyway. Alice stood up and she was in a strop. "Mam, I swear if I go and see my nana for the money then you'd better pay her back this time. She knows it's for you anyway. She's not thick you know."

Janice threw the cushion from the sofa over at her daughter and sat up in her seat. She dipped her head low and cupped her hands in front of her. "I want fuck all from my mother, so don't you be telling her about our troubles. She'll love that we're on our arses. I can just see her face now saying, 'I told you so'. No Alice, just tell her it's for you. Say you're going to a party or something."

Alice let out a laboured breath. She was talking back now with a cocky attitude. "If you didn't blow all your money on the vodka then we wouldn't need any hand outs from her would we? Isn't it about time you stood on your own two feet and got a job or something? You know like normal people do."

Janice gripped the corner of the sofa and closed her eyes, her chest was rising with speed and she was ready to blow. "Listen, smart arse, what have I told you about giving me lip. I don't work because I have medical problems. Not that you care anyway. I could be six foot under for all you care. I'm better off dead I am, nobody would miss me." Here it was, the usual everybody hates me campaign her mother used when she was feeling sorry for herself. Day after day Alice had to listen to this story, she was sick to death of hearing it. It was complete bullshit and all she ever heard when times were hard. Janice was in a bad way, her eyes and lips were swollen. There was a big gash on her lower lip that looked infected, green gunge was forming inside it. Her arms were covered in purple bruises too, she was lucky to be alive.

Alice sat down and pulled her legs underneath her and yanked her t-shirt over them to keep warm. "What happened with Darren last night anyway, is he coming back or what?" She sat waiting for an answer, twitching nervously.

Janice sprawled out on the sofa and touched the side of her cheek slowly, feeling the lumps and the bumps on her cheeks. "No, he won't be coming back here again. I've told him straight, I'm done. What, do you really think I'd have that cunt back in here after the way he treated me?" Alice stood and headed towards the door shaking her head. To the world, Darren seemed like a nice lad and he'd always bunged Alice a few quid whenever he was there. Silence money it was, to keep his dirty little secret, to never breathe a word about what had happened between them. Now that he was gone there was no money coming into the household. They were up shit creek without a paddle.

Alice looked at her collection of clothes scattered on her bedroom floor. This was her life and all she owned, no jewellery, no make-up, just a few items of skanky clothing that she'd had for years. She looked out of the window and rested her head in her hands on the windowsill. The estate was quiet today and nobody was about. In the distance she could see the notorious, Tavistock Square in the distance. Every night she'd watch the goings on there and was mesmerised by it all. Everything sounded so much better there; laughter, happiness, being part of something, being involved. Janice had always warned her from ever going onto the estate though, she wasn't allowed on the square, ever. Her mother said it was too dangerous for her there and always warned Alice if she was ever caught there her life would not be worth living. It was the forbidden land. A different world to what she knew. Janice kept her daughter under lock and key, she very rarely let her out of her sight. She just sat at home most nights, alone and bored watching her mother get pissed out of her head.

Alice got ready and headed back downstairs. The house stank of stale tobacco and everywhere she looked was dirty and needed cleaning. The pots in the sink were piled high and unless she cleaned them they would stay there forever. Janice was not house-proud - she was a lazy cow, bone idle. Alice couldn't invite any of her friends to her home, no way; she would never live it down. The place was a pigsty - in fact pigs lived in healthier conditions. "Mam, I'm going over to my nanas. I'll be back later; you know I'll have to stay there for a bit. I can't just go in there and get some money and leave can I?" Janice rolled on her side, she was shaking and every now and then she retched into her cupped hands. She was withdrawing from the vodka and drugs that she had consumed the night before. She desperately needed a fix. Janice only ever used drugs when her mood was low. A social user she called herself but over the last few months she was using them every day. Darren had seen to that, he was always giving her a quick bump to liven her up. Cocaine was her master and what started out as just a few lines for a livener was now an addiction. It was a filthy habit that ruled her life. Darren had always provided her with the drugs, he was a user too but now he was gone she was fucked - no money, no drugs, no more handouts. Janice put on her sympathy voice.

"Just hurry up, be as quick as you can. See if she's got any nice food in the fridge too, she always has loads of grub, she won't miss it. Just nick some cheese and bacon, anything you can get in your pocket."

Alice grabbed her coat and walked to her mother's side. She was going to kiss her on the cheek but stopped dead in her tracks. Janice didn't deserve any love, she was disgusting, a walking disgrace. Alice turned and walked away. Just before she left the room she paused. "So, were you lying when you said that you were pregnant or what?"

Janice chuckled loudly and held the bottom of her stomach. "I might be a lot of things Alice, but, I'm nobody's fool. Am I fuck pregnant! I just said that to Darren to hurt him. As if I would have another kid, get a grip will you. I can just about stand the sight of you, never mind another baby." Alice was relieved; she sighed and left the room.

The weather was bad outside and Alice zipped her coat up tightly. The wind was howling and leaves were floating up in the air. Her eyes focused on the journey in front of her. It would knock at least ten minutes from her journey if she cut through the square. She dug her hands into her pocket and headed towards it. Kids sat in doorways, shouting over to each other, music was being played from a parked car. There were strong smells of cannabis.

Alice stepped onto the square with caution. This was

forbidden land and she was scared of getting spotted. Her hood was pulled up and her eyes were scanning the area. She was nervous and picked up speed, head dipped low. A hand came from nowhere and gripped her from the side. Her legs buckled as a youth got into her face. A lad it was, with a scar on his left cheek. "Are you looking to buy some bud or what? I can get you whatever you want, come on, what do you need?" Alice swallowed hard and shook her head, she couldn't speak. Her arse had fallen out. This guy was scaring her he was touching her all the time he was speaking. The lad pulled her nearer and his hot stale breath was in her face. He asked her again and this time he wanted answers. "Oi, pretty lady. I said do you want any substances?"

Alice knew she was on borrowed time and she could hear voices nearing her from behind, she was being swarmed. "No thanks. I don't touch drugs." The male pulled her hood down and before she knew it she was in the middle of a gang of lads. Her heart was pounding inside her rib cage and she was white with fear. Why the hell had she come here in the first place, she knew the risks. "Have you got a boyfriend or what? I've not seen you around here before; do you fancy a quick bang or even sucking me off?"

The other men laughed, high-fiving each other as they poked her in the waist. Alice was bright red, her palms were hot and sweaty and she knew if she didn't speak soon she was in big trouble. Plucking up the courage she struggled to break free. She was pushing them out of the way. "Will you just let me go? I don't want any fucking drugs. I'm just on my way to my nana's, just move will you." They were touching her now, prodding at her, touching her hair, groping her breasts. Tears were forming in the corner of her eyes and she was ready for breaking down crying. She didn't know what else to do. Her rosy red lips trembled with fear and she had every right to be scared, this was a dangerous situation and one that could have been avoided. Why the hell had she come this way in the first place. She knew the stories about what happens here, she'd read the newspapers.

Alice was aware of how the square worked; everybody knew not to go there unless they wanted trouble. She'd dropped a bollock for sure. Alice was petrified and looked around the area hoping somebody would help her. Ready to sink to her knees she heard a loud husky voice shouting from behind her - footsteps pounded the pavement getting closer. The boys parted from her side and now she stood looking straight into the eyes of an older lad, quivering, shaking. "Leave her alone dickheads, just let her go. Stop being pricks, can't you see she's shitting it?" The youths left her side whispering to one another. None of them had the balls to confront the older man. This guy must have been top dog here because none of them questioned him, there was not a peep from any of them. They just obeyed his orders as if he was their master. Alice looked straight into her hero's eyes and her heart melted, her jaw dropped low. He was drop dead gorgeous. Nobody had ever stuck up for her like this, ever. She was just about to thank him when he left her side in a hurry, without a word; he just left her alone to get on with her journey. Her heart was beating ten to the dozen, had this really just happened? Alice kept twisting her head over her shoulder as she ran from the square. The lad who'd saved her was stood under some shelter in the distance away from the other group of youths. He smiled at her and nodded his head slowly. Alice had to thank him, she had to tell him how grateful she was for saving her. She could have been raped and pillaged if it wasn't for him. Slowly, she walked to where he stood. Once she got there she pulled her hood down. They chatted for a while and he was making her smile whatever he was saying to her. Once the conversation was over Alice ran as fast as her legs could carry her. She would never come back here again, ever. Her mother was right, it was way too dangerous. Alice looked over her shoulder and waved at Terry. He'd saved her life.

"Nana, it's only me, where are you?" Alice shouted up the stairs waiting for her nana to answer her. Pat come to the top of the stairs and dipped her head low over the banister. "Hiya love, go in the front room. I'll be down in a minute. I'm just getting ready. Make something to eat if you want because I bet you've had no breakfast again have you?" Alice peeled her wet coat off and headed straight into the kitchen, she was starving. Her nana was right, she'd had no breakfast. Her eyes scanned the fridge, she licked her lips, hunger pains crippled her stomach. She'd never see a fridge stocked this at home, hers was always bare and there was rarely anything worth eating inside it. Shoving pieces of meat in her mouth she grabbed the butter and placed it on the side.

Alice sat munching four pieces of toast; she was like a gannet, chewing rapidly. "Bleeding hell, watch your fingers love," Pat sniggered as she came into the room. Pat was a large lady and her face was worn, troubled. The deep set wrinkles round her mouth suggested she was a heavy smoker and thick deep tramlines all over her face.

"Has that lazy cow not fed you again then?" Pat knew the answer already. Alice had her mouth full of food and tried to slow down eating. Pat popped a cigarette into her mouth and joined her at the table, she patted her arm softly. "You look like a drowned rat, love. Is it still pissing down out there? I have to go out shopping too but I'll not bother if it's still raining," she glanced outside with a sour expression. "I can't be arsed anyway. I don't really need anything. I was just going to do some window-shopping really."

Alice licked the hot butter from her fingers and flicked her wet hair from her cheeks. It was like rats tails. "It's really bad out there nana. I'd stay in if I were you. If you need anything I could go for you."

Pat looked at her granddaughter closer, she always knew when she was upset and delved deeper. She sucked hard on her fag and crossed her legs before she began. "So come on then, spit it out, what's she been up to now? Don't lie for her Alice, just tell me the truth. She makes my blood boil she does," Pat bit hard on her bottom lip and reached over to touch Alice's arm. "I'll put that cunt six foot under if she carries on hurting you. I swear to you, I'll do her in." Pat was a right battleaxe and you could see where Janice got her foul mouth from.

Alice dipped her head low and chewed hard on her fingernails. Twisting the cuff on her tattered jumper, she tried to sound relaxed when replying "Oh, it's nothing really, just the usual crap nana. Nothing changes in our house. You know that more than anyone. I'm fine, I'm used to it." Alice was hiding something, her eyes clouded over and whatever it was she was finding it difficult to talk about. It was there on the end of her tongue but she just couldn't spit it out.

Pat snarled and gritted her teeth together tightly; she banged her flat palm on the table. "She'll never change that one. I've given her more chances than anyone. I've washed my hands of her," Pat welled up and pressed her hand firmly on her heart. "She made me ill you know. The doctor said it was all the stress from her that caused my bleeding blood pressure. She wouldn't care if I jossed it." Pat lit another cigarette and blew a large cloud of grey smoke out in front of her. "I can't understand her; she had everything and threw it all back in our faces. We tried everything, it was just hopeless." Pat reached into her handbag and pulled out her purse, she was snivelling. "Here, get this tenner and make sure you get something for your tea tonight. Don't tell your mother either. She'll have it away and spend it on drugs or beer. No Alice, you keep it hid well away love." Alice shoved the money into her pocket and smiled. She loved her nana and wished she could open up to her, to tell her everything, to confess her secrets. But, it was just so hard. Where would she start? Eating the crust from the bread Alice sat gabbing to her nana. She flicked the invisible dust from her pants and tapped her fingers on the table.

Finally she asked her, "what goes on in Tavistock Square nana? Why is everyone warned from ever going there?" Pat raised her eyebrows high and looked concerned. She snarled and her front teeth were showing like an animal under attack. Alice had hit a nerve, she was sorry she'd asked.

Pat went white and her nostrils flared. "You stay well away from there. It's nothing but trouble that place is. Your mother was around your age when she started sneaking on there too. I didn't have a clue either. Before that she was just a normal teenage girl." Pat sipped her cup of tea and her hands pressed hard against the side of the cup. "That place messed with her head, ruined her it did. It took every bit of innocence away from her, broke my bleeding heart to watch it too." Pat's eyes opened wide and she clutched Alice by the arm looking straight into her eyes, pleading with her. Making sure history didn't repeated itself. "Don't you ever go near that place, promise me you'll stay well away."

Alice dropped her eyes low, she couldn't look her in the eye. She crossed her fingers under the table and lied. "I won't nana, don't be daft. I'll never end up like my mother, ever. I'm different than her." Alice was intrigued now, the square was a magnet and it was drawing her in.

Alice sat with Pat for a couple of hours gossiping. She told her all the local news and how her neighbour had been caught with his pants down in another woman's house. Alice was warm and fed now, contented. Flicking her eyes to the clock on the TV she realised it was time to start heading home. Pat would have let her live there with her but she knew Alice would never rest knowing her mother was alone and she always declined the offer whenever she asked her to move in. She was stupid really, Pat would have looked after her and she could have had a good life with people who cared about her. Pecking her nana on the cheek she grabbed her coat from the radiator in the hallway. It was dry now and boiling hot. Pat watched her granddaughter heading towards the front door and her heart sank. She knew what she was heading home to and wished she could do more for her. She'd threatened so many times to report Janice to social services but she always lost her nerve and kept quiet just like everyone else did. Every night she tossed and turned wondering if her grandchild had been fed.

Pat ran to her side and hugged her; she was squeezing her harder than usual. As if this would be the last time she ever saw her. "Alice, make sure you go straight home. And, remember there is always a bed here for you."

Alice smiled and felt warmth rising through her. "I know nana, I know. Thank you, it means a lot." Alice headed out into the night, she zipped her coat up tightly as the wind picked up. Pat watched her heading down the street. She needed to do something and fast. She had a gut feeling that something bad was going to happen and she knew if it did she would never be able to live with herself. Pat walked back inside the house, she was troubled. Sitting at the dining table she was just staring into thin air.

The roads were busy tonight and everybody seemed in a rush to get home. It was a Friday, pub night, people were getting pissed and twisted and not giving a flying fuck about anything in life. Alice always dreamed of having a better life and wanted to change. She wanted a job and a car and maybe one day a boyfriend, a husband, someone who loved her. She'd never really had any interest in the opposite sex. Well, maybe one lad who was in her class at school but she soon lost interest in him when his teenage acne kicked in, he was a spotty greasy slob. The male sex scared her; she hated what they could do. The power they held, so much power over the opposite sex. They made her do things she never wanted to do, sick, twisted things that nobody ever knew about. Alice's attendance at school was poor. The high school where she went just seemed to have given up on her and with only a few weeks left to go before she left they never bothered her anymore. She was lost in the system, just a number on a very long list.

Alice could see the square in the distance as she headed home, stopping at the side of the road she stood gawping over at it, hiding behind a lamp-post, out of sight. Lots of people were gathered there, motor bikes skidding about, engines revving, girls screaming. Alice started to walk off slowly; there was no way she was going there again. She valued her safety. The lad who'd saved her was still playing heavily on her mind. He was her hero, her knight in shining armour. Alice headed in a different direction than her home. Where ever she was going she wanted to keep a low profile. She was ducking and diving and avoiding being seen.

Janice sat rocking to and fro. Alice had been gone ages and she was gasping for a cigarette. She sat biting the skin at the side of her nails. Standing at the kitchen window she lifted the grey net curtain up, peeping outside. The curtain was hanging and nearly falling apart, black mould clung to the top of it and it had a musky, damp smell that oozed through the house. Janice always kept a low profile when she owed money and today was no different. Lights off, curtains closed, nobody could see she was at home. Janice stood at the window talking to herself, she was anxious. "Where the fuck are you Alice, you'd better have got some money from that old boot otherwise you'll be in deep trouble. I wish you'd fucking hurry up. I'm gagging for a fag." She paced the kitchen floor in a right mood. Janice kicked the bottom of the door and melted to her knees. She was sobbing her heart out, ragging her hands through her hair. It was all just getting on top of her. She knew she'd made mistakes, but what could she do now? What was done was done. She just couldn't pull herself together anymore. Janice was in a bad place, a dark depressing place with no way out. All of a sudden her expression changed, she bolted up from the floor and searched for her mobile phone. Dialling a number she held her ear to the phone. "Hello, it's me. I know you said never to ring you again but I'm desperate. You owe me, remember. I've kept your secret for long enough. If your wife found out you were Alice's father you know what would happen don't you? I need some money and fast, don't fuck me about." Janice held her ear away from the phone and smirked. Whoever she was speaking to was going ballistic, she had them by the short and curlies by the sound of things. The call ended and Janice ran into the living-room searching for her shoes. She grabbed her keys from the coffee table and rushed to the front door. Janice was gone.

CHAPTER FOUR

Terry and Skid sat in the car watching one of the shopkeepers from the square getting ready to get into his car. Today he was banking and they were ready to grab the takings, break his fucking neck if they had to, knock the cunt right out. They knew he was carrying a fair bit of cash today. It was a decent wage that would put them back on their feet again. The Asian man was edgy as he popped his head out through the shop doorway. Asif kept checking the area and going back into the shop as if he'd forgotten something. He knew given half the chance he would have been robbed and beaten within an inch of his life for the money he was carrying. Harpurhey was well known for criminal activity and he was always reading pieces in the paper about someone getting hijacked and beaten for any cash they had. It was a dog eat dog world where only the brave survived. The shop keeper always made sure he carried a weapon with him when he was banking. He was willing to use it too, smash the fuckers up if they tried having his hard earned money away.

Skid was chomping at the bit and ready to go. "Look at the fat twat taking his time Terry. He knows something isn't right, his arse is twitching. Look at the fat cunt wasting time."

Terry kept his mind on the job; he was focused and never took his eye off the ball. "Just be quiet, for fuck's sake, just chill out and watch him. You're just spooked that's all, we'll be fine. He's banking today, trust me. He's not been all week and today is his last day to get it in the bank. It's Saturday and he won't rest knowing he's got all that money in the shop. Just trust me on this and relax."

Skid sat chewing on his fingernails, fidgeting, agitated. "Nar, something doesn't feel right Terry, let's sack it, we can have him again on another day."

Terry was livid and snapped. "Will you just shut the fuck up? We've been on him for weeks now and he's getting had, stop fucking flapping you're doing my head in. He's got pure cash with our name on it and he's being had over today, end of." Skid knew to be quiet. Terry was tapping his hands on the steering wheel and his breathing was heavy. The Asian man hooked the sports bag over his shoulder in the distance and after the last few security checks he sprinted to his car not far from where he was stood. "Look at him Skid, the daft cunt thinks he's safe. It's going to be like taking candy from a fucking baby. He'll shit a brick when I belt him on the head with this fucker." Terry lifted the silver claw hammer up from the side of his seat and kissed the end of it before placing it on his lap. "I'm going to smash his swede in, he'll give us no trouble, trust me." Skid clipped his seat belt into the socket and dipped his head low as they started to follow the silver Astra onto the main road. This shit was going down.

Asif Patel had been a shop owner in the square for years. He'd been a young lad when his father first bought the family business. He knew a lot of the lads from there but always kept his barriers up when he was in their presence. He knew they were scum and never trusted any of them as far as he could throw them, devious bastards they were who would stick a knife in him the moment his back was turned. These youths were not from his culture, they held no respect for nobody, not even their own parents, no family values. He spoke to them to have a quiet life, no other reason. They were not his friends and never would be. In his time as a shop-keeper he'd let his barrier down once before, he'd never do it again, ever.

Terry and Skid had secretly been watching Asif for over two months now, day in day out clocking his every movement. They knew his banking days in and out and as of yet they'd not been spotted. Asif never banked locally, no, he was too cunning for that, or so he thought. He travelled up to Rochdale town centre to deposit his hard earned cash. It was a twenty minute journey there but he never minded it, he just felt safer doing it this way. Skid turned the music down; he was concentrating and getting ready to strike. Small beads of sweat formed on his forehead and he was constantly rubbing his hot sweaty palms together. Terry and Skid had to be fast when the time came to fleece him. They needed him to be struck down with the first blow before he could raise the alarm. They were both ready to do whatever it took to get the money he was carrying, anything, even murder. Terry's jaw dropped. "Fuck me, where is the cunt going now, he never usually goes anywhere else. What the fuck is he up to?" He slammed the brakes on and parked up in an alleyway watching him with eager eyes. Asif drove into the drive-through for Kentucky fried chicken not far from them.

Skid banged his clenched fist onto the dashboard. "Greedy fat bastard he is. Fancy him eating Kentucky fried chicken. I thought Asians couldn't eat that kind of shit. I thought it had to be all that Halal crap."

Terry chuckled and shook his head. "What, do you think he only eats curry? They're just like us some of them. They're more modern nowadays and they wear the latest swagger. You know, like Armani and all that."

Skid looked puzzled, "What, so they don't have to wear all those pyjama dresses?"

Terry nearly choked and held the bottom of his stomach laughing. "Nar, like I said, they can wear what they like nowadays. I don't think the women can though, they're on lock down and have to wear them big tent dresses." Skid sat forward in his seat looking directly at Terry. "What do you mean them black ninja dresses that you can only see their eyes in?"

Terry scratched at his head, he wasn't sure. "I don't know, but the Asian culture has got it right. English girls should adapt that shit too instead of walking around with all their tits and arses hanging out. The Asian's have got it right in their belief that only their husbands should be able to see their true beauty, not every fucking Tom, Dick and Harry." Skid pushed at Terry's arm, eyes wide open. "Right, here he is. Fuck me, he's got a family bucket of chicken to eat. No way, is he going to scran that on his own, the fat porker?"

Terry flicked the ignition and gripped the steering wheel tightly; he was ready to rejoin the traffic. His heart was pounding in his chest and he knew the time was near for him to knock this guy right out. He was a big fucker too, a giant. They were both going to have to tune him in, take him off his feet and silence him when the time came. Terry and Skid sat watching the man eat his food in his car. He ate every single morsel of it too, the greedy bastard, he never left a single scrap. They watched him wipe his mouth and lick his fingers clean. It was time, he was ready to leave. Terry eased back into the traffic keeping his head low.

Asif sat in his car for a few minutes before he opened the car door. Terry and Skid were nearby and ready to strike. Dressed in black balaclavas, their identity was hidden. It was here, it was time to go. It was time to waste the fucker. Terry sprinted across the car park at speed and knew his first blow would have to be perfect. He was screaming and shouting at the top of his voice. He had to take him down, he had one chance only. Terry drew his arm back and smashed the claw hammer over his victim's head. You could hear his skull crunching. Asif fell to the ground and he was sparked, completely out of it. "Quick, get the fucking bag off him. Come on, before it's on top." Skid peeled Asif's large banana like fingers from the bag. He could see a large amount of blood gushing from his forehead. He was still breathing but he was in a bad way, his head swelled instantly. His eyes flickering rapidly. Terry and Skid motored back to the car with their heads low. Once the engine started they were out of there as quick as could be. Skid sank into his seat. "Fuck me, that was easy," Terry chuckled. His adrenalin was still pumping and he was in a zone. "It was like taking fucking candy from a baby. I thought it would have taken a few more belts to bring him down but I was spot on with my shot, no messing about. I hit the target in one"

The men pulled the black balaclavas from their heads and shoved them down the side of the seats. Skid was white and his heart was still pumping at speed. He was checking behind them making sure nobody had witnessed the crime. Through the back windscreen he could see Asif trying to get up from the floor, crawling he was, on his hands and knees. Once they'd been driving for a while Skid placed the black sports bag onto his lap and unzipped it slowly. Terry was still driving but he was aware of what Skid was doing. "Fuck me bro, we've touched down lucky here. I bet there's over ten grand here. Oh happy fucking days," he chuckled.

Terry nodded his head slowly; this was music to his ears. He'd been on jobs before and been let down with the wage from it, but not this time, he'd struck gold. "Right, we need to sort this cash out and get rid of any evidence. We'll ditch the car too, burn the fucker," Terry said. Skid was alive now and he was happy it was over. He was a grafter yes, but he hated that Terry was capable of ending someone's life at the drop of a hat. He scared him sometimes, he was so unpredictable.

Skid let out a laboured breath. "We'll go to our Janice's, she's sweet. We can give her a treat for keeping schtum and she'll be sorted. She's alright like that."

Terry had never met Skid's cousin before and he didn't trust anyone. His circle of trust was small and he never let anyone inside it. "Nar, fuck that. Are you right in the head, she might blubber under pressure. We need to keep this on the low. I don't want anyone knowing it was us. Do you get me or what?" Terry shot a look over to Skid that let him know that it meant telling nobody, not a soul.

Skid was a big mouth sometimes and he was always telling his business to people, bigging himself up. "Okay yeah I understand, just chill ya beans. It was just a thought that's all. Janice is alright though. I'll take you there tonight to meet her if you want, she's sound and on our wavelength. Ay, she might even let you slip her one if you're lucky. She's a bit of a cougar Janice, well; she was back in her day. She's just let herself slip lately, you know with the drink and that."

Terry was listening but still he was adamant that any of his business was staying between them two. "I might call around to see her with you later but first let's sort our shit out. The last thing we need is getting our collar felt. I've had enough of jail food to last me a fucking lifetime. And, I don't plan on having anymore any time soon."

Terry stepped into the shower and scrubbed himself, cleansing the guilt he felt inside. He hated what he had to do to keep his head above water but he had no other option. He needed to live. Anyway, after a few spliffs with the lads Asif would be out of his mind for good. The cannabis saw to that, it numbed his emotions, the pain he felt inside. The word on the street was that the dibble had been on the square all night long searching for any leads that might reveal the identity of Asif's attackers. They were trying to ask questions to the gangs there but none of them would give them the time of the day. They were the filth and nobody ever spoke to them if they knew what was good for them. Grassing was the lowest of the low. To be labelled a Judas in the area was a fate worse than death, house petrol bombed, the lot. A snitch never lasted long in Harpurhey. Everyone made sure they were driven out of the area as soon as could be, some grasses left in body bags.

Terry was heading onto the square tonight. He always went there to chill. They were his kind of people and he knew they had his back. A lot of the gang had grown up together and they all knew the score. A new lad came onto the square tonight. A good looking fucker he was and a lot of the girls there were already drooling over him. Terry didn't know anything about this kid but he knew he would suss him out and know instantly if he was a wrong-un. Terry was the alpha male in the group and everybody knew that. Nobody ever challenged him to his title. Spraying his new Diesel aftershave all over him he started to get ready. He loved to smell good, he loved that he smelt of money.

Skid was sat on a step rolling a joint as Terry bounced onto the square. Skid had all new clobber on and he made sure everybody had seen him, he looked dapper. Terry shook his head at him and snarled. "Fucking hell, I said don't bring any attention to us. Why the fuck don't you listen?" He kicked at his shoes and pulled at his clothes.

Skid lifted his head and chuckled, he was smirking. "Chill bro, it's a new pair of trainers that's all. My old ones were scruffy. No one's going to put two and two together are they? For fuck's sake stop going over the top."

Terry gripped him by the arm and went nose to nose with him. "Listen dickhead, what I say goes and if you don't like it, I'll start grafting with someone else. The police aren't daft you know. They'll be looking for stuff like this," he kicked his foot against Skid's new trainers again and this time he marked them. "And, let me tell you now, if my collar gets felt, it will be down to you."

Skid wasn't gobby any more; he dipped his head and tried to make amends. "Yeah, you're right. I wasn't thinking straight. I'll be more careful in the future. You know me I just get a bit giddy."

Terry turned his head quickly; the new kid on the block was walking over towards them. He had a few of the girls around him and he held a cocky look in his eye. "Yo, what's going down lads. I'm Nelson. I'm new around here and just thought I would introduce myself to you all." Nelson reached his clenched fist over to Skid. "Touch me down bro," he chuckled. Terry screwed his face up and stood with his back against the wall weighing this guy up and down. Nelson reached his fist over to him now. "Touch me down bro."

Terry snarled and blew his breath. "Nar, I don't do all that touch me down shit. I'm not black. So fuck off out of my face with your daft lingo shit." Nelson looked around and he was crumbling. He was around the same age as Terry. He was mixed race and his hair was shaved down to the bone. He knew he had to defend himself. He was on the spot and looking like a right clown. Everybody was waiting on his reply. "Yeah, I get ya. It's just something I do to break the ice when I'm nervous. I'm not from around here and don't know the script yet. I'm from Oldham. I think we're a bit behind the times up there if you know what I mean."

Skid sniggered as he looked him up and down. "Yeah, you better sort it out if you want to start chilling on the square. We don't have any hillbillies on here. We have street cred." Nelson agreed and he never took his eyes from Terry. He knew if he was ever to be accepted on the square he had to lick his arse, he was doing his best to win him over. "Here, check this bud out, it's pucka shit. Our kid got it for me. It will blow your fucking brains out." This was it, he had Terry's attention. Skid was by his side instantly. He loved new bud and was always looking for something better to blow his mind. Terry watched carefully as Nelson revealed his bag of weed. There was loads there and he knew the others on the square would be around him like flies around shit until every last bit was blazed. Terry watched as another spliff was made, they all sat down in the doorway and passed it around getting stoned. Terry kept his distance from Nelson though. He didn't trust him, there was just something about him that he didn't like, he just had a gut feeling about this guy.

The square was busy tonight. Nicked motorbikes sped across the square doing wheelies and a few girls were arguing in the distance. Drunk as skunks they were and the gobs on them were loud, filthy. Skid nudged Terry in the waist. "Do you fancy coming to my cousin Janice's. I said I'd do her a borrow until her pay day?"

Terry gazed about the square, nothing really was going on and he'd been bored out of his head for the last hour. "Yeah, fuck it. I'll come with you for a bit. I'm going to get Tina on the phone anyway. She can be my bed buddy for tonight."

Skid nodded his head as they both set off walking. "I thought she carted you, that's what you told me anyway."

Terry flicked some invisible dust from his collar and spoke. "Nar, she's always saying it's over but she's gagging for it really. She never refuses me. Just watch this." Terry pulled his mobile phone from his coat pocket and searched for Tina's number. He held the phone to his ear and waited for her to answer with a cocky look on his face. "Yo Tina, it's me Tez. Are you coming around tonight for a quick knee trembler or what?" You could hear her loud voice screaming down the other end of the phone and judging by her tone there was no way he was parting her tash tonight or any other night for that matter. She was like that Tina. One minute she'd be all over Terry and the next she couldn't stand the sight of him. They had a kind of love-hate relationship.

Skid roared laughing. "That's what you get for being a show off, you thought Tina was in the bag and she's just carted you. You'll have to have a wank tonight then bro. A self service." Terry growled, how dare she turn him down the dirty little slut. She was going to pay for this humiliation, pay big time. She would never get a booty call again, never.

Skid hammered on Janice's front door with his clenched fist. It was late, but Janice was always up at this time. Where the hell was she? Skid bent his knees low and shouted inside the letterbox with his mouth pressed inside it. Terry leant against the wall looking bored. A light came on in the hallway and he could see a shadow approaching the door. "Fuck me Alice, was you asleep. I've been knocking for ages. Where's your mam?" Alice yawned and pulled her t-shirt down over her legs, she'd been in bed fast asleep and her hair was all over the show. Alice went to close the front door after Skid came inside but a foot appeared at the bottom of it stopping it from shutting. Skid shouted behind him as he made his way towards the front room. "This is Terry, he's my mate. He's sorted, Alice let him inside." The two of them stood looking at each other, eyes locked.

Alice stuttered as Terry walked passed her. A warm feeling circled her heart and she was blushing. "I don't know where my mam is Skid, she wasn't in when I got home. I'm a bit worried about her really; she's never out at this time. I bet she's gone to see Darren, they had a blazing row the other night and he nearly half killed her." Alice followed them both into the front room. She straightened her hair and tried to look half decent. Skid pulled two bottle of brandy from his pocket and plonked it onto the table. "This is for your mam when she gets home. It's my treat tell her," he scratched his head as he checked his wristwatch. "Have you tried her mobile, try ringing her and tell her I'm here." Alice sat down and lifted her legs up to the side of her. She could feel Terry's eyes all over her and didn't feel comfortable. He was trying to get a glimpse of her knickers, she was sure of it. Men were such perverts, always out for something to put in their wank bank.

Alice looked worried. "I've been trying her phone all night Skid, but it keeps going to voice-mail. She is just doing this for attention, to teach me a lesson because we had words, she always does this."

Terry pulled the coffee table nearer to him and smiled at Alice. "Is it okay if I skin up," he never waited for an answer and carried on building a joint. Something was happening to Alice, her lips were dry and her cheeks were beetroot. Skid opened one of the bottles of brandy he'd brought and passed it to Terry. After a few gulps of it he looked at Alice and held the bottle out in front of him. "Here, get a gob full of that, it will warm you up, you look perished." Skid screwed his face up and reached over to grab the bottle from his hand. "Ay, she's only fifteen, she's not like the girls on the square Terry. Our Alice is a good girl, she's not into all that shit."

Alice sat forward and from nowhere her words came flying out. "Skid, I can have a few mouthfuls. It's not going to kill me is it?" Skid watched her carefully as she held the bottle to her mouth and necked a mouthful, perhaps he'd been wrong about Alice, perhaps she wasn't as clean cut as he first thought. The front door slammed shut and Janice came storming into the front room, her nose was bleeding and she looked in a bad way. Skid jumped up and ran straight to her side. "Who the fuck has done this to you? Look at the state of you, come on, give me a name and I'll sort the cunt out."

Janice took her coat off and spotted the booze on the table. She plonked down on the sofa and wiped the blood still dripping from her nose. "I just banged it Skid, me and Daz was fighting last week and it's still sore that's all. Every time I catch it on something it just starts bleeding. You know me love; I'm as hard as nails."

Skid sat back down, he knew she was lying. She was a fool to herself and there was no way he was beating himself up about it, secretly he knew she probably deserved it for being such a big mouth. Janice held the bottle of brandy in her hands and screwed the lid from it, her hands shaking. "Mam, Skid's brought that for you, so make sure you say thank you."

Janice winked over at Skid. "Top one for this, you always come at the right time. I've had a shit day and this is what I need to help me chill out."

Terry looked over at Janice, she was as rough as a bear's arse and where Skid had got that she was a good looking woman from he'd never know, she was minging, rough as they come. A has- been. Janice nodded her head over at Terry. "And, who are you stranger?" She licked her lips slowly and played with her hair at the side of her face as she waited for him to answer.

Terry sat back in his chair. "I'm Terry, nice to meet

you."

Skid sat chugging on his spliff and passed it over to Janice. "Terry is a top grafter Janice, me and him are top of the rung when it comes to crime around here. Ruthless fuckers we are."

Janice was impressed and as she took her shoes off she smirked over at him. "You're a good looking lad too. I bet all the girls are falling at your feet aren't they?"

Terry blushed and he could feel Alice hanging on his every word. "I don't bother with the girls around here anymore, they're all the same. They're just after a free ride and drugs. I'm saving myself for somebody special, "he smirked over at Alice.

Janice examined him closer and peeled her crusty socks from her feet. "I see the square hasn't changed much then. It was like that when I used to go on there. I suppose you're right, the girls are sluts."

Alice looked at her mother, she was a right hypocrite. She'd preached to her for as long as she could remember about stepping foot on the square and yet here she was openly admitting she spent time there when she was younger. Alice watched Terry from the corner of her eye. "Mam, where have you been? I've been worried about you; you could have at least rung me to tell me where you were."

Janice snarled, blaming her daughter for her pain. If Alice would have been home quicker with the money in the first place she would have never have had to go out to see him, to beg Alice's father for more money. Janice hissed at her. "Well, I had to go out didn't I? Anyway, did you get the money from your nana? Fuck me, you were there long enough. I thought you were staying the night."

Alice pointed at the TV. "The money's there, I told you I wasn't just going to my nanas for money then just leaving straight after I'd got it, that's just cheeky. I had to stay for a bit."

Janice stood up and walked in front of the TV. Picking the money up she shoved it down the front of her manky white bra. "Better late than never I suppose. What did the old cow have to say anyway? Was she slagging me off like she always does?"

Skid knew if left, Janice would have gone on all night about how her own mother had turned her back on her in her time of need, he jumped into the conversation cutting her short. "So, why were you and Daz arguing? He's a top guy him, he's laid back and all that."

Janice reached for the spliff and sucked hard on it. "Don't be fooled by him Skid, he had me over too. He was bad on the sniff and all that, he was trying to get some money from me and when I told him no, he snapped and done this to me."

Alice was gobsmacked, her mother was lying through her front teeth. She wanted to tell them the truth but the words were just stuck in her mouth just as they always were when she tried to tell someone what was going on. And, Skid saying Darren was alright guy, what the fuck was he talking about! He made her blood boil. She wondered if he would have changed his tune if he'd known the truth about Darren. That he'd been abusing her during his time there. He was a cunt, a sex case who needed his balls cutting off and ramming down his throat.

"Can we get our head down here tonight Janice or what, it's late and we can't be arsed walking home at this time."

Janice nodded, she didn't sleep much anyway and a bit of company would stop her brain from working overtime. "Yeah, no worries. Terry can jump in with me if he wants?" She chuckled and patted Skid on his arm. "I'm joking, I'm joking. I bet you shit your pants then didn't you Terry. I love a joke me, Skid don't I? Go on, tell Terry how I'm always messing with people's heads."

Skid sighed and looped his arms above his head. "Yeah Tez, just ignore her, she's a right head the ball sometimes. Game for a laugh our Janice is."

Terry screwed his face up and you could see she disgusted him, she was vile. He wasn't even willing to take one for the team. She made his skin crawl. "I'm going to get off Skid. I've got to be up early and I like my own bed. You know me, I'm a creature of habit." Terry stood up and nodded his head over at Janice. "Nice to meet you anyway." He headed towards the door and turned his head back slowly. "Bye Alice, see you again."

Alice couldn't speak; the cat had got her tongue, a hot flush passed through her, she was beaming. Janice took the main stage now and walked up behind him, needing some attention. "You can always change your mind you know. I'm not that bad really. I'm just a bit rough tonight. I scrub up well if you ever fancy taking me out on a date."

Terry looked over at Skid and nodded his head, not even acknowledging her. "See you tomorrow."

Janice was pissed off he'd not replied to her. She was sexy, she was good-looking, why on earth hadn't he took her up on her offer, she was putting it on a plate for him here. The front door banged shut and Janice listened to make sure he was gone. Once she knew the coast was clear she whispered over to Skid. "He's a strange one isn't he? I mean, where's his sense of humour. I was only joking with him you know."

Skid knew she was a man- eater and pretended to go along with her for a quiet life. "He's shy Janice that's all. You would eat him up for breakfast and spit him out of your arse. He went under that's all. I bet he says to me tomorrow that he fancied you. You just wait and see." He was lying of course. Terry had no interest in her whatsoever.

Janice stroked the side of her face, nursing her bruises, she was feeling sorry for herself now, her eyes clouded over ready to start blubbering. "I'm not looking my best though am I? Look at the state of me, no wonder he blew me out. I'm a disgrace."

This was Alice's cue to go to bed. If she sat there for a second longer she would have been subjected to hours of her mother's self pity. How the world was against her, how nobody loved her. She stood up and walked to the door. "I'm off to bed mam, see you in the morning, goodnight Skid." Janice ignored her and carried on swigging from the brandy bottle taking large mouthfuls. Skid was watching Alice like a hawk, licking his lips slowly and tickling his chin with the end of his fingers. "Night sweetheart," he shouted behind her. Alice looked at him a little longer than she should have and left the room.

Alice lay asleep in her bed. The moonlight shining through lit up the room. Alice always slept with her head under the duvet and tonight was no different. She'd always slept this way to keep warm and in a way she always felt secure if she was hid away under her cover. It was a safe place where no one could hurt her, where she could feel no pain. The bedroom door creaked open and the light from the hallway shone inside. Footsteps, creaking slowly towards her. The duvet was lifted up and Skid sneaked inside. Alice stirred under the cover but before she knew it Skid covered her mouth with his hand and pressed down with force. Alice was wide awake now and she knew what lay ahead. This wasn't the first time he'd been into her room and she was shaking from head to toe. The covers were kicked from the bed as she tried to break free. It was no good, he held her in a grip and mounted on top of her. His teeth gritted together tightly and his voice was chilling. "Shut the fuck up, one more word out of you and I'll end your fucking worthless life. I said, button it." Tears streamed down Alice's cheeks as she turned her head looking at the moonlight. He was inside her now and groaning as his cock penetrated deeper into her. This abuse had been going on for months. There wasn't a single thing she could do either. Nobody would have believed her, nobody cared about her. It all started by him asking to lie on her bed with her. Just for a chat he said. Alice just thought it was normal and liked that he showed her some affection. But then it went horribly wrong, he started touching her, rubbing at her, making her touch him. She hated him with a passion. Skid was always bunging her cash, getting her little gifts but she knew that was to keep her mouth shut, it was guilt money. Alice had often thought of telling her mother but would she ever have believed her? Skid provided her mother with drugs and booze, there was no way she would have had a bad word said against him, about any man she brought back to her home.

Alice inhaled, she could smell stale tobacco and body odour. Skid brought his lips to meet hers and pressed them down with force. "Kiss me," he snarled. Alice kept her lips sealed; there was no way she was responding to his request. It was nearly over anyway, he was moving rapidly on top of her, pounding deep inside her. "You're a dirty cunt you are Alice, you are always begging for it. I saw the way you looked at Terry too, do you want him to bang you." Skid was horrible with his mouth, hurtful. "You're lucky I stuck one up you tonight. You're hanging, no one will ever love you. Your own mother can't even stand the sight of you. You should count yourself lucky that I'm even here with you." Skid rolled off her and pulled his jeans back up. He bent down towards her and growled. Suddenly he froze, he thought he heard someone outside the door. Quickly he ran over to it and opened the door slowly. His head must have been playing games with him, he couldn't see anyone. He tiptoed back over to Alice who was lying in the bed. "One word to anyone about this and I'll hurt you. Remember, nobody would believe you anyway. Keep it shut." He gripped her hair in his hands and ragged her about a bit. Before he left the room he spat in her eye. What a horrible bastard this man was. He pretended to everyone that he was Mr Nice guy when in fact he was nothing but a dirty kiddy fiddler.

Alice was alone, she sobbed her heart out, blaming herself, wishing she would have screamed out for help. Wishing she was dead. How could she ever make it stop, he was right, no one would ever believe her anyway. Somehow, some way, she had to make it all go away, end the pain she was feeling in her heart. Footsteps outside her door, somebody was there. Pulling the duvet over her head, she hid away from the world. She wanted to be dead, she wanted all this misery to end.

CHAPTER FIVE

Janice was running about the landing in a panic. She was still half asleep and wobbling about. "Fuck, it's the rozzers at the door," she shouted at Skid. He emerged from the bedroom and he was white as a sheet as he sprinted to the window in a panic.

"What the fuck do they want," he cursed. "Fuck, fuck. I hope it's not for me."

Alice sat on the side of her bed and rubbed her knuckles into her eyes. "Mam, who is it at the door, why are they banging like that?" she shouted.

Janice crept to her bedroom door and popped her head inside. She held one finger over her mouth. "It's the fucking police, just stay in here until they've gone. Fuck knows what they want. I think they're after Skid."

Alice lay back down on her bed and dragged the covers over her. She was feeling sick and her head was banging. She could hear them both talking outside the door. "Skid, I've done fuck all wrong. I don't know why they're here, it must be for you," Janice whispered.

Skid stood thinking for a few seconds. "Just go and open the door then. At least we'll know then won't we? Fuck me I hope it's not for me. I'm fucked if I get arrested I've got a few ounces of weed on me."

Janice crept down the stairs and stood facing the door debating her next move. She straightened her hair and opened the door slowly. "Bleeding hell, why are you banging like that, people are in bed asleep you know?"

The two officers stepped forward and put their hand on the doorframe. "Can we come in please?"

Janice was up in arms, she never did anything by the book she always caused a commotion. She clocked the care worker at her car facing her. "Nar, what do you need to come in for. Say what you have to say and fuck off? Anyway, do you have a warrant because if you're looking for something I need to see a search warrant? I know the law and I know and my rights."

The female officer came closer to Janice and her voice was firm. "We're here about your daughter Alice. We need to come inside and speak to you about her."

Janice let out a laboured breath. At least she was in the clear now and she started to relax. "What do you want with my Alice she's a good girl, she's not done anything wrong, trust me, she's not like that. You're barking up the wrong tree if you think she's a criminal."

The male officer had had enough of being polite. Day after day he had to deal with dead-legs and know it-all's and he'd had enough. He was here to do a job and he was wasting no more time. He barged passed Janice and headed straight into the front room. Janice was hysterical and ran after him. "You daft bastard, you can't just come in here. Get the fuck out of my house. Where's your warrant. I want to see the paperwork."

Skid was dressed now and he was stood on the stairs watching closely. He'd plugged the weed up his arse and knew it was safe for now. The female officer clocked Skid from the corner of her eye and any attempt of him getting off was foiled. "Can you come and sit in here sir? Is anyone else in the house before I do my search?"

Skid swallowed hard and raised his eyes. "Yeah, our

Alice is in bed. She's asleep though."

The female officer ran upstairs and she was checking each room for the child. Janice popped a cigarette into her mouth and yanked her tracksuit bottoms up as she lit her fag. Her gut was still hanging out and she was doing her best to cover it. She sat down and blew a thick cloud of grey smoke from her mouth. "You have no respect for anybody's private lives. This is why nobody likes you, hurry up and fuck off out of my gaff."

The officer looked at a small bag of weed on the table and shot a look at Janice. "Is this yours?"

Janice knew more than anybody that she could get away with having marijuana for her personal use, she wasn't supplying it, she was just blazing it. She stepped forward and still held her cocky attitude. "Yeah, it's mine. I use it for my pain, to numb it. Go on shoot me for trying to live a pain free life."

The officer shook his head and started to place it into a big plastic bag as evidence. "Who lives here with you Janice, is it just you and Alice?"

"Yes, what's that got to do with you?" Skid sat facing her and cringed as he listened to her going on, she was making things ten times worse. He had to do something; he had to shut her up before they all ended up getting nicked.

"Janice, the officer is just asking that's all. Stop making things worse than what they are already."

The male officer sneered at Skid. "And, who are you? Do you live here too?"

Janice never gave him chance to speak; there she was again with her big gob. "Don't tell him fuck all Skid, he's a nosey twat," she stood up and placed one hand on her hip. "Listen Mr Plod, ask what you have to and piss off. It's not good around here to have you lot inside your house, my neighbours will think I'm a grass."

The living room door opened and Alice stood there with the female officer. She was fully dressed and zipping her coat up. Janice bolted over to her and grabbed her face, squeezing her cheeks together. "What the fuck have you done, if you've been up to no good then you'll see what I'm all about. I'll knock you to kingdom come lady."

Alice was tearful, I don't know if it was tears of relief that someone had finally come to help her or tears of a young girl scared of how her life would turn out. The female officer stared directly at Janice. You could see the disgust on her face. This woman didn't deserve kids in her eyes, she was a scruffy piss-head who cared about nothing except drink and drugs. She stood tall and looked Janice directly in the eye, she didn't scare her, she was ready to take her down if she needed to. "Alice will be coming with us. We've had several calls now about the way she is being treated and she will be taken into care until we have sorted everything out. Once the investigation has finished we'll know more."

Janice was speechless; she ragged her fingers through her hair and ran over to Alice. This wasn't right, she was a good mother. What the hell was happening here? Janice gripped Alice's hands. "Tell them love, go on, tell them you're fine here with me. I'll tell you what officers, whoever is poking their nose into my business will soon be seeing me at their door," Janice held her hands up in the air. "Skid, tell them it's all been a bad mistake."

There was a silence and all you could hear was the scream from the pit of Janice's stomach, the realisation, the guilt. Alice was being escorted out of the room. "No, don't take my baby, she's all I've got. I'll be a better mother. I'll stop drinking, just leave her here with me." Alice should have said something to the officers, told them everything was fine at home but she never did, she kept quiet. At the end of the day they were right she had been mistreated, more than anyone would ever know. Janice was never one to take things lying down. She was up in arms, throwing things about, hurling shoes across the room at the officers.

Skid ran over to her and held her back gripping her arms, she was strong and she was fighting back. "Just calm the fuck down Janice. We'll get a solicitor on this and Alice will be back with you before you know it. They can't just take your kid from you. You're right. Liberty taking twats they are. Who've got nothing better to do than harass innocent people."

The male officer turned his head slowly before he left the room. Skid was known to him and he'd had trouble with him in the past. He went nose to nose with him and spoke. "I'd keep quiet if I was you, son. You know more than me that I can have you arrested at the drop of a hat, so think before you make any more snidey remarks."

The front door banged shut and Janice sank to her knees. "My baby, bring my baby back, please, she's all I've got."

Skid placed his arm around her shoulders as she broke down crying, he was helpless. His voice was low as he tried to console her. "We'll sort it out Janice. We'll sort it all out. She'll be back home with you in no time."

They both knew now that Alice was in the care system. Their battle was going to be long and hard if they were ever to get her back, the days ahead were dark and

Janice knew in her heart her daughter was gone forever. She was fighting a losing battle.

Alice sat twiddling her thumbs, her head dipped low. She held so much sadness in her eyes; loneliness, desperation. Should she tell them she was fine? Should she say all the complaints they'd heard about her were lies? Her mind was racing and she had some big choices to make. This could be her big chance, her only chance of escaping the life that was set out in front of her, to never see her abusers again, to start with a clean slate.

A lady came into the room and sat down next to her. She gripped her hand in hers and smiled gently. "It will get better Alice, this is for the best. I'll make sure you are safe. Will you come with me while we have a chat, just so we both know what's going to happen next?" The lady was around thirty years of age, good looking and had the biggest brown eyes Alice had ever seen in her life. "My name is Christine and I'm going to be your case worker. That means my job is to make sure you're never in danger again."

Alice choked up; the emotions she'd stored for years seemed to flood from her eyes. At last somebody cared, someone would help her out, save her. Christine passed her a tissue and led her to a room at the side of the corridor. She left her alone for a few minutes and came back shortly after with a hot cup of sweet tea and a plate of biscuits. A female officer came into the room to join them both. Alice snivelled and her shoulders were shaking. This was it, it was time to open up and tell the world how she was living her life. Hold nothing back, tell them all. Christine held her hand and comforted her again. She was so nice and understanding. Kind of like a big sister to her. "Alice, just take your time and tell us what has been going on. We know your mother has not been looking after you properly and that's her fault not yours just remember that. We're here to help you, not to judge you."

No one was prepared for what Alice was about to reveal. They had no idea of what her life was about and when she began speaking you could see the two women looking at each other in disgust. Alice's voice was low and she kept her head dipped, never having any eye contact with them. You could have heard a pin drop at that moment. "It started when I was ten years old. My mam always had men back at our house. She was drunk most of the time and usually passed out on the floor somewhere," Alice closed her eyes and folded her arms tightly around herself, guarding herself, protecting her broken heart. "His name was Dave. He was an old man with grey hair and I could never understand why she was even with him, she told me he was her sugar daddy." Alice swallowed hard and took a moment to regain her breath. "He was crafty, he never touched me when my mam was in the room, he'd wait until she went to the toilet or something. Just come here and sit on my knee, he'd say. At first, I liked it and he was always showing me affection. I thought he cared about me, loved me even," Alice gripped her knees and shook her head. "But, then he did things to me. You know, bad things." Alice clenched her fists together and her knuckles turned white, her chest rising with speed. She lifted her head up and her teeth clenched together as the words came out of her mouth. "He put his fingers inside me, hurting me, telling me to keep quiet. Not to move, to smile and carry on as normal." Christine chewed on her bottom lip and closed her eyes. She held onto Alice's hand even tighter now and shook her head as she looked over at the female officer. Alice sobbed and looked at them both for forgiveness. "It wasn't my fault. I never asked him to do it. I told him to stop but he never listened."

The atmosphere could have been cut with a knife, both women felt sick and disgusted, that some old man could ever do this to a child. "Do you know what he said to me after it," she looked over at the policewoman and twiddled with her hair. "That I was gagging for it just like my mother was." Alice pulled her hand away from Christine and hugged herself, rocking to and fro. She dragged at her skin, squeezing at it, scratching it. "I wanted to hurt him. I wanted to tell everyone what he'd done to me but I was too scared. He said he would kill me if I whispered a word to anyone. He said he would tell my mam that it was me who came onto him. I was a child, a fucking ten year-old child. He should have never have touched me. I'm not wrong am I? Tell me it was his fault and not mine." Alice broke down sobbing her heart out and Christine told the officer that they should have a break for a while. This was too much to take in, even for her caseworker. Alice was shaking, teeth chattering together. Christine left the room and she was alone. The rage she felt inside her was strong and from nowhere she snapped. She ran at the door punching and kicking at it, head-butting the walls, she'd lost the plot. She was doing her best to hurt herself, ragging at her hair, dragging at her skin.

Christine heard the commotion from outside and ran back into the room. She gripped the young girl in her arms. She was strong enough to hold her and fell to her knees with her. "Alice, take deep breaths, breathe, come on girl just take deep breaths. You're going to be fine, you're safe now. The worst is over; you've been so brave in telling us what has happened." The red mist was clearing and Alice was coming back to the real world. She yanked her knees up to her chest and sat in the corner of the room. She dragged her hood over her head and sat sobbing, she wanted no comfort from anyone, she wanted to be left alone. Christine had dealt with lots of abuse cases in the past and was used to dealing with girls in this kind of circumstances. She just sat with her and just tapped her arms softly. "Together, we'll get through this. I will get you all the help you need. You never have to go back home."

Alice kept her head covered and mumbled softly. "Am I mental? My mam said I'm not right in the head. I'm not insane am I?"

Christine fought to keep her own tears back as she spoke. "No, you're not insane Alice. Your mother has let you down. She should have protected you against paedophiles. You're a child, an innocent young girl who has been groomed by your mother's lovers." Alice calmed down and the officer came back into the room. Alice stayed sat on the floor and she kept her hood up as she told them about the other men who'd molested her. It was strange though, she never mentioned Skid's name once. She kept him out of it. Why was she protecting him? This was the ideal time to put the kiddy fiddling bastard behind bars for good, lock the cunt up, make sure he never did it again. What the hell was she doing? The interview lasted for another forty minutes. And some of the things she told them would have made your toes curl, sick twisted things that happened in the dark of the night. The police had more than enough evidence now to make sure Alice never went back home again. The names she'd given them were written down and it was only a matter of time before the police picked them up and charged them with the offences they'd committed.

At last, Alice was safe thanks to her nana's phone call to the police. Pat had searched her soul long and hard before she made that call and she knew in her heart of hearts that she'd made the right choice. Her daughter was an unfit mother and now she had to pay the price for her actions.

Later in the evening, Alice looked like an emotional wreck. She had dark circles around her eyes and her hair was stuck to her cheeks, her eyes were bloodshot. "I'm going to take you to the care home now Alice. There are lots of girls there like you. Nobody will hurt you again, or judge you. Our job is to protect you and that I can promise." Christine hugged Alice tightly. She couldn't help but get attached to the girls she worked with, she was a kind, caring person and her background was similar to the girls whose cases she managed. Christine had spent much of her youth in the care system too and knew more than anybody how it felt to be abused. They left the police station and headed to Christine's car. Alice was numb, drained of any emotion. Her eyes were tired and for the first time that day she felt hungry. Once they were in the car Christine started the engine. She turned to face her. "You're so brave Alice to do what you've just done, some people never tell the truth and those slimy bastards just get away with it." Christine realised her foul language and covered her mouth with her hand. "Oh, I'm sorry for swearing but I just get so angry. Please forgive me."

Alice smirked and looked out of the car window. She didn't mind her swearing, her mouth was filthy sometimes too. "What about my mam, will she know what's gone on now. She'll hate me now won't she? I just know she'll blame me. She's like that you know, she'll turn all this round and say I'm lying."

Christine pulled out from the car park and indicated to go right. "Your mother has some demons to face Alice. If she wants to live in denial, then that's her problem nobody else's."

Alice wanted to protect her mother, to find the reasons why she was the way she was. "She's not well Christine, she drinks a lot, when she's sober she's kind of alright. She's just had a bad time lately, she gets so down sometimes."

Christine was listening but there was no way she was ever condoning what her mother had done. "How often is she sober Alice, does she drink every day?"

Alice sighed and her heart sank low. Who was she kidding, her mother hadn't been sober for years, she needed to face it, her mother was a piss head who was incapable of ever looking after her. The radio was low in the car and Alice spent the rest of the journey in silence. This was a lot to take in, changes were happening around her and for once in her life she could see light at the end of the tunnel.

Alice and Christine pulled up in a car park at the back of a road. The traffic could be heard speeding by. Before them stood an old Victorian brick building. It looked like one Alice had seen on an old film she'd watched with her nana. Christine could feel Alice's fear bubbling and turned the engine off. She faced her. "I know exactly how you are feeling Alice. Believe it or not, I was in the same place you are when I was younger. I was abused by my uncle. I know everything that you are feeling and believe me it does get better. You'll put all of this behind you one day." Christine shivered and she rubbed her hand slowly over her arms as she continued. "Life is hard sometimes Alice but it doesn't mean it will stay bad. I'm working alongside you and no matter what, no matter where you are in life, you will always have a friend in me." Christine was getting emotional; she just couldn't hide her own pain. And it was pain you could see it in her eyes as she choked up and held the tears back. Christine took a deep breath and lifted her eyes to the roof of the car. "I can never have children because of the abuse I suffered. My uncle took that away from me, he took away my innocence and my right as a woman to have children. I've found inner peace by helping girls who have lived like I did. Each one of you is my baby now and I'll always be there in your time of need."

Her words were endearing and straight from the heart. Nobody had ever spoken to Alice like this before. Christine offered real friendship and hope. Alice let out a laboured breath and somehow she realised she was not alone in the hurt she was feeling inside. Christine opened her door. "Come on Alice, let's get you settled and get you something to eat. I bet you're starving aren't you?" Alice pulled herself from the car and followed Christine to the entrance they could see not far from them. It was late now and only a small light outside the door gave them the guidance they needed. Christine pressed the intercom button and spoke into it. "Hi, it's me Christine; can you open the front door?"

Alice had no belongings with her. All she had were the clothes on her back. The front door opened and a woman stood there dressed in pyjamas and a purple housecoat . "Come on, get inside, its freezing out there tonight."

Christine followed her inside and Alice closed the front door behind her. The corridor was long and doors were situated all along it. "Doris, can we get Alice something to eat before we show her up to her room, she's not had a bite to eat for hours."

"I'll make her some chips and a burger if she wants. I've got a few left from teatime," Doris smiled at Alice. "Is that what you would like my dear?" Alice nodded her head. This sick feeling inside her was getting worst and at one point felt faint, her face turned green and she had to sit down for a few minutes sipping on some cold water. Doris stood cooking as Christine sat at the dining table with Alice. "Just get something to eat and you should start to feel better. I always get like that when I'm hungry too. I've made a point now of not skipping meals. I try and eat snacks throughout the day too." Doris placed the food in front of Alice. Home-made chips and a burger on a bun the size of Mount Everest. She'd put cheese on it too and lots of salad. Alice picked a chip up and slowly munched on it. Once the taste tickled her pallet she was away and started to scran the lot, she was hungry, starving.

Christine led Alice up the stairs and along a small corridor. She could hear low music from inside the room.

"Here you go sweetheart. You'll be staying here with Sharon. She's a nice girl and she'll help you get used to things in here. She's one of my favourite girls and I love her to death." The door opened slowly and Alice clocked a young girl around the same age as her lay on the bed listening to some music, her feet were tapping as she hummed along to the track. "Sharon, this is Alice. She's going to be sharing a room with you. I'll be back here tomorrow Alice; you just try and get some rest it's been a long day for you."

Christine smiled at her and patted her softly on the arm as she left. Sharon was clocking Alice as she sat down on the bed. She was watching her eagerly. Alice unzipped her coat and placed it at the side of her. She had no nightwear and was willing to sleep in her clothes. "I've got some spare pyjamas for you if you want to lend some," Sharon said. Alice hunched her shoulders and you could see she didn't know what to say. Nobody had ever been nice to her before and gave her anything without wanting something back in return. A grey pair of bottoms and a vest top landed on the bed next to her. "Go on, get them on you can't sleep in your clothes can you?"

"Thanks," Alice whispered back to her.

"I'm getting my head down now but we can chat in the morning if you want?"

Alice smiled and nodded her head. Once she'd got ready for bed she slid her emaciated body between the sheets. The fresh, clean bedding smelt of flowers and the crisp white sheets wrapped around herself. Alice tossed and turned and the only comfort she got was from the moonlight shining in through the bedroom window. The sliver light of it calmed her; it always had. Ever since she'd been a small child the moon had been her best friend. Alice closed her eyes and a single bulky salty tear fell from her eye. At last, she was safe and away from her abusers, away from her mother.

CHAPTER SIX

Janice was a lost cause, drinking more, getting off her head every night, she was a walking disgrace. It was late at night and she was walking the streets searching for cigarette stubs from the pavement to crave her nicotine addiction. What a skanky bitch she was, she had no pride. Janice stopped near her parent's house and sat on the brick wall facing it. She hid away in the shadows, hiding her shame from the world. She'd often come here when her mood was low and watch her family home from a distance. She had so many regrets at how her life had turned out. Her parents, Pat and Ted, lived a quiet life and every day they followed a strict routine. They ate at a certain time, went to bed at nine o'clock each evening and never really had a social life; they were set in their ways, old fashioned. Don't get me wrong they used to do lots of things in their early days, go out drinking or out for meals but that all stopped after Janice was carted from the family home when she was younger. Ted could never admit what had happened to his daughter; she'd shattered his heart into a thousand pieces, made him lose the will to live, disgraced him. He'd always wanted so much more for her and he blamed his wife for the way she'd turned out.

Janice looked at the four cigarette butts in her hand and unfolded one slowly. She squeezed her lips together tightly holding the fag in the corner of her mouth before lighting it. Kicking her legs against the wall she hummed a tune. Janice was sat in deep thought when she saw a light flicker across the road in her parent's house. She could see the silhouette of a man stood near the window. "Dad," she whispered under her breath as she watched with eager eyes. Her heart melted and her jaw dropped low. Janice stood up and wobbled over the road, swaying about, pissed as per usual. She needed help and if anyone could help her it was her father. He was her last hope. Sneaking up the garden path she edged closer to the living room window doing her best to keep out of sight. She could see him now; she could see her dad sat in his armchair with his head held in his hands. Ted had never been a good sleeper and if anything was lying heavily on his mind he'd toss and turn all night long. Perhaps, he'd got up to make a warm drink; he usually had hot milk when he was restless. Janice pressed her cold lips onto the glass and held her flat palm against the window, she closed her eyes. The years had passed and words had been said between them both; horrible, sick, hurtful words. She'd wished him dead and told him to rot in hell for all she cared. Janice wished she could turn back time and right the wrongs in her life. She held so many regrets about how things had turned out. Her dad had been her best friend at one point in her life, she told him everything, she trusted him. He was her hero and she was his princess, she could do nothing wrong in his eyes. The Square had changed Janice Goodman and everything was lost from the very first moment she stepped foot onto it. It was an evil place that held so many dark, spine-chilling secrets that few ever spoke about.

Janice inhaled deeply and was ready to knock on the window to get his attention. But, where was her mother, the old battleaxe. Was she downstairs too or was she asleep upstairs? She wasn't ready to face her too, one step at a time. Janice tapped her fingers on the glass and stood back to watch. Ted heard the noise and his head twisted about the room like a barn owl. He was hard of hearing and Pat was always telling him to get a hearing aid. She called him cloth ears as he struggled to hear anything unless it was up close. Janice kicked her foot into the ground in frustration. She could see Ted still sat down in the living room, oblivious to her being outside. This was it, she was going to give it one last go and if he didn't hear her this time she was getting off. It was a bad idea anyway, what was she even thinking. Janice casually knocked on the window again but this time it was loud and Ted heard her. She watched him head towards the front door dressed in his dressing gown and his tartan slippers. Janice prepared herself, she was making her way to the front door to meet him. It was do or die time.

Ted stood at the door and his eyes squeezed tightly together as he tried to focus. "Who's out there," he growled. "Come on, show yourself before I ring the bleeding police. I'm not scared of you you know. I'll rip your bleeding head off if I find you." Ted was the neighbourhood watch man in the area and his vigilance had helped him capture many active criminals. A plant pot his wife called him, he never missed a trick he was always up at the window peeping outside in search of criminals. Ted stepped out of the front door and tied his belt around his waist. He was a have a go hero and he still thought he could have a fight. In his day he used to train hard at the gym but lately his ailments had curbed his thirst for a toned fit body. He repeated himself but this time he was louder. "I said is anyone out there?" Ted stood scanning the area, neck stretching down the garden path.

Janice was nervous, her feet seemed glued to the floor, she couldn't move. She could see him from where she stood too. Swallowing hard she moved forward. "Hello dad, it's me Janice." Ted held a flat palm to his chest and his legs nearly buckled from underneath him. He was speechless and his jaw was swinging low. "Dad, it's me Janice," she repeated.

Ted shook his head and his eyes clouded over as he saw her for the first time. She'd taken his breath away and he was in complete shock. Checking over his shoulder he made sure his wife was still in bed and the commotion hadn't woken her. "Janice, what the bleeding hell are you doing here? You know if your mother sees you she'll have your guts for garters. You need to leave. Go on, piss off, you're not welcome here."

Seeing her father after all this time really got to Janice. He was old now, hair thinning, deep set wrinkles all over his forehead. Her emotions kicked in and there was no way she could stop the tears from flowing. She needed somebody to talk to, someone to help her. "Dad please listen to me. It's Alice, they've taken her."

Ted stood frozen, he loved his grandchild but as for her mother, he couldn't forget the heartache she'd caused him in the past. The money she'd stolen from him, the tears he'd cried, the times he'd stood up for her and she let him down. Janice moved closer to him, she could smell his aftershave. Ted always wore the same one for years, a man of habit he was. "Aramis" was his favourite aftershave and every time she smelt it, it reminded her of him. Ted's face creased at both sides. There was so much pain in his heart and he was struggling to breathe, his emotions were strangling his windpipe. He stared at his daughter for a few seconds and his heart sank. She looked like a woman twice her age, with greasy shoulder length hair, spotty complexion and she stank of stale alcohol and tobacco. Taking his time to digest what she'd just said he ragged his fingers through his hair. He knew what she was capable of and knew given the chance she would have had his eye sockets away at the drop of a hat. She was a cunning cow; sly, deceitful and he didn't trust her as far as he could throw her.

"What's wrong with Alice? Who's taken her?" he said at last.

Janice was hyperventilating; she gripped her hands around her throat and pushed her fingers deep into her skin. "Social services have taken her and they won't give her back to me."

Ted realised Janice needed help, she was going to have a heart attack. Without thinking further he took her by the arm and led her into the house. Once he'd sat down he ran into the kitchen to get her a cold drink of water. "Fuck, fuck," he mumbled as he searched for a glass. He had to be quick before his daughter started rooting around the house for something to have away. Janice sat with her head hung between her legs. She'd not eaten for days and any money she'd had was spent on drugs and booze. Ted stumbled back into the front room and passed her the glass of water. Sweat was pouring from her and even when she took the glass from his hand he could feel her warm sweaty palms. Janice dipped her fingers in the glass and wet them, she placed them on her forehead and tried to cool down. Her cheeks were on fire. Ted was edgy and his eyes were constantly on the door. If Pat found her here she would knock ten tons of shit out of Janice. She wasn't as forgiving as him and she would have never allowed her inside her home no matter what.

Ted sat on the arm of the chair watching her. "Why are you out at this time of night, there are some sick bastards walking the streets at this hour. You should be at home in bed."

Janice lifted her head slowly, her pupils were dilated and he knew straight away she was stoned. "Dad, can you help me. I'll never ask you for anything again. Just help me get her back, please just this one last thing."

Ted licked his lips slowly. Was she lying? Was she trying to have him over? What was the real reason she was here? It wouldn't have been the first time she'd come up with some cock and bull story to get what she wanted. The list was endless. Ted spoke in a low voice still unsure if she was lying or not. "There must be a reason why they've taken her Janice. Social services don't just get involved unless they have reason to believe she's in danger."

Ted knew the life Alice was living and in his heart he was glad his granddaughter was now safe. He knew all about the kid being starved most days and he also knew about Janice and her list of endless men. Dead beats the lot of them, none of them were worth a wank. Everyone knew about Janice in the area, she was the talk of the town, a cheap dirty slapper who would spread her legs for anyone offering a few quid. Ted had had many a fight in his local boozer regarding his daughter and her filthy habits. The lads knew she was his weak spot and whenever they'd had a few beers they always brought her into the conversation. Ted wasn't a big drinker anymore, he kept away from the pub and many of the friends he'd made over the years. He couldn't stand that they knew he'd failed as a father. Janice sat forward in her chair, playing with the cuff from her stinking coat. She had bad body odour and she was stinking the house out. "They said they had a phone call from someone saying she was at risk. Come on dad, even you know she's never been at risk, I looked after her. I tried my best."

Ted blew a laboured breath and sighed, he'd heard enough of her bullshit. He snapped, why should he agree with her, he owed her nothing. He told her the truth and held nothing back. "She's been at risk for bleeding years love, come on, we all know that. You've neglected our Alice and put your own drug addiction first. That kid has had fuck all off you. No love, no stability, fucking nothing."

Janice's eyes were wide open. His words shocked her, she wasn't that bad. She did love her daughter and she cared for her in her own way, everybody knew that surely? "Dad, don't say things like that. You know more than anyone how much I love her. I always have. It's just sometimes I go off the rails a bit, not all the time though."

Ted was giving it out now and his words were firm. "You loved yourself Janice and that kid has suffered every day because of it. Don't you think that I've sat here and watched her when she's been here? There's so much pain in her eyes and I know that look because I have the same look in my eyes too. Yeah, you broke me in two, left me with nothing except a broken bleeding heart."

Janice broke down crying. These were real tears for once – she'd been presented with the truth. She fell to her knees and held her hands out to her father. "She said she's been abused too."Ted froze, the colour drained from him and he ran from the room retching into his cupped hands. Janice could hear running water in the kitchen and she tried to stand to her feet to go and see if her father was alright. Hands on the floor she pressed hard trying to get up to her feet. Her eyes shot to the bare toes on the floor in front of her, red painting thick toenails staring at her. Janice looked up slowly and there she was, growling at her, ready to pounce on her, her mother.

Pat bent down and gripped Janice by the scruff of the neck. "Get your flea bitten arse out of my house. How dare you step a foot inside my door. How many times have you been told that you're not welcome here? You're a dirty drug addict who's got no morals. Get out of my house now before I drag you out by every hair on your bastard head. Go on, get out!"

Janice scrambled to her feet as Ted came back into the living room. He held the top of Pat's shoulder and pressed his fingers deep into her collar bone. "Pat, just be quiet for a second. Just listen to what she has to say. It's our Alice, social services have taken her. She said she's been abused."

Pat ran at Janice and grabbed her by her hair. "You dirty cow, you dirty slut. How could you let someone do that to your own flesh and blood? I should have known this would happen. Oh my Lord above, you knock me sick. Ted !! Get her out of here now."

"Mother, I didn't know anything. I swear to you. I never knew. She never told me anything. If she did, I would have done something about it. I would have stabbed the cunt, I swear to you."

Pat paced the front room gagging for breath. "You won't know fuck all about her when you're off your head will you? Didn't I say to you Ted that our Alice wasn't safe living there with her? Didn't I say something was going to happen?"

Janice was trying to calm Pat down. She didn't want to fight with her anymore she needed her on side. "Mam, please help me. I'm nothing without her. I'll change. I'll get help. I'll sort myself out, please believe me."

Pat ran for her fags, she was chain a smoker and any sign of stress and she smoked like a chimney. She collapsed into her chair and crossed her legs tightly jerking them in front of her. Her face was stern as she took a deep drag from her cigarette. She growled at Janice and made sure she heard her. "I was the one who rang social services on you. Alice deserves better in life and I'm not sitting back here watching her lead the life she was living. The poor girl has nothing. I'm glad they took her. I'll sleep better at night now knowing she's nowhere near you. Fucking scum you are."

Janice gritted her teeth together tightly, she was a ticking bomb. Her fists curled into two tiny balls at the side of her legs, she was ready to let rip. She was doing the only thing she knew how to when the chips were down, she was ready to fight. Ted saw the signs and pushed her back down into her seat with his hand against her head. "There will be no scrapping in this house lady. Have some bleeding respect will you."

Pat's eyes were wide open and she was ready to scratch her eyeballs out too. They were two of a kind, they both had a temper on them. "Ted, let the silly bitch do whatever she wants. I'm used to the way she is by now. There's no respect, nothing ever changes. Let her do what she's doing. If she lays one finger on me and I'll have her arrested again. See how she likes that ay," she shot a look at Janice and spoke with a sarcastic tone. "She'll be rattling, sat in the cells for hours. She'll be begging for drugs. Go on, let's see how long you last smart arse."

Janice stood hovering; she had no fight left in her. Something had changed; she ran to her mother's side and broke down crying. "I'm sorry. I'm so sorry for everything I've done. I know you don't believe me, but honest, I'll do anything to get Alice back. Please believe me."

Pat had heard it all before, it was the same shit just a different day to her. If she had a pound for every time Janice had promised her she'd change she would have been a rich woman. Her heart was numb and she was immune to any bullshit Janice was throwing at her. Ted however, he was different; he always saw the best in people and wanted to believe her, give her the benefit of the doubt. He hugged the pair of them close and screamed at the top of his voice. He was at breaking point. "No more, just no more fucking fighting. I can't take it anymore. It's killing me." Ted was crying, he was a grown man falling apart, sinking to his knees, unable to go on. "I've had enough. I want some peace in my life, just a bit of bleeding normality, is that too much to ask?"

Pat hated to see her husband upset, he was always her rock and never broke down. She owed it to him to quieten down. Pat started to calm down for his sake. She sat facing Janice and Ted was sat near them both just in case it kicked off again. And, it could of you know, they were both short-tempered. At the drop of a hat they could have switched and clawed each other's eyes out. Pat licked her dry cracked lips "Ted, will you get me a glass of brandy please, make it a large one. I need it to calm my nerves." Janice was just about to request one too when Pat stopped her dead in her tracks. "Don't even think about asking for a drop either. As long as you're sat in my house the strongest thing you can have is a bleeding wine gum." Pat still had her sense of humour, despite everything that had gone on in her life, she'd never lost that. Ted passed Pat a tall glass of brandy. Janice sat licking her lips as she watched her knock back a large mouthful. "Can I have a cigarette please mam? I've been smoking these but they're burning my mouth." She opened her hands and revealed the squashed cigarette butts in her palm.

Pat sighed and shook her head. "Fucking disgusting, what are you now, a bleeding dimp- picker. Didn't I tell you you'd end up with nothing, and look," she pointed her finger at Janice and waved it about. "I was right. God, you've let yourself go. I mean, at least you used to have a bit of dignity, but look at you now, a bleeding disgrace. A stinking sweaty skank." Pat was never one to hold back her words and she was a straight shooter, right from the hip. Ted coughed and reminded Pat about sorting things out. He wanted answers too; there were so many questions he needed to ask his daughter. Pat was the one who got the ball rolling. She's waited a long time for this day. "So come on, you owe us an explanation. We gave you everything, you wanted for nothing. I could understand if you were mistreated or had fuck all but you had everything. Come on, I've waited years for this day. You owe us the truth. Start bleeding talking."

Janice sank her head in shame. The things she'd done over the years came flooding back. Her shoulders hunched over, she thought about her life. And, there were bad things, dark secrets she could never reveal to her parents, never. They were just too bad. Janice was a prisoner to drugs, they were her master. She just didn't function without them, she didn't feel normal. "Mam, I just got mixed up in so much shit in a world I knew nothing about. Before I realised how bad it was getting. I was in too deep."

Pat just couldn't be quiet she had to say something, years of frustration just pumped out her. "We were here for you. We would have helped, but you pushed us away, abandoned us. For crying out loud you came home pregnant at fifteen years of age and wouldn't tell us who the father was, even to this day we don't know his name. Are you going to come clean now and tell us the truth? For once in your life tell us the fucking truth. Go on, how hard is it?" Pat popped a cigarette into her mouth and threw one over to Janice. "Here, get a cig before you start and calm yourself down. Look at you, are you withdrawing from drugs or something?"

Janice sucked hard on her fag, both cheeks sinking in at the sides. Her fingers were yellow at the end and Pat shook her head when she clocked them. Her parents were listening now, hanging on her every word. "I was a good girl when I first went onto the square. It was him, Martin Jones who made me the way I am. At first, he was in love with me or so he said and he kept buying me gifts to show me his undying love for me. All the girls fancied him, but do you know what, he wanted me."

Ted sat back in his chair and he held a proud look in his eye. "And, so he bloody well should, you were lovely. Stunning you were, everyone always said so."

Pat hissed at him and blew a laboured breath. "Ted, this isn't the time or place to be reminiscing about days gone by. This is serious."

Ted sighed. "I was just saying that's all Pat, she was so innocent and pretty. She had a look of you."

Janice smirked over at her dad, he always had her back when she was younger and despite everything that had happened he was still fighting her corner in his own way. "Right, can she carry on Ted. I want to go back to bed. I've not got all bleeding night."

Janice played with the dangling thread from her tattered coat, not once did she lift her eyes up. She knew this story should have been told to her parents years ago and she regretted she'd never told them. "Martin Jones told me I needed nobody but him, he said he would give me everything I could ever dream of having. And, he did dad. I swear, he looked after me at first. All the girls on the square were jealous of me and I was so proud to call him my boyfriend. I loved him so much, he was my world."

Pat shook her head. "Love, you didn't know what love was at that age, fifteen years of age you were, a bleeding child. What did you know about love?"

Janice retaliated. "I knew that my heart skipped a beat every time I saw him, every time he kissed me my legs melted away. That is love isn't it? I know it was or at least I thought it was. He was my life and I let him get inside my head. At first, I was so happy but as the time passed away the cracks began to show." Ted was gripped by the whole story he sat on the edge of his seat cracking his knuckles. Janice swallowed hard and dipped her head low. "He gave me the drugs you know. He made me believe I needed them to chill out. He said I was a stress head and I was ruining our relationship," she paused and looked directly at her mother. "I was stressed because I knew he was seeing one of the other girls behind my back. When I confronted him he never denied it, he just told me straight that he needed sex and if I wasn't giving it to him he was going to get it somewhere else. I loved him dad. I couldn't stand that he was slipping away from me. I had no other option than to sleep with him."

Ted smashed his fist onto the side of the sofa and a cloud of dust rose up in the air. "You did have a choice. I wish I would have known. I'd have cut his dick off and shoved it up his arse for treating you like that. How old was he anyway, he was older than you wasn't he?"

Pat folded her arms tightly across her chest. "Yes, he was older than her and he should have known better. Liberty taker he was preying on young girls."

Even to this day Janice wouldn't have a word said against him. She was under some kind of spell that he'd cast upon her. "He started to hurt me, hit me, make me cry after a while. I'd done everything for him to make him happy, I even slept with him but that was never enough. He just plied me with drugs and left me on my own. That's when I started drinking. The guy in the shop knew I was underage but he liked me and always supplied me with what I needed to get wrecked. When I was twisted, I felt good, numb, nobody could hurt me then."

Ted was in tears as he listened to his daughter pouring her heart out. He never knew the half of it; he just thought she was going off the rails. He had no idea that she was being abused by her boyfriend. Domestic violence was something he associated with married couples, people who'd been together for years. He wasn't aware that it could start so young in a woman's life. Janice licked her lips slowly. "He put me in the boot of his car once and locked me away there for hours. He said I was paranoid and I should learn my lesson for asking too many questions. When he finally let me out he nearly killed me. I swear if the shopkeeper hadn't saved me I would have been a gonner."

Pat was on the fence with all this, was this the truth or just something she was making up to get a bit of sympathy. "What and nobody ever helped you on the square? You had friends didn't you; surely they would have told you to cart him, to see sense."

"Mam, Martin Jones was the main man there, nobody messed with him, he was evil, fucking disturbed in the head."

Pat delved deeper wanting to know the ins and outs of a cat's arsehole. "So, what happened when he knew you were pregnant, did he want the baby, did he want to try again?"

"No, he told me he wished I'd died in childbirth. He got with my best friend then and completely blanked me. He said when the baby was born he would sort me out but he told me to never contact him again and he said he'd kill me if I told his new girlfriend the baby was his."

Ted was bouncing about the front room now, cracking his knuckles, wanting to rip somebody's head off. "What a fucking wanker! Why didn't you say something to me? I know a few lads who would have put a stop to him. Put him in a body bag. I do you know, I'm not lying. I've had dealings with some very dangerous men in the past, murderers, people who will do anything to earn a few quid. That's straight up, no word of a lie." Ted was on one now mumbling under his breath, swinging punches about in the air.

Pat was watching her daughter carefully. Perhaps this might have been the truth, she didn't know if she believed her or not. Anyway, what did it matter now, the past was in the past and nothing could be changed. It was obvious Janice was holding something back, she had more to say about the story but she just couldn't tell them. Pat turned to the present. "Well, so now we know about you. Let's talk about Alice, she's my main concern here, not you and your fucked up life."

Janice had some colour back in her cheeks now, she looked like the worries of the world had been lifted from her shoulders and somebody had listened to her. She'd always wanted to confess to her parents the truth about what had happened in her youth but she was young back then, challenging, rebellious and she didn't care about anyone but herself.

Janice swallowed hard, she'd had some reports from the social services and she relayed them to her mother with caution. "She said Darren was a nonce and old Dave too. Alice said they'd touched her, done bad things to her." Janice was heaving now, green looking and looked like she was going to pass out. She looked her mother directly in her eyes. "I would have known if anything suss was going on, why would they do that to her? I don't know what to believe anymore. My head's done in with it all."

Pat seen her arse and she wanted to throttle her daughter. Why was she even doubting her own flesh and blood. "You believe your bleeding daughter. Don't you ever say she's making this up! Do you know what, I should rip your fucking head off for letting this happen. Poor Alice, my poor girl. How must she be feeling? I should have done something sooner. I should have put you six foot under you worthless piece of shit."

Ted was bright red. His blood pressure was up and he ran to the drawer to find his tablets. Turning his head slowly he gasped for breath. "I'll have that Darren sorted out. I know where the dirty cunt drinks. I'll teach him to mess with little girls, the dirty bastard."

Pat was white, she felt guilty about not doing anything sooner. Looking at Janice she stood up and poked her finger into the side of her head, ramming at it, causing her pain. "You're nothing but a daft twat. How could you let this happen? She'll be ruined now you know, her head will be messed up and it's all your fault. You weren't just happy with destroying your own life was you?"

"Mam, I've come here for help. I've got nobody else to help me. You're my last hope," Janice shrieked.

Pat stood back and placed her hands on her hips. Ted was standing close to her ready to grab her if she started to lash out. "I care about Alice and I'll do my best to make sure she's alright. But as for you," she paused and made sure Ted was listening. If he wasn't backing her he could leave with her too. "You can rot in hell. You had your chance with us. For years you've caused us nothing but misery, but no more. You're dead as far as I'm concerned. I'll never forgive you for this. Now take your skanky bony arse and go and crawl back under whichever rock you crawled out from. Ted, show her out. And, don't you ever darken my door again."

Ted knew which side he was batting for, there was no way he was disagreeing with his wife. In his heart he knew she was right and even though he wanted the family to come back together he knew it would never happen. With a lump in his throat he showed Janice to the door. Pat collapsed into the chair and her heart broke. First thing in the morning she was going to find her grandchild, she would do whatever it took to make sure she was never in any danger again.

Ted stood at the door and peeled Janice's fingers from his arm. "Dad, speak to her will you. I'm not the same person I was. Trust me, I'll never let you down again, please, just go and talk with her. I'll wait here. Dad, don't turn your back on me when I need you." Ted made one of the hardest decisions of his life and turned his back on her. He slammed the door shut and slid the bolt along the top of the door. Holding his back against the wall in the hallway he sobbed. Janice pressed her mouth through the letterbox and pleaded with him, she could see his feet. "Dad, don't give up on me please."

Pat ran into the hallway and banged her fist onto the door. "Fuck off, leave us alone. If you're staying there I'm ringing the police, go on piss off."

Janice knew not to stay around. She smashed the letterbox hard against the door and scrambled to her feet. "I'll show you, I'll show you all," she screamed as she left the garden.

Pat ran to her husband's side and cradled him in her arms. She had to be the strong one now, he was inconsolable. "Sssshhh Ted. Come on now. We'll sort this out. We'll make sure Alice is alright. Nobody will hurt her again."

Janice headed home to her empty house. It was pissing down, big fat blobs of water falling from the sky. She shivered as she ran down the main road. Cars honked their horns at her as she weaved in and out of the traffic; she had a death wish for sure.

Opening the front door she ripped her wet coat off and flung it on the floor. Running upstairs she stood outside Alice's bedroom and gripped the handle on the door. She was scared; petrified to open the door and see that her daughter was gone. Slowly she pulled the handle down. She melted to the floor as her eyes met the empty bed. Crawling over to the other side of the room she dropped onto the bed. Janice cried here eyes out, sobbed her heart out. "I'm sorry Alice." Pulling the crusty blankets over her head she hid away from the world, she wished herself dead, to never wake up again. Life was hard for her and the days ahead were full of sadness and misery, she needed a miracle to happen, a bleeding big massive miracle.

CHAPTER SEVEN

lice was awake, she'd had her eyes open for ages just lying there staring into space. Her stomach was churning and something didn't feel right, she was nervous, jittery. Sharon was in the other bed not too far from her and she was yawning. She stretched her arms over her head as she tried to relax. Alice wasn't good at making friends and she'd never been a big talker, her confidence was low and she lacked self belief. Sharon threw a sock over at Alice's bed to get her attention. "Oi, shit the bed, what time have you been up since?" Sharon chuckled as she folded her pillow behind her. She looped her hands just over her head and shot a look over to Alice. "Bleeding hell, you don't say a lot do you? I hope you're not one of them mental cases. I'll go mad at Christine if she's put a crank in here with me." Sharon was so old-headed; she spoke like a woman twice her age.

Alice snarled over at her, who was she calling mental? There was no way she was having this. She hated being labelled an oddball. "I've just opened my eyes haven't I? What do I need to talk about anyway, there's nothing to say?"

Sharon's back was up, she was only trying to have a bit of conversation with her. "Whoa there, Mrs hormonal. I was just saying that's all. There's no need to bite my head off. Relax, and take a chill pill."

Alice retaliated. "Well, don't call me mental then. I'm not much of a talker that's all, so you'll have to be patient with me. What do you want to talk about anyway?"

Sharon sucked hard on her gums. "Nothing really, I just like talking," she rubbed at her stomach. "I'm starving. I hope Doris has got some bacon on the menu today. I've had porridge now for three days. I'm sick to death of it. Do you like porridge?"

Alice rolled on her side and rested her head on her folded arms. She'd never tasted it before and the most she'd ever had for breakfast was a piece of toast, well, that's if there was any bread in the cupboard. She answered her softly. "I don't know if I like it to be honest with you. I've never tasted it before."

Sharon sniggered and kept a low voice. "It's minging trust me. It tastes like mush, thick, stodgy white muck, like a pile of sick. But don't tell Doris I said that though, she'll go off her trolley if she thinks I've been slagging her food off."

Alice was starting to relax and it was nice to have someone her own age to talk to. "How long have you been here Sharon?"

Sharon had bright ginger hair and freckles, she had so many freckles scattered about her face that you couldn't put a pin between them. Sharon had pale skin, like vanilla ice-cream and the biggest green eyes she'd ever seen in her life. She wasn't pretty; she was plump and had an ugly mush, like a bulldog chewing a wasp. "I've been here for two months now. I've been in care though since I was fourteen years old, so all in all," she held a finger to her mouth thinking. "About a year or thereabouts in the care system."

Alice sat up and held her back against the wall. She pulled the blanket up and wrapped it around her shoulders. "Why are you in care? You don't have to tell me if you don't want to?"

Sharon sighed and chuckled. "I'm not arsed who knows why I'm in care. It's life isn't it? Shit happens and we have to deal with it the best we can." Alice liked her outlook on life and smiled over at her. Sharon rolled on her side and played with her hair, twisting and turning it, it was like a fox's tail, big and bushy. "It was my dad, he was ill. Depression he had, bad mood swings and all that. He was a bit nutty at times. My mam just walked out on us when I was two years old so it was only my old man we had to care for us. My brother's in care too but he's got a foster home now in Stockport, so hopefully he'll get adopted or at least they will keep him until he's old enough to leave."

Alice looked concerned. "Why aren't you two together, how can they split you up when you're brother and sister, that's not right is it?"

Sharon sighed and rubbed her finger slowly across her lip, it was dry and chapped. "I wasn't bothered at first but getting a good foster home is like winning the lottery in places like this. They only wanted a boy as the family had girls of their own, so I had to take it on the chin and let him go. He needs a family more than me anyway. I'm not arsed any more I just get on with it. Anyway, that's enough about me, what's your story?"

Alice was tongue-tied, what was her story? Was she going to tell her the truth, the whole truth or just make something up? Her life was her business and nobody else's. She didn't want people judging her when they didn't even know her, she lied. "Same as you except it was my mother who was depressed. As for my father I don't even know who he is. One day my mother tells me he's dead and buried and the next she said she would tell me when I was older. I still don't know the truth; she just messes with my head. I'm not bothered who my dad is anyway. I've never had one, so I'll never miss one will I?"

Sharon giggled. "Mad isn't it how life can turn out. At least you have your looks, where as me, you don't have to tell me I'm no oil painting. I just hope my personality is big enough for someone to love me in the future." Alice shook her head slowly. This was such a shame. How could Sharon be saying things like this about herself? Alright, she wasn't the prettiest of girls but there was something about her that was pleasing to the eye. Sharon jumped out of bed. "Come on I'll take you to meet the other girls. Some of them are right bitches so just keep away from them ones."

Alice popped her pale legs out of bed and she was shivering. Sharon threw a housecoat over to her and chuckled. "Here, get that on frozen arse. They'll sort you out some clobber later. It usually takes a few days but you'll get a grant for some new clothes and toiletries." Alice didn't know if she was kidding or not. Why would they give her money? They didn't even know her. They weren't her family. She put the housecoat on and followed Sharon out of the door.

There were girls chatting and pots and pans were being clashed together as they walked into the kitchen. There was silence and an awkward moment as all eyes were on the new girl. Alice found a space at the table and sat down. It didn't take long for mouth almighty to start either, she was a right gobshite and Sharon sat snarling at her. Annie Hargreaves was as rough as they come, she thought she was black the way she talked and as she looked over at Alice she flicked her two fingers together. "Yo Sharon, who's the new bitch?"

Doris heard her from the other side of the room and stopped what she was doing. "Annie, what have I told you about the way you speak to people. Alice is new here and you're probably putting the fear of God in her already. Speak to her properly and stop talking like a bleeding gangster." Doris had her back up, every day this girl was pushing her buttons and she was at the end of her tether. She really wanted to slap her one, big mouthed cow she was.

"I'm just asking that's all Doris. Wind your neck in and get cooking me some pukka grub. Can't you see this girl is wasting away here?"

A few others laughed at Annie's remark to Doris, arse-lickers they were. The kind of girls who laughed when she laughed, they were brown-nosers. Doris walked back to the stove and shook her head, she was mumbling under her breath. Alice was bright red and this Annie girl was just staring at her waiting for an answer. "Derr, do you have a name then or what?" Sharon dropped her head; there was no way she was getting involved. The last time she'd opened her mouth to Annie she got a slap right in the gob, lip bleeding and everything. Alice was on her own, she had no back up.

"I'm Alice," she answered in a low voice.

Annie slammed her hand on the table making sure she held everyone's attention. "What's your name again, Alice in fucking wonderland," Annie chuckled loudly and she turned her head to make sure Doris hadn't heard her. Who did this girl think she was Bernard Manning?

Alice felt her temper boiling and she could feel her fist curling up under the table. She had to stop her, put her in her place. Before she knew it words just leapt from her mouth.

"And, who are you Arsehole Annie?"

Oh the shit was going to hit the fan now. Nobody had ever stood up to this girl, she had her reputation at stake and she wasn't taking this lying down, no way. "Ay, fucking have a go hero. I'd button it if I was you. Do you want to sort this out later or what?" Annie shot her eyes over to Doris who was singing and unaware of the commotion behind her.

Alice was on the spot, what the hell had she got herself into. It was her temper you see, once she got to this point she couldn't let it go. Her face creased and from nowhere she stood up and leant over the table. "Never mind later, let's have it now. I'm not scared of you. You're a bully."

Sharon had to do something, Alice was a new girl and she wasn't doing herself any favours. Annie threw a piece of toast over at her and she was ready to fight. To kick her head in, to batter her in front of everyone to show her who was the boss. Sharon pulled Alice back and looked over at Annie in desperation. "Orr, don't be starting on her Annie. She's new here, just give her a break. You know yourself how it feels to be the new girl. I'll have a word with her and sort her out."

Annie sat back down, this was her excuse not to fight and her reputation was still intact. "You'd better had Sharon. She's lucky you're here with her otherwise I would have ripped her head off."

The girl next to Annie patted her arm and spoke to the other girls. "And, you know what Annie's like when she snaps Sharon, she's a right head the ball."

"Okay, okay, just let's have breakfast and I'll sort things out." Sharon sighed.

Alice sat back in her seat and her breathing was returning to normal, she was white and her nostrils flared wide. Doris placed some bacon and eggs on the table and everybody was grabbing at it. It was like feeding time at the zoo, what a load of starvers they were, gannets. Alice wasn't eating anything and Sharon leaned over and got her some food to put on her plate. She covered her mouth and whispered to her. "For crying out loud girl. You don't want to make an enemy out of Annie Hargreaves. Just get some food down your neck and let's do one. I need to fill you in on how things work around here. Phew, you need to know about the pecking order."

Alice placed some bacon in her mouth, salty, crispy strips. The food tasted strange to her, she'd had bacon at her nanas house in the past but that was months ago. She sat munching it, chewing on it, enjoying all the flavours dancing around on her tongue. The other girls were talking and every now and then Alice locked eyes with Annie across the table. This battle was far from over. The worst was yet to come. The girls finished eating within minutes and none of them were waiting around. One by one they headed back to their rooms to get ready for the day ahead.

Christine came into the dining area now and she made a beeline for Alice. Her feet clipped along the vinyl floor. "Good morning, how are you finding things, I hope Sharon has been looking after you?" Alice didn't have much to say, she was still thinking about the top girl here and how she would deal with her. Alice was strong; she was used to getting hammered by her mother when she was pissed so she knew she could take a good hiding if the worse come to the worse. Time would tell, but there was no way she was backing down. She was sick of being the underdog and people walking all over her. Christine started talking. "I've had a word with the team Alice and I'll have some money for you this afternoon. You can go and get some new clothes and the stuff you need, you know, girly stuff."

Sharon nudged her in the waist and chuckled. "Told you didn't I. I'll come shopping with you, if they let me that is."

Alice was coming round now and the colour was returning to her cheeks. "Thanks Christine. Will I be staying here for a long time?" Alice asked.

Christine held a concerned look in her eye. Alice had only spent one night here and already she was asking when she was leaving, something was going on, surely. Christine studied her for a few seconds and touched her hand softly, she was a right touchy feely person, always hugging and kissing people, invading their personal space. A bit over the top really but she was harmless. "It's early days yet sweetheart. Just give it time and you'll be happy here once you've settled down. Sharon, you tell her how you were when you first came here." Sharon didn't even get time to answer her. Christine was a right gasbag and she continued talking. "Sharon was a loner for days; we couldn't get a word out of her. Honest to God, it was like getting blood out of a stone."

Sharon jumped into the conversation, she was annoyed. "I wasn't a loner Christine. I just took time to get used to people that's all. Bloody hell, you're making me out like I was a non-coper."

Christine hugged her and smiled. "Orrr, you know what I mean darling. You know I love you to death really." Christine was forgiven and she watched as the two of them walked out of the kitchen. As soon as they left she walked over to Doris who was stood washing some pots. "How did Alice go on this morning, was everything alright with her?"

Doris dried her hands on a pot-towel and rubbed her damp hands on her jeans at the front. She made sure nobody was in the room with them and spoke. "Annie was having a pop at her. I told her straight to zip it but we both know she's nothing but trouble that one. She really does my head in you know. I know she's had a hard time too but she doesn't make things easy for herself. It's like she's pressed the self-destruct button and all she wants is violence, to fight, to smash someone's head in, twenty-four seven."

Christine leant back on the kitchen side and folded her arms. "You get that sometimes with the girls in here. It's like they want everyone else to hate them too, just because they're not happy inside. I've put Annie's name forward for some anger management classes but the way she's heading she'll be in big trouble before she even goes on them."

Doris held nothing back and her views were firm. "She needs bringing down a peg or two she does, a good kick up the arse. She has the girls running around her like flies around shit. And, the girls do it too, what's all that about? They treat her like bloody royalty."

Christine flicked the switch for the kettle. Doris was angry and she needed a quick cuppa to take the edge of things. The care home was a hard place to work. Each day brought a new challenge to the workers here. Girls addicted to drugs, girls who had been raped. You name it they had it there, even prostitutes and drug dealers. Doris had been working at the home for over six years but every now and then the job got the better of her. Stress came with this kind of work and everyone working here had their own amount to deal with. Yes, they had team meeting and ways to cope with the stress but that still didn't stop them wanting to punch someone's lights out that was constantly doing their head in. These people were normal human beings. Doris had a family of her own, two boys and three girls. They were all grown up now though and she'd always made sure they had respect for the people they spoke to. Perhaps, this is why she was finding it hard to understand some of the girls and their bad attitudes.

"Shall we have a couple of chocolate biscuits Doris with our brew? I know you're dieting but you deserve a treat for all your hard work."

Doris inhaled deeply and her rant was over. "I do work hard don't I Christine. Go on then, I will have a treat. In fact make it four biscuits. I've worked my bleeding socks off this morning." They sat giggling. They were great friends and both had helped each other out in times of need. When Christine was upset about not being able to have children Doris sat with her for hours consoling her telling her everything would be alright. That's how it worked in the home; they all had each other's back.

Doris sat munching on her biscuits, licking her fingers, sucking the thick creamy dark chocolate off the top of it. "Do me a favour Doris, just keep your eyes and ears open around here for a few days and see what the script is with Alice. I just get a feeling that something is going on. It might just be me, but just keep your eyes open anyway."

Sharon sat on her bed and watched Alice combing her thick dark hair. She had lovely hair but all she ever did with it was shove it back in a ponytail. Sharon loved being creative and stood up looking at Alice. "Give me the brush and I'll do you a style. I'm pretty good at hairstyles. Just let me get my clips."

Alice sat on the edge of her bed and pulled the bobble out of her hair. "I don't ever do anything different with this mop. Ponytails are all I know how to do."

Sharon got everything she needed and started to clip pieces of hair back from Alice's face. "Orr don't take it all from the front, it's my comfort blanket. I hide behind it when I can't be arsed with people."

Sharon sniggered. "Sssshhh, while the master is at work. I'll leave you a bit of hair at the front but stop stressing until I've finished. You have a lovely face you should want to show it off." Alice dipped her head. She twiddled her thumbs and swallowed hard. Nobody had ever called her pretty before. Her heart melted and for the first time ever she felt like she had a friend. Sharon was spraying hair spray all over the style she'd created. Alice was choking as the mist dropped onto her skin.

The bedroom door opened slowly and there she was, stood tall, Annie Hargreaves. "So, what's going down then Alice? Are we going to sort this shit out or what. Nobody speaks to me like you just did." Sharon slowly backed off and moved to her own bed. If she could have got

out of the door she would have ran for help but her exit
was blocked by the other girls stood at the door. "Well,"
Annie hissed. Alice turned to face her and just stared at
her, she never blinked once, it was spooky. Annie was
getting frustrated but for some reason she never moved.
There was something about this new girl that she wasn't
sure about. The other girls in the home just gave into
her straight away but this girl had balls, big ones at that.
Alice had always been taught that you needed to stand up
to bullies and in the past she'd smacked one right in the
eye for trying to belittle her. Alice licked her lips slowly
.Perhaps, if she wasted her she would be the new top girl
in the home, Queen of the castle. Did she really want that
though, to be disliked, to take advantage of the weaker
people around her? But, to sit back and let this girl make
a show of her, no, her mind was made up. She was ready
to fight. Sharon sat on her bed chewing her fingernails,
her chest rising frantically. Alice's bed creaked as she stood
up. Sharon closed her eyes and shook her head. She made
the sign of the cross across herself and prayed her friend
would still be breathing at the end of this.

"Listen Annie, you started this. You don't even know
me yet you were having a go at me. If you want to get
it on then let's do it. Like I've said to you before, you
don't scare me." Annie had no other option, she was being
watched by everyone, to walk away she'd be classed as a
shit-bag, a yellow-belly, she had to fight. Annie bounced
over towards Alice and they were nose to nose pushing
each other. From nowhere Alice swung her fist around
and jawed Annie. What a knockout blow this was, she'd
put her on her arse. There was giggling from the doorway
from the other girls. They were whispering, sniggering.

Annie screamed out in pain as Alice jumped on top of her. She was ragging her about now really kicking ten tons of shit out her, she was going for it.

Sharon opened her eyes and without thinking she started shouting at the top of her voice. "Fucking waste her Alice, give her a belt from me." "And me," somebody yelled from the doorway. Annie curled up in a tiny ball on the floor and she had her hands over her head protecting herself.

Alice had a flash back of her home life and she visualised it was her mother on the floor and one of her many men were beating her. Now, she knew what it felt like to be the one in control, she liked the fear she could see in her opponent's eyes. Alice swung her leg back and surged it deep into her ribs, a crippling pain and a scream from deep within made Annie sound like a wounded animal. Sharon could see she'd had enough but although she deserved everything she was getting she just couldn't stand back and watch this massacre.

"She's had enough Alice, just leave her now, you've proved your point, "Sharon stressed. "Just let her go. You've won."

Alice dropped her bleeding fist down to the side of her legs and looked around at everyone. Her teeth were gritted tightly together. "Anyone else fancy a go?" she roared.

Annie scrambled out of the bedroom and one other girl helped her to her feet. There were no more threats now. No, I'll do this to you, I'll do that. Annie was silent. Her title was gone, she would never cross Alice again. Sharon waited a few minutes and chuckled. "Wow, where did all that come from. You were like a wild woman. If I hadn't stopped you, you would have finished her off for sure."

Alice was calming down, she could hear people talking again, she was starting to focus. Her eyes dropped to the red blood dribbling down her fingers and she ran to the bathroom to wash them. Hands shaking she bolted the door behind her. This rage she held inside her was out of control. It just got a grip of her and there wasn't a single thing she could do about it. She stood looking at herself in the mirror and sobbed. She was a monster now, just like her mother was, a brutal, callous bully who had inflicted pain on another human being. There was banging on the door and she could hear Sharon's voice from the other side of the door. "Alice, what are you doing in there? Are you okay, just open the door. I want to talk to you."

With her back pressed firmly against the cold wall she answered her. "Just give me a minute. I'm just getting cleaned up." Sinking to her knees she rocked to and fro, this wasn't good, this wasn't good at all.

Alice opened the bathroom door that led to her bedroom and her jaw swung low when she saw the other girls sat on the bed waiting for her. She thought they were Annie's soldiers, under her rule, why were they still sat here? One of the girls stood up and walked over to her. "It was bang on that. It's about time she was knocked down off her high horse. I couldn't stand her anyway if I'm being honest. I just did what she wanted for a quiet life. I think we all did. Anyway, you're top girl now and we follow you."

Alice's lips were moving but nothing was coming out, she was shell-shocked. "Listen," she mumbled. "I'm not being any top girl or anything. I don't want you to follow me. I did what I did because she was a bully so just treat me as you would anyone else in here."

Well, this was a first, a home with no number one ruler, no one bullying anyone. This was heaven and you could see the relief on a few faces. Sharon came to her side and patted her shoulder. "That's so nice that is. It's been a long time coming for that cocky cow to get her block knocked off. I'm proud to call you my friend."

Alice was tearful and as all the girls shared a moment, nobody noticed Christine come into the room. "What's going on girls? Jesus Christ , Alice you're bleeding." The other girls left the room in a hurry, nobody wanted to be a grass. Sharon would have left too but Christine walked over to her for some answers. "And, come on Sharon. I know you know something."

"Christine, I don't want to get involved, it's nothing to do with me. Just keep me out of it, speak to Alice."

Alice folded her arms and chewed on her lip. She was in two minds whether or not to walk out too. Why should she answer to anyone here, she was the victim, the innocent party in all this. Christine could see she was getting upset, her eyes clouded over and her face was bright red. She placed her hand on the girl's shoulder and spoke in a calm voice. "Just take a deep breath and tell me what's going on. I'm not saying you're to blame. I just have to follow procedure and make sure everyone is alright." Alice didn't look well at all, the colour drained from her cheeks and she fell to the floor like a lead weight. She was lifeless, her eyes were open but she was in some sort of trance. "

"Sharon go and get me the nurse, quick as fast as you can," Christine yelled, "tell Betty to bring her first aid kit too."

Sharon stood gawping for a few seconds until Christine yelled at her. "I said get Betty." Sharon sprinted out of the room and headed down the corridor. Christine lay Alice on her side and put her in the recovery position. Small beads of sweat were visible on her forehead, she didn't look well. Christine rushed to the sink in the bathroom and got a glass of cold water. She sprinkled bits of it onto Alice's face. Slowly she was opening her eyes. Betty rushed into the room. She looked like a bigger version of Snow White, jet black hair, pale skin and two rosy red cheeks. She didn't speak to anyone, she went straight to the patient. Sharon sat on the edge of the bed. This girl seemed to be more trouble than she was worth, she'd only been here two minutes and she was already causing her stress. Alice sat up and rubbed her knuckles into her eyes. Her lips were dry and she seemed to be having difficulties swallowing. Betty passed her the glass of water. "Here you go, just sip at that. Christine can you open a window and let some fresh air in."

Christine walked to the other side of the room and stretched her hands over her head to open the window. The gentle breeze rushed past her and flicked her fringe up at the front. Christine needed to take control now, get things back to normal. "Sharon, can you come with me down to my office. I need to take a few details from you. Alice, I'll come back soon to see you. You just take it easy until I return."

Sharon stomped across the room, she hated being a grass. Betty sat talking with Alice she was asking her questions trying to rule out a few things. "When was your last period," Betty asked. Alice shied away from the question, she very rarely talked about her periods and nobody knew she had started them not even her mother. She stole what she needed for her monthlies and she only knew what she'd learned in school about them. "I'm not sure. I think I had one about two or three months ago. I'm not regular and I don't keep a record of them."

Betty frowned. "You should always know when the painters are in my dear, how else will you know if you're pregnant or not. Have you ever had sexual intercourse sweetheart? I just need to rule it out?" Alice dropped her head low. Did this nurse not know her background, the abuse she'd suffered? Why the hell was she putting her through this all over again? Betty knew how girls hid the fact that they'd been sexually active and dug deep in her medical box. This wouldn't be the first time a young girl had turned up at the home with child and she was sure it wouldn't be the last. Passing her a small strip she gave her a gentle smile. "Just go and have a wee on that for me. Once you've done that I can look at other areas to see what's causing this sickness and fainting."

Alice took the test from her hand and walked inside the toilet. Once inside she dropped her knickers and placed the pregnancy strip between her legs. From outside she could hear that Christine was back in the room. Listening closer she heard them whispering. The job was done and she returned back into the bedroom. Betty didn't say much and just took the test from the young girl. Christine knew what was going on and her head kept twisting over to Betty. Alice still felt weak and rested on the bed, her eyes were closing slowly as tiredness took over. Christine tiptoed quietly over to Betty and she was eager to know the test results. It was such a crying shame that she could never have children, never have the joy of reading a positive pregnancy result. The world was cruel sometimes and she'd been dealt a bum deal this time around for sure.

"It's positive Christine. Alice is pregnant."

They both gasped; this was such a tragedy, such a waste of life. There was no way Alice could stay at the home now. She'd have to be moved to another home where young mothers stayed until their child was born, a place nobody liked to speak about. Christine shot her eyes over to Alice sleeping in the bed. Somebody had to tell her, somebody had to break the bad news. Betty left the room, there was no way she was staying around here. She was already feeling a bit down herself and to watch more misery unfold in front of her eyes, she just couldn't take it. She left the room and slowly closed the door behind her.

Christine stood still for a minute thinking. She edged closer to the bed. "Alice, are you awake? I need to have a chat with you." Alice stirred in the bed but she wasn't waking up. The last few days had taken it out of her and she was exhausted mentally and physically. Christine sat for a moment pondering with her own thoughts. After a few minutes she tried waking her up again and this time she got a result. "We've found out why you've been feeling sick and fainting." Alice licked her lips, she was listening. Christine took a deep breath and got ready to break the news, this wasn't going to be easy. How on earth do you tell a young girl she had a baby growing inside her. "Alice you're pregnant." Not a single sound, nothing.

Christine was waiting for a reaction and knew any time soon the young girl was going to blow. "Get it out of me now. Christine, help me, get it out of me." Alice dragged at her skin and ragged her fingers through her hair. There were tears falling from her eyes at a rapid speed dripping onto her cheek. Christine turned her head away and a single tear fell from her eye. This was a mess, a nightmare that needed sorting out as soon as possible.

CHAPTER EIGHT

Asif Patel sat with his brothers and his nephews in his shop. It was late and the shop should have been empty. Something was going down. The men all sat around like witches around a cauldron. Asif was still in pain and his head was still swollen even though the attack had been sometime ago. A large gash at the side of his head was still visible; it looked sore and painful to touch. Sharif was Asif's younger brother. He was a cocky bastard and had double standards, a smarmy twat who very few people really liked. He was a modern Pakistani. Yeah, he'd had the arranged marriage and the children like his brothers had but he had another life separate to that, a life he kept secret. In the past he'd helped his brother Asif deal with a situation similar to his. Asif was lucky he was there to help him otherwise he would have lost everything he owned, the shop, the money, his family, everything. He wasn't careful, he never covered his tracks and it all came back to bite him on the arse. He owed Sharif a lot. Asif's nephews were in the shop too. They were dressed in Armani tracksuits and top of the range trainers.

Things had changed so much in this culture for the men especially. They were able to live a great social life with no questions asked. Whereas the women still had to live by the rules of her husband and his family, they were like prisoners. It wasn't fair really; the Asian women were like second class citizens compared to the men. Night after night they would hear their husbands coming home late. They never asked any questions, never confronted them, it was just something they had to live with. "I need someone on the square to start talking. All we need is someone who will point the finger at Skid and Terry. I swear to you dad, I'll do the cunts in once I get told it was them." Sharif nodded his head at his son Gugz. He was a chip off the old block he was. He loved working out and keeping himself in tip-top condition just like his dad did. He'd made a name for himself too; he was well up there with all the main heads in the area where he lived. If you needed something or a problem sorting out he was the man to talk to, ruthless he was.

Gugz Patel looked out of the window onto the square and pressed his nose against the cold glass. He could see Skid and Terry sat on a wall close by. He knew who they were, everyone did on the square. Gugz shouted behind him, his head never moved. "Asif, who's close to them two pricks, do they have women? There must be someone who's willing to talk."

Asif struggled to stand up from his seat. He held a strained look in his eyes as his hand gripped the counter as he tried to steady his grip. Asif peered out of the window and grinded his teeth together as he looked more closely. "Terry sees a girl called Tina, "he pointed him out to his nephew. "Tina is a gold-digger, she'd do anything for money or so the other girls say. I've heard them slagging her off in here. She's into the sniff she is, you know cocaine."

Gugz nodded his head slowly and smirked. "Leave her to me then. I'll sort her out. If she's a coke whore she's going to love me. She's the weakest link and I'll get onto her straight away."

The other nephews chuckled loudly as Sharif stepped forward. He nodded his head slowly as his head dipped looking onto the square. "We all know how these white bitches work, that's why we never make them our wives." He shot his eyes back at his brother and Asif looked uneasy. He was fidgeting and nervous and he changed the subject quickly. Asif had been married since he was seventeen years old. He hated that his family had arranged his marriage and he'd refused to marry his chosen bride at first. He hated her as soon as he set eyes on her, she made his stomach turn, there was no feeling involved and there never would be. "She's ugly as fuck," he had screamed at his family as they held a gun to his head demanding that he was marrying her no matter what. "My heart will never be hers. I will never love her," he had ranted to them as the tears gushed from his eyes. Those words were stuck in his mind forever. He had repeated them to his family every time there was a problem, every time he wanted to walk away from his marriage. Sharif was younger than Asif but he was the head of the family. He made sure his brother never stepped out of line and kept his family name safe. Asif had made one mistake in the past and he wasn't letting him make any more. Asif loved women. He loved white women and was a well known face in the Cheetham Hill area of Manchester. He kerb crawled most nights there seeking the fix of a white woman's flesh next to his. He loved the young girls too, they were his guilty pleasure. Most of the prostitutes tried to avoid him. He was the last resort for them to make some money. His sexual activities were sick and twisted. There was something not right in his head.

Gugz paced the shop's floor and cracked his knuckles slowly. "It's payback time. It's only a matter of time before our money is back. Nobody messes with us Patel's, fucking nobody."

Skid sat rolling a joint. He was sat next to Terry on a wall in the square. Skid was snappy and kept jumping down Terry's throat for nothing. He was so stressed and the slightest little thing was doing his head in. Terry watched him closely and knew it was time to put him in his place. "Oi, fucking Chief Black Cloud you need to sort your mood out. You're doing my head in now and I'll end up twisting you up if you carry on chatting shit to me." Terry was ready to take him down, he dangled his legs further from the wall and he was ready to pounce on him if he gave him any back-chat.

Skid let out a laboured breath and shook his head as he sucked hard on his spliff. "It's our Alice. I can't stop thinking about her. Fuck me, she's been taken into care. Our Janice is a pill away from a breakdown. It's all doing my head in. I've not slept proper for days with it all," Skid dipped his head and inhaled deeply. "She said she's been abused, you know, fiddled with by Darren."

Terry gripped his knees and looked straight into Skids eyes. "Why haven't you done something about it then? If that was my relative who'd been nonced I would be going through the cunt's door. That Darren is still walking the streets and you've done fuck all about it. Why haven't you put the sick bastard in a body bag?"

Skid was nervous, edgy, thinking before he spoke. He was a cunning bastard and he played with the end of his chin as he spoke, he was up to something. "Alice might be lying. You know what girls are like. She might just be saying it to get back at her mam."

Terry's face creased at the sides, he nearly choked. "Am I hearing you right here or what? When we were in jail and we wasted that beast on K-wing did you ask him any questions before we done him in or did we just give it him? For fuck sake Skid, if this was our Sandy I wouldn't sleep until the dirty prick was six-foot under." Terry rubbed at his arms as a cold chill passed over him. He loved his sister and he'd not seen her for a while now. The last time he had any contact with her she gave him a fluffy brown teddy, a big furry one. That bear meant so much to him and he always kept it close by. He had Rolex watches and as much money as he could spend but this teddy bear meant more to him than any of that. He never told anyone what the bear meant to him, nobody ever knew that deep down he was a bit of a softie where his sister was concerned, she was all he had left. The only person he cared about anymore. Terry often thought about the family he'd left behind and some nights he cried. Well, after he's been on a bender for days and he was on a come-down. That was it with the drugs, it was great when you were out partying but by the time the weekend was over the depression crept in, the low mood, and feeling sorry for yourself, suicidal. Terry missed his mother and he knew his father was the one calling the shots. They'd left on bad terms and he always said if he ever saw him again he would blow the fucker up. There was no love lost between them, none whatsoever. Sandy was different though, he loved her unconditionally. She melted his heart; she always thought she could change the world. Her outlook was positive and she always saw the good in everyone, even Terry.

Skid ragged his fingers through his hair, it was all getting too much for him and these days even the weed couldn't block it out of his mind. "Do you fancy coming to our Janice's with me later pal? I could do with the support if I'm being honest with you. Janice is on suicide watch and I really think if Alice isn't home soon she'll do herself in."

Terry sighed, he hated going to Janice's. She was a sex-starved bitch just like the rest of them, do anything for a hit or to get stoned but Skid needed him, he had no option. "Yeah, no worries I'll come with you but I'm not staying there for hours. I've got things to do."

Skid seemed to liven up. A loud voice from the other side of the square made them look at each other. They both knew the voice and Terry cringed as they spotted Tina heading towards them. This girl was good looking but it was the drugs that had ruined her, she always after a free bump, a line of the white powder. They watched as she wobbled towards them. She was dressed to the nines and there was no need for her high heeled shoes and skinny jeans. She couldn't even walk in them. Why on earth would you wear something like that when you were in danger of falling over every time you took a step forward? Terry met her eyes and she snarled at him. She was like that Tina, she blew hot and cold. One minute she could be all over you and treating you like her best friend and the next she was acting like she'd never met you, a crank she was.

"What's up with your kite," she hissed over at Terry. "You look like you've found a penny and lost a pound.

Cheer up it might never happen."

Terry jumped up from the wall. He knew she could switch at any time and he wasn't sticking around to find out. Her jaw was swinging, she was wired. "Tina, I'm not in no mood for your mind games. What do you want anyway?"

Tina smiled and walked closer to him, her warm breath in his face. "I want to sit on your face all night long if you're up for it. You know you like that."

She made his skin crawl as he looked at her. Before she started taking drugs she was a prize catch, everyone wanted her but now she was old news. She'd had more bangs than a front door and everybody knew she was just a gold-digging bitch. "Nar, I'll pass on that Tina. Been there done that so to speak."

Tina hated rejection and Terry always made her feel so cheap and dirty. She knew what she was without anyone telling her and over the last few months she'd told everyone she was going to get clean. It didn't look like that was going to happen any day soon though. It was a shame really she could have been so much more. The square did that to people; it took their innocence away and involved them in world of dark secrets, drugs and crime. The youth from the area came to the square at some point in their lives but it was only the clever ones who got away without any addiction or a criminal record. People felt part of something here, they were a family, there was a bond with everyone they met here. The council had threatened to knock this place down and build more shops but the residents kicked up a fuss and it was never done. I bet they could have kicked themselves now though. Times had changed and the once peaceful area was just a meeting place now for all the local thugs in the area. The police did try and manage the criminal activity here but no sooner had they solved one crime then another one had been committed. It was a never-ending circle, nothing ever changed.

Tina knew she'd have to up her game, she was after scoring some sniff but she was potless. Terry had told her in the past that she would never get tick again for drugs after she ripped him off for over two hundred pounds and until this day he had kept to his word. In the past he'd just let her work her debts off. She sucked his dick regularly and anything else he wanted from her, even anal sex.

"Terry, stop being nasty to me will you. We had something special you and me, so why are you treating me like this. Give me a bit of respect please."

Skid knew it was just a matter of time before Terry would snap and kick her arse all over the place and he stepped in to save her bacon. "Tina, you know the rules, no money, no drugs. What do you think we are fucking Brighthouse or something. You'll be asking if we do direct debit next."

Terry smiled and he was glad Skid was back to his normal self. When he was on form he was so funny and he often had Terry in stitches laughing at his one liners. Tina flicked her hair back and made sure the top of her breasts were on show. She was desperate and willing to do anything to get what she wanted. "What about us three going back to your place Terry and having a bit of fun. We're all consenting adults so let's do it."

Skid swallowed hard, his cock stood to attention in his pants and this was one of the best offers he'd ever had. He shot a look at Terry hoping he was up for it too. "You can go and bang Skid on his own Tina but as for me I'm looking for something with a lot more class. You need to get a grip Tina and stop putting it on a plate for everyone, where's your respect girl?"

Skid looked gutted and even though he was dying for a shag he stood by what his mate had said. Tina plonked down on the wall and his words had cut her in half. "Come on Skid, are we getting off or what?" Skid looked at Tina and something inside him wanted to comfort her, she was in a bad way but friendship came first. He walked away and followed Terry.

Tina sat on the wall and her mascara was running down her face. She was sobbing and knew Terry was right. She was a mess and she needed some help. The wind was howling now and she could feel speckles of rain landing on her shoulders. She lifted her eyes up to the night sky and she sobbed her heart out.

Gugz walked slowly towards her. He's been stood watching her for the last ten minutes. He'd already had a grip of a guy called Nelson from the square and he'd already told him who the culprits were who'd had his uncle over. He had no loyalties, none whatsoever. As he neared Tina she lifted her head up and looked at him. "Hiya sweetheart, why's a pretty girl like you crying? If you're crying over a man he's not worth it. It's his loss."

Tina snivelled and wiped the tears from her eyes. Once she started to focus she could see Gugz properly for the first time. He was tasty and not her usual type. "I'll never cry over a man," she lied. "I've just got a lot going on at the moment, you know with work and that." Wow, this girl was such a liar. She'd not had a job since she'd left school. What the hell was she talking about? Gugz dug in his pocket and pulled out a bag of weed. He was watching her from the corner of his eye and knew she was interested. "You want to have a smoke with me. I'm Gugz by the way."

Tina studied him and a smile appeared on her face. "Yeah, why not. I'm Tina." Gugz moved closer to her and took his coat off and draped it around her shoulders. He was such a charmer, such a bullshitter. He was a player for sure and he knew which boxes to tick when he was trying to impress a woman.

Tina wanted to know more about her new found friend, she'd not seen him around here before and wanted to know a bit more about him. "So, why are you on the square? I've not seen you around here before, where you from?"

Gugz popped the joint in her mouth and flicked his lighter underneath it staring at the bright orange flame. "I was just coming to find my mate but somebody said he doesn't live around here anymore."

Tina sucked hard on the spliff as he passed it to her. "What's his name, I know most people who live around here, so I might know him."

"Nar, he's not lived around here for long. He's just got out of jail and he said he was moving on soon anyway."

Tina sat thinking, it was strange that he hadn't said who he was looking for. "Do you want to get in my car and smoke that? Its freezing here and my arse is frozen."

Tina twisted her head trying to see his car but she couldn't see anything. "Come on then," she said desperate to get warm. Gugz walked across the square onto a small car park at the side of them. He pressed his alarm button for his vehicle and Tina nearly collapsed on the spot when she saw his motor. This guy must have been wadded to be driving something like this. It was a black Audi, top of the range, sports wheels and everything. Tina rubbed her hands together. What a result, just what she needed to lift her mood. Gugz opened the door for her and waited for her to get inside, he knew exactly what he was doing and could tell she was impressed by his manners. Tina inhaled the sweet fragrance inside the car. The new leather seats were shiny and as she sat down she shivered at the thought of being treated like a princess. Yes, she'd had men with cars before, but they were old bangers or ones they'd nicked, this was the dog's bollocks. Tina pushed her seat back and looked over at Gugz. His hazel eyes were enchanting, she seemed lost in them. The smell of his expensive aftershave tickled her nose and she knew then this was no shit scent, this guy had money and she couldn't wait until she got her claws into him. The engine started up and Gugz smirked as he tapped his fingers on the steering wheel. "You want to go for a spin?"

Tina didn't have to be asked twice she clipped her seat belt into the socket and reached her hand over resting on his knee. "Yes, why not. I've got nothing better to do. It's shit around here anyway and I'm due a change." The car screeched out from the car park, the smell of burning rubber filled the air and Tina could see a few lads in the distance watching them. She felt special, cared for. She was going to do her best to keep hold of this guy no matter what it took. He was a Godsend and just what she needed.

★

Skid sat looking at Janice. She was all skin and bones

and her eyes seemed like they were popping out from their sockets. Terry sat flicking through the TV stations and he was already bored. He didn't do emotions and when Janice broke down crying in front of them he just switched off and blanked her. "Janice, she'll be back soon. Stop getting upset. It will all work out, trust me."

"Skid, I've let her down. That dirty bastard Darren abused her and I didn't know about it. What kind of a mother am I to have let that happen? It wasn't just him either and there's probably more that she's not even told us about. I was off my head and most days I didn't know what fucking day it was. I want to die Skid. What do I have to live for anymore?"

Skid's eyes clouded over and he turned his head away from her so she couldn't see him getting upset. Terry clocked him and sat back in his seat. Was Skid going soft or what? This was so out of character for him. Terry listened in to them talking and couldn't stand it any longer. He had to say something. "Let's go and do Darren in then. Fuck me, it's not rocket science is it? Poor Alice probably thinks nobody cares what's gone on with her. It's the least we can do something to show her we care about her."

Janice's eyes opened wide and she agreed with him. "Yes Skid, cut the pervert's nob off. And that Dave, the old cunt. Why didn't I think of that? At least Alice will know I believe her then and that I'm not just sat here getting twisted."

Terry nodded his head, at last, a problem solved. "We can go and get Alice back too. She won't be locked up in that place forever, surely she has to go out and all that. We'll just kidnap her and bring her back here so you can tell her that you care about her and you're going to sort your napper out. That's all she wants you know, some love and attention."

Janice stood up and wobbled over to where he was sat. She bent down and kissed him on the cheek. He cringed as her stale breath hit his nose. She stank too, the dirty crusty bitch she was. Janice was alive; they had a plan now. A light at the end of the tunnel. Alice was coming home, they were going to right the wrongs she'd done to her. Terry sat forward with his hands on his knees. "So Skid, let's get this sorted then. The sooner we get that fucker done in the sooner Alice will come home."

Janice was excited she had life in her again, hope. Skid blew a laboured breath, something was wrong. His arse was twitching and he shook his head slowly. "Okay, we'll sort it. You're right Terry we need to twist these fuckers up."

Terry stood up and zipped his coat up tightly. "You know it makes sense Skid. Give me a bell tomorrow and we'll go and find Darren. Take it easy Janice, I'll see you tomorrow." Janice popped a fag in her mouth and watched as Terry left. It was time to get her ship in order and sort her life out. As from today she was on the wagon, no drinking, no drugs, she was getting clean. Skid seemed in a deep trance, he never spoke a word.

CHAPTER NINE

Alice sat with Christine and she was extremely quiet. The news of her pregnancy had knocked her for six, she was devastated. Christine kept looking at her but she had no more words left to say to heal her aching heart. She'd done all she could. There was nothing more to say about the matter. A woman walked out of the office and came to talk to Alice. This place was eerie and Alice wasn't sure she'd made the right choice by coming here. It was her only solution though; the doctors had told her that if she wasn't willing to have an abortion then adoption was the only option she had left. Alice thought long and hard about her choice and after days of thinking she knew she could never end her child's life. Christine was eager to get things moving. She stood up and started to make her way to the office. Alice was trudging behind her. This was a mother and baby unit and like her, other girls were residing here. Once inside, Melanie the centre manager sat down behind her desk and dipped her glasses low on the edge of her nose. To her Alice was just another slut who deserved everything that was happening to her. Melanie was a bible-basher and hated that so many young girls were so willing to spreads their legs at the drop of a hat. Alice stood gawping at her and she wasn't sure about her. She looked evil, with small beady eyes, thinning hair and brown stumpy teeth and stale coffee breath.

"Alice, I know I've spoken to you before about your

options and I'm glad you have come to the decision regarding an adoption. When the time comes I will explain things further. Lots of young mother's take this road and just think how much happiness you will bring to a childless couple." Alice sat twisting the cuff of her sleeve. Melanie was so up her own arse and she knew deep down inside she didn't give a flying fuck about her, it was just about the baby she wanted. This place had a reputation and Sharon had told her all about it before she left. Okay, they were only rumours but judging by the look of things so far this place was living up to it.

Christine wanted to know more about the care of Alice whilst she was there and started to delve deeper. She knew about this place too and wanted it out in the open. "Melanie, I don't know if you're aware but people have been bad mouthing this centre. They're saying things happen here, bad things."

Melanie dabbed the tissue at the side of her mouth and pushed her glasses back up her nose. "I can assure you that our centre is one of the best mother and baby units in the area. Some girls come here with the attitude that pregnancy is something they will sail through but as we all know each case is different."

Alice turned her head and looked about the room. It was a modern office and all she could see were files stacked high on every cupboard. Is that all she would be soon, just a file, just another case of a young girl having a baby. Alice had been quizzed about the identity of the baby's father but her lips were sealed. Nobody could make her talk and nobody was going to, she kept her cards close to her chest. She felt different now, a rage boiling inside her, the need to explode. Every now and then she had to sit on her hands to try and pull her out of the state of mind she was in, she was a ticking bomb. Janice had been in touch with the authorities to try and contact her but Alice refused any contact with her. As far as she was concerned her mother was dead. She never spoke about her and blamed her for everything that had gone wrong in her life. Come on, Janice deserved it, she was no mother of the year and how could she could even try to make amends after what had happened - she was guilty as charged.

Alice's eyes shot to a drawing on the wall facing her. It was a sketch really more than a painting. It was a man's face, Alice was intrigued by it. She loved art, she loved drawing too. Her teacher at high school said she had an amazing talent and hoped one day she would produce some of her work for others to see. When Alice was drawing she was taken to a peaceful place where all she could hear was the sound of the pencil scrolling across the white sheet of paper. Portraits were her favourite. In the past she'd drawn a few of her friends at school. Eyes were the windows to the soul and even when she was concentrating on her model she could tell if they were happy or not. Her artistic skills were a gift from the Gods, or that's what she told herself. Alice had drawn her own portrait once by looking in the mirror, it was a masterpiece and she only ever showed it to her mother. Janice said it was shit though and to stop wasting her time on things that wouldn't get her a decent job. What a cow her mum was. She should have been praising her and urging her to continue in the craft she had found. Alice never listened of course and every night when she was alone in her bedroom she'd spend hours drawing. All her work was under her bed still, hidden away from the world.

Melanie could see Alice looking at the picture and coughed to get her attention. "One of the girls created that. It's so calming isn't it? I look at it every day and it seems to change in some way, her eyes look sad one minute and the next they are filled with happiness. I'm sure the portrait is alive," she chuckled and sipped on her cup of coffee. Christine glanced at the picture but it never grabbed her attention like the others. It was just a woman looking out from a rain splattered window, nothing special. "Do you like art Alice," Melanie asked. "Because if you do, we have some great artists on board here at the centre. They hold classes a couple of times a week and help the girls with their artwork."

Alice smiled, at last something she liked. She thought the months ahead would just be spent in a room lying on a bed. Christine watched her smile and started to relax, perhaps the rumours weren't true and it was just some girls trying to put the fear of God into anyone who came here. Alice's stomach was still pretty flat, maybe a little fatter than usual but nothing where you could say she was with child. "Alice, you know your nana is coming tomorrow don't you. She knows where you are now and knows about your situation." Melanie was such a straight talker and just said it how it was.

Alice was looking forward to seeing Pat. She'd spoken to her on the phone and knew when she saw her for the first time she would break down crying. Pat had been the one who'd saved her from any further abuse. How hard must it have been for her to do this? She knew she'd want some answers when she came face to face with her. Oh yes, Pat would leave no stone unturned. She'd want to know it all. Christine rolled her sleeves up and glanced at her watch, it was time to leave. For some reason she was finding it hard to say goodbye, she hesitated before she stood to her feet. Melanie couldn't wait to see the back of her if the truth was known. This was her centre and she would run it the way she wanted to. So what, she cut corners and never did things by the book, it was her way or the highway. "Christine I can assure you Alice will be fine here. Once she gets her feet under the table she will love it here. I'll get one of the girls to look after her and before long she will have this problem sorted and she can get on with her life." Christine held her head to the side. The way this woman was referring to Alice's pregnancy was doing her head in; her situation, her problem. Melanie shook hands with Christine and opened the office door. "It's been nice speaking to you Christine and feel free to pop in whenever you are around these parts."

Christine was stuck for words, but one thing for sure was that she would call here again, without any appointment either, she would just turn up. Alice watched her leave and she was already holding her bag ready to be showed to her room. She just wanted to get settled into this place, to have somewhere she felt safe. A cold chill passed through her as Melanie returned back to the room. She rushed to the window and peeled the blind back; she was secretive and made sure nobody could see her. After a few minutes she turned around and stood with her hands on her hips. "So, what have you been saying about this centre. Its girls like you, that give this place a bad name. Keep your trap shut in future otherwise you'll see what I'm all about. Get yourself stood up and I'll take you to the main building where the bedrooms are." Alice wanted to give her a piece of her mind, why was she talking to her like this? She wasn't the one who'd started the rumours, she needed to get her facts right. Melanie shot a look to her and hissed. "Girls like you are the scum of the earth, so eager to take your knickers down for the first boy who tells you they love you."

Alice walked to the door and snarled back at her, she couldn't hold her tongue. "I'm not scum, and I don't drop my knickers for anyone so get your facts right you dick-head."

Melanie rushed to her side and leant her head into hers. "I would keep your comments to yourself my dear. I can make your life a misery while you're here so it's up to you how you want to play this." Alice held her head back and her face was white, she never replied. "This is Lizzy, Alice and she'll be showing you how things work in here. This is your bed and that's where you put your belongings. We run a tight ship here and everything is kept clean. I'll see you later when you're settled." Melanie rubbed her hand on top of a nearby wardrobe and looked at the dust on her fingers. "Lizzy, sort this out. It's a shit-tip in here."

Alice plonked down onto her bed. She opened her bag and started to put her belongings in the wardrobe. She could feel Lizzy watching her and turned to meet her eyes. "What are you gawping at," she sneered.

Lizzy looked shocked and shook her head. "Ay, don't be coming here with that attitude. I've been asked to show you the ropes so stop stressing at me. I didn't ask for the job." Alice carried on folding her clothes and she could see another two girls from the corner of her eye sat on the other side of the room. Every girl was with child here and Lizzy looked liked she was going to pop. "How far are you," Lizzy asked trying to make a friend of her.

Alice realised she was being nasty and tried to calm down. "I don't know yet, I just know I'm preggers. How far are you?"

Lizzy rubbed the side of her stomach and blew her breath. "I'm anytime now. I'm due tomorrow but I think I'll go into labour tonight. I've had pains for days, really bad pains in the bottom of my back. It feels like I'm going to shit my knickers every time I bend over."

Alice started to relax, she lay down on the bed to ease her aching legs and spoke to Lizzy. "What's that Melanie all about, she's a horrible bitch. You should have just heard what she said to me. Scum, she called me the cheeky cow."

Lizzy shouted the other girls over and introduced Alice to them. There was strength in numbers and she knew once they filled the new girl in about what goes on here she would be onside. "Melanie is a bitch, just try and keep out of her way. She's a devil dodger and likes to think just because she goes to church every Sunday that she's some kind of saint. Honest, you don't know the half of it Alice."

Lizzy, who was now sat on the end of Alice's bed, introduced herself, she was around the same age as Alice and her stomach wasn't that big either. "Melanie is an evil twat. I've been here for three months now and all she keeps saying to me is to have my baby adopted. She does some work with the convent down the road and I'm sure they have something to do with the adoptions. I told her though, I said, I'm keeping my baby and there is no way she can make me change my mind. That fucked her up, you should have seen her face."

Lizzy sucked hard on her gums. "Just keep an eye on her Jenny. You know how devious she can be."

Alice was scared and she had every right to be, this place was hell. Lizzy's hair was short and cropped, kind of like a basin hair cut. As Alice looked at the other girls here they all had the same hair style too. Was this the fashion, was she missing out on something here. The girls all sat chatting when Jenny stood up and walked to the window. She flicked it open and sat with a fag hanging from her mouth. "Orr Jenny, do you have to do that in here. If they smell it we'll all be in trouble," Lizzy moaned.

Jenny blew large smoke hoops from her mouth and smirked over at them. "Does this face look like it gives a fuck? There is nothing they can do about it. It's my choice to smoke, not theirs."

Lizzy who was slightly older than them all, sat down with her arms folded tightly across her chest. "Smoking can harm your baby Jenny. Have you not read all the books about it?"

Jenny blew a cloud of thick grey smoke from her mouth and sniggered. "I'm not keeping it anyway, so what do I care. This kid is going to get adopted and once it's out of me I'm going to start my life again. I never want to see it or even hold it. As far as I'm concerned the sooner it's gone the better."

Alice twisted a piece of her hair that was dangling near her cheek. This girl knew what she wanted and she felt there was something more to her story. There were so many questions she wanted to ask her. So many things she needed to know. "So what happens when the baby is adopted? How long after they're born do they take them?"

Jenny flicked her cigarette butt through the window and walked towards them. "They've told me that it could take up to six weeks or even longer if the adopted parents are coming from abroad. They're already searching for parents for it now, they just have to find the right ones."

Lizzy wanted to know more about Alice's story. Was she keeping her child or was it getting adopted like Jenny's. "Alice, what have you decided to do when your child is born? Do you have a boyfriend or was this just a mistake." Alice was on the spot they were all waiting for her to answer. There was no way she could tell them the truth, no way in this world, she made it up. "I've been with Terry for over six months. He wants to marry me he said but I'm not ready for all that. I've got plans to go to college and to be an artist. He was devastated when I told him, so no." What a load of cock and bull this was, she was lying through her teeth. She didn't know what else to say.

"So, you're not keeping your baby then?" Lizzy quizzed.

Alice remained calm and she played a role that any actress would have been proud of, she deserved an Oscar. "No, I'm going to give it away to a couple who can't have children. I'm too young to be a mother and I've got dreams I want to follow. I want to be an artist."

Jenny was excited; she loved to hear about girls who put their career first. Lizzy was old-fashioned and thought she was above the rest of them all because she was keeping her child. She was no better than them and Jenny wasn't afraid to tell her that every time she got above her station. "Will you draw me Alice? I've always wanted a portrait, but only do my face, not my body. I don't want this fat stomach on anything." Alice was accepted into the group and they sat on the bed chatting.

The door opened and Alice could see a woman stood there with a face of fury. She was a large woman and all her hair was greased back from her face. She looked like a Russian shot putter. "Alice, can you come with me. You need to get your hair cut and gather your uniform." Alice looked at the others for some kind of guidance. She didn't need her hair cutting and what was she going on about saying her uniform. The woman shrieked as she stampeded across the bedroom floor. "Oi, cloth ears. Did you not hear me? I've not got all day. Move your arse now." Jenny growled as she watched May standing at the end of the bed. She'd had a few run-ins with her in the past and knew what she was capable of. She'd locked her in a room for two full days without so much as a phone call or anything one time. May was Melanie's younger sister and the pair of them ruled the place like two sergeant majors.

Alice was tired but used the last bit of her energy to jerk herself up from the bed. She stood facing May and awaited her instructions. Jenny whispered into Alice's ear as she was leaving. "Don't take any bullshit from her. She doesn't own you; she's just a worker here. You have rights, make sure you remind her about that." Alice followed May down the corridor and she waited for her outside a door at the end of the corridor. Once she took her inside she placed a bundle of clothes onto the table. It was a grey pinafore and white shirts. Alice looked at her and decided she needed to ask some questions. "Why have you given me these clothes? I don't go to school anymore so I don't need a uniform."

May chuckled and held her head back as she picked her teeth with her fingernail. "All the girls wear a uniform inside the centre. You are no different, so don't think you are." May held a serious look on her face and walked to the back of the room she was searching inside a box. When she lifted her head she held some silver scissors in her hand. "Will you take a seat so I can trim your hair? I have to check you for head lice too. You'd be surprised how many girls come in here with nits. We had an outbreak last month and everybody was crawling with nits, itchy heads the lot." Alice felt dirty as she scratched at her scalp. Just the thought of head lice made her skin crawl. There was no way she wanted nits and she was eager to sit on the chair to get her hair checked. May was a cunning cow and this was a trick to get Alice to sit on the chair in front of her. There was no such thing as an outbreak of head lice, she was making it up. May put some disposable gloves on and started to separate Alice's hair in sections. She wasn't checking for nits she was just gazing out of the window. All of a sudden she let out a scream. "Oh, bleeding hell you're crawling with them."

Alice jumped up out of her seat and panicked. She hated spiders and the thought of something crawling about in her hair made her hysterical. "Get them out, please get them out," she shrieked.

May held a cunning look on her face, she was up to something. "Just take a seat and I'll do my best to get them out." Alice sat down on the chair and covered her eyes with her hands. May brought the scissors from behind her back and she started snipping away at her hair. Before long Alice's dark locks were on the floor and she too now had a basin hair cut. Alice opened her eyes and looked at all the hair on the floor, she was devastated. As she stood up she could see May smirking in front of her. The crafty cow had had her over. The nits story was just made up so she could cut her hair off. Alice was fuming and she was ready to attack this woman. May stood tall and shot her eyes to a big baseball bat not far from where she stood. "Don't even think about it because I'll put you on your arse. Just take your things and go back to the dorm. I expect to see you wearing your uniform at all times. If you don't, you'll be punished and you don't want that do you?"

Alice didn't wait – she was heartbroken, really upset, sobbing. She needed out of this place and as soon as Christine returned she was telling her exactly what was happening. She was right; the rumours were true, this place was a nightmare. Alice ran back to the bedroom and as soon as Jenny saw her she chuckled loudly. "I see you had nits too then. I fell for exactly the same script. Don't worry about it Alice we're all in the same boat here, we've all got short hair." Alice threw her clothes on the bed and dragged the covers over her head. She wished she was dead, she didn't want to live any more, she'd had enough.

★

Pat lay in bed. She'd been crying. As if the abuse wasn't enough for Alice to take on, she now had an unwanted pregnancy. It was like history repeating itself and it was all too much for her to take in. She questioned her own parenting skills and although she tried not to, she was blaming herself for everything that had gone wrong. The pains in her chest were as bad as ever, she told nobody about them as she didn't want to involve anyone. She didn't want her husband worrying. The doctor had sent her for tests and she was still waiting for the results. Ted came into the room holding a cup of hot chocolate in his hands. He walked over to Pat's side of the bed and placed it on her bedside cabinet. "Come on now love, you need to get some sleep. We're going to see Alice tomorrow and we'll put things right, I know we will. No matter what has happened we can't change it can we?"

Pat sat up in bed and placed a pillow behind her head. She straightened her nightie and smoothed the blankets out with a flat palm. "Why Ted, what have we ever done to deserve this? We've worked all our lives and we've never caused anyone any trouble, why, just tell me, why us? Look at them scruffy bleeders down the street they've never have any bad luck and not one of them has done a day's work in their lives?"

Ted got into bed next to her and stroked her forehead softly. "I know love, I know. Things will turn out alright. Our Alice is strong and believe it or not she will come through this."

Pat reached over and picked up her hot chocolate, she blew at the top of the cup slowly. "It's all Janice's fault Ted. I bet she's asleep in her bed now off her head on drugs. I can't ever forgive her for this, never. And, I don't think for one minute that Martin Jones is the father of Alice either, she's hiding something as per usual."

Ted kissed his wife's cheek with his warm wet lips. He held her hand tightly. "Come on now, try and get some sleep. You're going to make yourself ill if you carry on like this." Pat snivelled. "I want Alice here with us. We're the only family she has that cares about her. I'm going to tell her tomorrow that she's coming home with us. And, if Janice thinks she's getting to see her she's got another think coming. She's our granddaughter and it's our job to make sure she's cared for. I've sat back for long enough now and I could kick myself for not doing something sooner. It's my fault she was abused. I should have done something sooner and got her out of that shit-tip."

Ted held his own guilt too and he was gutted just the same as his wife that he'd not done something sooner. If his daughter ever set foot near his home again he was going to end her life. There was no more pity for her any more, none whatsoever. She was a lost cause and as from today he'd washed his hands off her. Ted flicked the bedside lamp off and snuggled up to his wife. He could hear her sobbing and there was nothing he could do to make things better. His heart was heavy and as he turned to the window his eyes met the moonlight. He was going to fix things; he was going to start first thing in the morning. God help anyone who crossed him. He was a man on a mission.

Alice lay in her bed and something was stirring inside her stomach, butterflies, some kind of movement. Her eyes were wide open as she placed her flat palm on her stomach. She was in a panic. She was right, the child was moving about. Her hands froze as she pulled her t-shirt over her stomach, fingertips slightly touching her skin. She would never touch this child again, never bond with it. From across the other side of the bedroom she could hear Lizzy sobbing. She'd been in labour for a few hours and the staff had told her to get back in bed and stop being a mard-arse. Couldn't they see she needed help? Alice sat up and looked over at Lizzy. She couldn't just leave her on her own when she was in so much pain, she had to do something. Slipping her pale legs out of the bed she sneaked over to the other side of the room. "Lizzy, are you okay? Can I do anything for you?"

Lizzy rolled on her side and her knees were held up to her chest as she struggled to talk. "They said I'm not ready yet and I can't have any painkillers. I'm dying here, look at the state of me."

Alice watched her closely and she could see the pain in her eyes. Alice stood up and walked over to Jenny's bed. She shook her rapidly and tried to wake her up. "Jenny, get up. It's Lizzy she's in a bad way; honest you need to see her. We have to do something, we can't just leave her like this." Jenny rubbed her knuckles into her eyes and sat up in her bed. She wasn't awake yet and it took a few minutes to come round. She fell back onto the bed. "Jenny, wake up," Alice screamed at her. "We need you."

A shrieking voice came from the other side of the room and Jenny was wide awake now, alert and aware of her surroundings. She jumped out of her bed and ran to Lizzy's side. Alice stood frozen for a few seconds and she was unsure of what to do next. She'd never seen anything like this in her life. Jenny flicked the light switch on and shouted over to Alice. "Go and get help, tell them she's in a bad way."

Lizzy was panting and she was trying to talk, her words were mumbled and hard to understand. "They said I can't have any pain relief Jenny. Melanie said if I wake her up again tonight she's going to put me down the corridor in the room."

Jenny knew exactly where the room was, she was talking about. She'd been there herself on numerous occasions. A small windowless room with just a bed in it. A thinking room they called it. "Oh, did she now. Alice, you stay here with Lizzy while I go and get that fat cow out of bed. Who does she think we are some kind of fucking animal?" Jenny rushed from the room and Alice was left to deal with Lizzy. With each pain surging through her, she gripped her hand with force turning it white. She was squeezing her hand that hard that it was stopping the blood from flowing. Lizzy's forehead was wet and her lips were dry and cracked, she was gagging for a drink. There was a look in her eye that told Alice she was petrified of what lay ahead, fear like she'd never seen before. No matter what she'd read in the books about childbirth, nothing was ever going to prepare her with what lay ahead.

Jenny was shivering, her teeth chattered together as she rubbed at her arms. Her flat palm hammered on the door in front of her. Melanie opened the door and she was furious, she hated being woke up in the night and once she was awake it would take her hours to get back to sleep again. She snapped as soon as she saw Jenny standing there. "What the hell do you want at this time of the night? Piss off back to bed and come and see me in the morning. I don't know what you girls think I am. I need my sleep just like you lot do. Go on, back to bed."

Jenny wasn't going anywhere, no way; her feet were firmly fixed to the floor. Her blood was boiling and this woman was getting told. "It's Lizzy, she's in pain and the baby is coming. She needs your help, something to take the pain away." Melanie was just about to close her door when Jenny stuck her foot inside stopping it from closing. "If you don't come and help her now I'm going to make sure everyone knows how you treat us in here. All the girls are sick to death of it and the first thing in the morning we're going above your head and reporting you. You have a duty to attend to us here, now do your fucking job."

Melanie growled at her and stepped out of her bedroom. "You know nothing; go back to bed before I call for May. You're a load of sluts who deserve every bit of pain you go through. Now leave me alone."

Jenny knew she couldn't back down now, she'd come too far. It was all or nothing. She stood with her hands on her hips. "I've got signed statements from all the girls about a few of your antics. I'm going back now to attend to Lizzy doing the job you're supposed to be doing. If you're not there in a few minutes I'm phoning for help. You're a disgrace you are. You know what some of us have been through and yet you're treating us like dogs. I've had enough of it and I won't stand for it any longer," Jenny leaned in towards her. "You can do what you want to me, lock me up, have me moved out of here, but be sure of one thing. I'll make sure everyone knows about you and your sister. You're a disgrace." Jenny turned on the spot and headed back down the corridor. She was watching her back all the time and was aware she could be attacked at any time soon. Melanie was a cunning cow and often stuck a blow from behind on her victim.

Lizzy's screams filled the corridor. She sounded like a wounded animal, howling at the top of her voice. As Jenny came back into the room Lizzy's legs were wide open and she was bearing down, her chin dug deep into her chest, sweating. "Help me. I can't breathe, somebody help me," she gasped. Jenny didn't know what else to do; she wasn't a midwife, she had no training, she didn't have a clue.

Jenny gripped Lizzy's hand and held it tightly. She turned her head and looked behind her. "Right Alice, we're going to have to do this on our own, them bastards are still in bed and Melanie won't help. Wake Sally up, she's helped deliver a baby before I'm sure of it. We need to do all we can." Alice was like a headless chicken, her head was doing overtime and she was running one way, then the other. Jenny pointed her finger over to Sally's bed. "Hurry up, for crying out loud this baby is coming." Sally was awake and sat up in her bed. Nobody could sleep through this noise everyone was awake and watching in horror. This was it, the baby was coming. Lizzy wriggled about on the bed and it was Jenny's job to keep her still. Sally was between her legs and she was the one telling everyone what she could see. Alice was white as a sheet as she stood at the bottom of the bed. She could never go through this pain, ever. Lizzy sat up in bed and held the top of her knees, fingernails dug deep into her pink hot flesh. Sally was urging her to push; the baby's head was in view. This was one hell of a mission and they were all pulling together.

"Push," Sally yelled. "Just push and it will be over soon. I can see the head."

Everyone was around the bed and from nowhere Melanie appeared. "Move out of my way, she better be ready for having this baby and not pissing about again. I've left my bed for this." Melanie pushed Alice and Sally out of the way. She bent down and assessed the situation. Something was wrong, her face said it all. Panic, pure panic was visible and she was stuttering. "Go and ring an ambulance fast, get May too. The cord is around the baby's neck and we need to get it out as soon as possible."

Jenny stomped her feet and snarled at Melanie. "Well, it's your fault this is and if anything happens to this baby it's your neck on the line. Lizzy has been in labour for hours and you've just left her like a dying fly. You call yourself a woman of God; you should be ashamed of yourself."

Melanie shook her head and bit hard on her bottom lip. She knew Jenny was right but this wasn't the time or place to discuss it. She'd deal with her later. Things weren't looking good and because of Melanie's negligence it didn't look like this baby was going to make it either. Lizzy gave one last final push. Her hands sank deep into her head as the last bit of strength soared through her body. There was an eerie silence as Melanie took the baby to a nearby bed. There was no crying, the baby was still. Alice was watching everything that was happening from where she stood. She could see the infant lying in the white towel, it was a girl. Lizzy sat up and shot a look over to where Melanie was. "Why's my baby not crying Jenny? See what's going on. Sally, go and get my baby."

Melanie wrapped the child up in the white towel and left her on the bed. She came back to Lizzy. She never said a word to her, she just started to clean up. May, her sister was here now and she was trying to calm things down. "Girls go back to bed. Lizzy is going in the ambulance now. Thanks for your help but please get back into bed." No, this wasn't going to be that easy, the girls were up in arms. Lizzy tried getting out of bed and blood was gushing from her all over the floor, thick red claret. Alice was stood alone and her eyes never left the infant. She reached over and picked her up and walked slowly over to the bed. Lizzy froze then slowly took her child in her arms and opened the towel fully. "What's wrong with her, why is she not moving about? Someone help her, please, somebody do something."

The girls huddled together as the medics entered the bedroom, each of them stricken with grief. Lizzy was assessed and the baby was taken away by another female medic. Alice had never seen such a look of heartbreak before in somebody's eyes, such a look of desperation and loss. This was heart-wrenching and she had to close her eyes to stop her mind from doing overtime. She would never forget this day for as long as she lived; it would stay with her until her dying breath. May pushed her along now, fingers digging deep into her waist. "Come on, I said get back in bed," she flicked her eyes behind her and watched Lizzy leaving the room on a stretcher.

Lizzy was up in arms and all she kept repeating was. "I want my baby, please, she's all I have, bring her back to me."

Jenny was livid and there was no way she was obeying any words May spoke to her. The girls all gathered together and Jenny was the spokesman. "Oi, there's no way you're getting away with this. You killed Lizzy's baby, you and your bible- bashing sister. I'll make sure you both pay for this, we all will. Won't we girls?" The girls backed her up and each of them voiced their opinion. The shit had hit the fan and May didn't know what to do. They were closing in around her. Usually she would have given them a backhander but there were too many of them, each looking like they were ready to kill her. May ran to the bedroom door and searched deep in her pockets for her keys. She stuck the gold key in the lock and waved her finger about inside the room. "No one will believe you. You're all the same you lot are. A dirty load of whores."

Jenny rushed after her but it was too late the door was slammed shut. She hammered her clenched fist on the door and kicked the bottom of it, screaming at the top of her lungs. "You just watch, your days are numbered here. Mark my words everyone will know what's happened here tonight." Alice sat on the edge of the bed and her head dropped into her hands, she had nothing left, no fight, no strength to carry on, she was broken. This place was worse than anywhere she'd ever stayed before. She'd never been so scared in all her life. She needed something to give, something to change. She was at her wits end.

The next morning in the centre the door opened and Melanie and May stood near the doorway hovering. All the girls were awake and ready for war. Jenny barged passed the girls and went nose to nose with Melanie, she was a loose cannon. "Do you think you can keep us locked up in here forever ay?"

Melanie was quieter than usual and she knew no matter what, her time here was nearly over. Her voice was low. "It was all a big misunderstanding girls. Lizzy had been coming to my room every night for a week saying she was in labour, when all that was wrong with her was that she had wind. Night after night I sat with her and nothing happened, she had indigestion that's all. Last night was unfortunate and I know I should have listened to you all but I was drained, honest. I've not had any sleep all week. You can't hold me responsible for Lizzy's baby. Even if she was in the hospital it would have still been the same outcome. It's a tragedy and our staff are as upset as you lot. I need you all to calm down and let's move on from this." Melanie had something up her sleeve she moved forward and held a single finger up to the corner of her mouth. "I mean, without this place where else will you girls go. You'll all end up back on the street, probably homeless."

Jenny held her head back and chuckled. Did this woman think she was green or what? She might be pregnant but she certainly wasn't thick. "Don't you dare try and blackmail us all. You know we will all stay here no matter what. It's you and your slob of a sister who'll be out on your arses. The truth is getting told and I know for sure, justice will be served from you two murdering bitches."

Alice was watching with eager eyes. The two of them were like gunslingers at dawn. Jenny turned her head and shot a look at Sally and the other girls. "You'll all tell the truth won't you. Everyone knows what went on here don't we?" This wasn't looking good; there wasn't a peep out of any of them, no back up nothing. Jenny growled at Sally. "What the hell is up with you? Are you going to let her get away with what she's done? Last night you were all of the same mind as me and look at you now, come on, where's the support."

Melanie knew she'd won. "Sally could you and the other girls go down for breakfast. Anyone who feels the same way as Jenny stay behind and we can have a chat about it."

May stood tall and she was flexing her knuckles, someone was getting a good hiding. Sally dropped her head low and walked from the room with the others. Her arse had gone and yes, she was a coward but there was no way she could go back home to her previous life, this was her home now and the only stability she'd had in her life for ages. Perhaps the other girls felt like that too. The outside world frowned upon teenage pregnancy and for some of them this was their last hope. Jenny was up shit street for sure. She watched as the girls left. "Fucking sell outs the lot of you. What happened to sticking together ay, what about Lizzy and her baby? Do none of you give a flying fuck about her or what?" Jenny shot a look over to Alice who was sat on her bed. "Go on, you go too. These two don't scare me. I'll give as good as I get. So what, I'll be homeless. I'm not one bit arsed what they do to me."

Alice didn't want any trouble, she just wanted peace. She'd only been here a short time and she didn't want to make any enemies. May came to Alice's side. "Come on Alice you don't need to be any part of this do you? You look like a clever girl to me so make the right choice and leave the room." This was a threat, May sucked hard on her gums as she helped her up from the bed. Jenny was alone, it was two against one. This girl had balls and she wasn't going to go down easily, no way. May pointed at Jenny's stomach with her eyebrows raised. "Are you sure you want to do this. Think about your child, could you live with yourself if anything happened to it?"

Jenny rolled her sleeves up; she didn't care what happened to her unborn child. It was getting adopted anyway and what did she care if it lived or died she had no feeling for it whatsoever. Jenny ran at May, she had to bring her down first because she was the biggest, the meat in the bunch. She didn't stand a chance; May just threw her to the floor and pinned her down snarling into her face. "You're a trouble causing tart and nobody will believe a word you say. Did anyone listen to you when you said your uncle fiddled with you ay?" Her eyes were evil as she spit in the young girl's face. "Girls like you are what makes this world bad. You deserve everything that's happened to you." Melanie knew she would have to step in. May was a head the ball and wouldn't have thought twice about laying into her. She was ex military and built like a brick shit house. "Get on your feet, come on, get up you piece of worthless shit," she cursed. Jenny was ragged to her feet and she was still trying to swing a punch.

Melanie stepped in and grabbed her clenched fist. "It's like this Jenny. I can easily tell everyone you're a bare faced liar and none of the girls will back you up. Where as me, I have May to tell my side of the story. Do you want to go back home, back to where nobody wants you, back to your abusers?"

Jenny clenched her teeth together; she wasn't giving up that easily, no way. She knew what the difference was between right and wrong and there was no way these two witches were getting away with it. "I'm telling them everything. You don't scare me. Just wait; everyone will know what happened here." May dragged Jenny out of the room. She was going to the thinking room, the block, solitary confinement. Nobody would know she was there and by the time they let her out all this mess would be smoothed over.

Alice was hidden away, she'd seen everything; her heart was in her mouth as she watched Jenny being frog-marched to the other end of the corridor. She had to do something, she had to help fix this mess, what the hell was she waiting for?

Pat sat at the reception in the mother and baby home. Ted was by her side and he was constantly fidgeting. He was nervous and kept jerking backward and forward. It was annoying his wife and she was ready to tell him to stop it. Melanie had sent one of the girls to get Alice from her room. She'd been gone for ages and they were wondering where on earth she'd got to. Alice lay down flat on the bed. She was kicking her legs out behind her and she was drawing. This was her escapism. The time when nothing else mattered in the world to her, she could be anybody she wanted to be without being judged. When she had a pencil in her hand she drifted away and it was so peaceful. The white pieces of paper was spread out on the bed and Alice's tongue was hanging out a bit as she concentrated. The noise of her shading was like waves crashing against the shore. This was a masterpiece. The portrait was of a baby, Lizzy's deceased baby. Closing her eyes she remembered every detail of the frozen child she'd seen the night before. She'd got every crease of skin right on too, the fingers, the toes, the dark hair on the child's head, everything. Once she'd finished it she sat back with the pencil hanging out from her mouth, tapping it slowly against her teeth. Alice touched the portrait with her fingertips and a single salty tear trickled down her cheek. This was the child she'd seen last night; it was the double of her. Instead of the white towel around the infant she'd drawn a blanket instead, a thick knitted blanket where every stitch was visible. In the bottom right hand corner she wrote a small message. "To Lizzy we'll, never forget." She signed the portrait and rubbed her hand across it for the last time to remove any loose debris. As soon as Lizzy was back at the home she would give her to her. At least then she would have something to remember her child by.

Alice jumped as Sally stormed into the room. "Bleeding hell, I've been looking for you for ages. Your nana and granddad are here to see you," she stood looking at the paper in Alice's hand. "What's that you've done there, let me have a look at it then?" Sally snatched the portrait from her hands. Alice wanted the floor to open up and swallow her. She wasn't confident that her work was any good and hated people seeing her artwork for the first time.. Her work was personal and private. "This is amazing," Sally whispered. Her eyes looked closer at the sketch and she lifted her head up slowly. "This is Lizzy's baby isn't it?"

Alice nodded. "I just thought that I needed to do something to help ease her pain. She has nothing left. That baby meant the world to her. Life's so cruel sometimes isn't it? Why wasn't it my child that died? Why did it have to be Lizzy's baby?" This was all getting a bit too deep for Sally and she wasn't going to open a can of worms that could have had her there for hours. Each girl there had their own reasons to forsake their baby and she wasn't getting into it now, she didn't have time. "Alice, come on, we can talk about this later. I'll ask Melanie for a frame for the picture. I'm sure she'll bend over backwards to get us one now. She knows it only takes one word from us and her world will fall apart."

Alice stood up and placed her artwork on the side of her bed. "Someone needs to make sure Jenny is alright. Can you go and see her while I go and see my family.

Tell her I'm sorry that I didn't back her up. I just lost my bottle. I'm sick of fighting, I've got nothing left."

Sally hurried her along. "I know what you mean. I'll go and see her soon. She might have calmed down by now with any luck." Alice picked her grey cardigan up from the end of her bed and ran her fingers through her short cropped hair. With caution in her step she went to see her family.

"Well, where is she?" Pat asked Melanie, "Twenty minutes we've been sat here. What are we waiting for?" This was just extra stress that Melanie didn't need. Alice's family were doing her head in. She was flustered and twisted her head behind her looking down the corridor. Pat was on one; she was never shy at coming forward and if she had something to say, no man, nor beast would ever stop her. Here it was, the abuse that always followed when she was annoyed. "What kind of a place is this anyway when you can't find my bleeding granddaughter? I want to see her and I want to see her now. Don't you be giving me any more excuses love, because I'll knock your bleeding block off. I've shit bigger than you, smart arse. Now go and get her before my foot goes right up your arse." Pat was giving it out for sure and Melanie was gobsmacked. Her cheeks were bright red and she was just about to call for help when Alice appeared at the other end of the corridor. There was no way she was being spoken to like this, she demanded dignity at work.

Ted grabbed Pat's shoulder, aware that she could lash out at any second. He hated her when she was like this, she was a right handful. "Can you just keep it shut for two bleeding minutes Pat? Bloody mouth almighty you are. Here's Alice now. I don't know what's up with you

sometimes, you always have to take it to the next level."
Pat flicked the invisible dust from her sleeve and shrugged
her shoulders. There was no way she was apologising.
Melanie could suck a fart out of her arse if she thought
she was getting one too, it just wasn't in her make-up.
Pat would never admit when she was wrong, stubborn
cow she was. Pat held her arms out wide and her eyes
clouded over as she saw Alice for the first time. Ted gave a
gently smile to Melanie and tried to smooth things over.
He kept his voice low and made sure his wife didn't hear
him. "Excuse my wife, she's just upset. She get's like this
sometimes. I think it's her hormones."

Melanie didn't want any more trouble today; she'd
had enough grief to last her a lifetime. She'd only just got
off the phone to the big wigs at head office and she knew
her neck was on the line when they told her they were
coming to the building to take some statements. Melanie
cleared her throat and spoke. "If you would like to follow
me I'll show you to the visitor's room. I'll get some tea
and coffee brought over to you all. Would you like some
biscuits too?"

Pat ignored her. She hated authority figures and you
could see where her daughter had got her rebellious streak
from. Ted nodded his head. "Please can we have two teas
with two sugars in each? Thanks for your hospitality and
once again I'm sorry about my wife's outburst." Melanie
walked off in a huff. Common they were in her eyes, they
were the reason their granddaughter was in here, there
was no question about it.

Pat hugged Alice; she was hurting her she was
squeezing that hard. "Pat, let her go will you, she can't
breathe" Ted said at last. Alice was turning blue as Pat

released her just in time. Ted shot his eyes to her stomach and his heart sank. There it was, the sin, the bastard growing deep inside her. If he'd have had his way he would have terminated the pregnancy. He didn't care how far gone she was, he would have dealt with it. She was a young girl and he knew her life was ruined even before it had started. Adoption was the only option left for his granddaughter. He knew that, he'd thought about it for days on end but what would happen when the child was born? What if she wanted to keep it? What if the years passed and Alice found happiness then the child grew up and he or she came looking for her? He had so many questions floating about in his head and no matter which way he thought about it, the ending was never good. Alice was fucked, one way or the other, she was fucked.

"I want you to come home with me Alice. We're your family and I'll make sure you're safe," Pat said in a stern tone. Alice swallowed hard, she did have somebody who cared about her and she was loved by her family.

"Nana, I need to stay here until it's done. I can't be seen at home with a child in my stomach. People will ask too many questions and I can't answer them right now. I love you both with all of my heart and once it's over, I'll come and stay with you both."

Pat let out a laboured breath and she wasn't holding anything back. Typical, so bleeding typical, she never thought before she put her mouth into gear. She shot her eyes to Alice's stomach. "That thing inside you will be gone soon. You can hide away at our house; nobody will ever know you're there. You should tell us who has done this to you and I'll have his dick cut off, the dirty bastard." Pat studied Alice and sighed. "I can tell by your eyes you know who the father is and I don't know why you're protecting him. He's a no good dirty bastard and they should lock him up and throw away the key. Isn't that right Ted, go on, tell her she should tell us his name."

Ted dipped his head. This was history repeating itself. They'd had the same conversation with Janice when she was this age, she was a stubborn cow too and never once did she breathe a word about Alice's father. Ted had his own suspicions of course but he had no proof. Janice was a dark horse and he never believed a single word she told him, she was devious and sly. "Pat, just leave Alice alone. If she wants to stay here until it's over then we need to respect that." Ted was thinking about his own family name, his neighbours and his friends. He wanted no more shame brought upon his household. Alice gave her granddad a gentle smile, she was the apple of his eye and he would have done anything for her.

Pat continued. "I've heard your mother is off the beer and drugs now. A few people have told me but I don't believe them. She's too far gone to ever get clean in my eyes. It's probably just another cunning plan of hers to get something she wants."

Alice sat back in her seat as Melanie returned with the drinks. There was no conversation between them and she just placed the tray on the table and left. Pat waited for her to close the door and her face creased. "Oh she looks a right one she does. She's got a face like a smacked arse. I've just had a right go at her, tell her Ted, didn't I tell her straight."

Ted raised his eyebrows and his eyes closed slowly. "Yes love, you did tell her." He was so henpecked and he very rarely answered his wife back.

Pat reached over and took a sip from her drink, her expression was sour. "Has the bleeding cow died or what in this place. She must have only put a drop of milk in each cup the tight cow. I bet she spit in mine too," Pat chuckled and crossed her legs. She was back at Alice now. "Please come home with us love. I've spoken with your case worker Christine and she's looking into it for us. There will be no problems. You'll be safe with me I promise you."

"Pat," Ted shrieked. "I said leave her alone. Just back off, and be quiet for once in your bleeding life."

Pat folded her arms and looked about the room in a huff. She looked over at Alice and her eyes were wide open. "I'm not being funny love but what the hell has happened to your hair. It makes you look simple, honest to God, the moment I looked at you I thought what the bleeding hell has she done to her hair. You know me love; I have to say it how it is." Pat smirked and tried to make light of the matter. She playfully pushed her over. "You remind me of one of them lesbians from down the bottom of our street." She pointed her finger over to Ted and waved it about. "You know the ones don't you Ted, the women who look like two blokes. On my life Alice, I had to look twice at one of them. She had more muscles than your granddad."

Alice touched the side of her hair and you could see her pain. She knew if she'd told her nana one word about them cutting her hair off she would have had the place up. Oh yes, Pat would have scratched their eyes out. Alice nibbled on a biscuit; she didn't know what to say now, her words were stuck in her mouth. Pat examined her further. She wanted to know more about the abuse; how, where, and when. She just couldn't sweep it under the carpet; she needed to know no matter how much it would hurt her. Pat moved closer to Alice and placed her arm around her shoulder. "Tell me about it all love. I want to know what happened so I can understand what you're going through. I know it's hard but I'm your family I need to know what they put you through."

Ted bolted up out of his seat, there was no way he could listen to this, it disturbed him so much and if he would have sat there any longer he would have killed somebody stone-dead. He had to leave, he had to get some fresh air and clear his head. He stood up and grabbed his coat. "I'm going to pop out for a fag, Pat. I won't be long it will give you two time to chat."

Pat dismissed him and carried on talking to Alice. The door slammed shut and Ted was gone. "I'm sorry to bring it up Alice but you need to tell me everything, you can't deal with this on your own. I know you've spoken to people about it all but I need to know. I want to help you."

Alice swallowed hard and her emotions were high. To go through it all again, to relive every single detail of her abuse, she just wasn't ready for it. She tried to brush her off. "Nana, can we just forget about it for now. I need to blank it out of my mind. I've got bigger things to deal with at the moment," she shot her eyes to her stomach in hope she would back off.

Pat wasn't giving up that easy, she had to get her talking, she was worried about her. "Please Alice, for me. I need to know."

Alice covered her face with her hands and sobbed. "It wasn't my fault, honest. I never did anything to encourage them."

Pat blew her breath and pulled a fresh tissue out of her pocket, she passed one to Alice. This was going to be hard. Pat had to search her inner strength to find the courage to hold it together. Alice twisted the tissue in her hand slowly, her eyes were dipped low and she was heartbroken. "Dave was so nice to me at first. Whenever he came to our house he brought me sweets and even once he brought me a doll. He treated me like I was his daughter. I've never had a dad and this was the closest I was ever going to get to having one," she snivelled. "I wanted to be somebody's princess, nana. You know like all the other girls I know. I wanted to feel a father's love." Pat wasn't ready for this; she swallowed hard and carried on listening. "He gave me everything, he played with my hair when we watched TV together and he took me places, you know to the pictures and that." Pat growled and her fists clenched together at the side of her legs. "My mam was always too pissed to talk to him when he came over to our house and most nights she'd just fall asleep on the sofa. This happened quite a lot, well, every time he came over. She was just using him for the money I think."

Pat hissed and played with her neck scarf. "Yes, that's your mother all over. She thinks about nobody but herself."

Alice lifted her head up and looked directly at Pat. "I was sat on his knee when it happened. We were watching a film and we were cuddled up close as the scary bit came on. It was cold and we had a blanket wrapped around us both. My mam was asleep, dead to the world she was snoring. And that's when he did it." Pat sat forward in her seat and she looked like she was going to leave, her face was white and she kept ragging her fingers through her hair. She turned away as Alice continued. "He put his fingers inside me. As I tried to scream he covered my mouth and held me still. I couldn't do a thing, nothing. Afterwards he left me money to get a new toy, he told me it was our secret and if I ever told anyone he would make sure he would find me and kill me. This went on for a few more weeks. I always made sure I was never sat near him after that. I did everything to keep my mam awake at night and when I heard her screaming at him one night after an argument I knew he was history." Alice closed her eyes and shook her head slowly. "That was one of the happiest days of my life and I was so happy he was gone."

Pat snapped, her guts were turning and she was retching into her cupped hands. "Right, that's enough. I thought I was strong enough to listen to you but I'm not. Oh Alice, you poor, poor creature. Why didn't I just take you from her when you were born? It's my fault; I should have done something sooner." There was so much guilt in the room; remorse and regrets that things hadn't been different. But nobody could change the past could they? It had happened and no matter what, things would always be the same.

Pat cried, oh she sobbed her heart out and it was Alice who was consoling her now. She took her granddaughter's face into her cold hands and looked directly into her eyes. "This is far from over, I don't know how, or I don't know when but those bastards will pay for what they've put you through and that means your mother too. She's evil, and no daughter of mine. I swear to you now Alice, I wouldn't piss on her if she was on fire. I've washed my hands of her for good and you're my only concern now."

Ted walked back into the room and he looked

uncomfortable. He watched his wife wiping her eyes and knew whatever had been said in this room had affected her deeply. This family was falling apart, there was so much pain, so many tears. Were they ever going to find happiness?

Skid sat in his car with his head dipped low. He'd followed Pat and Ted here and now he knew where Alice was staying. It was only a matter of time before he had her in his grip. He needed to silence her once and for all. Starting the engine he crept out from the lay- by and joined the traffic. One last look in his rear- view mirror and he smirked. Alice was his for the taking and he'd make sure she never told anyone his seedy little secret. The clock was ticking and she was living on borrowed time.

CHAPTER TEN

Tina looked about the bedroom and couldn't believe her luck. She'd hit the jackpot this time, this guy was rolling in cash. His pad was mint, all the latest gadgets and more than that, all the drugs she ever needed to feed her filthy habit. Gugz walked into the room, he'd been in the shower. His chocolate coloured torso was still wet and there wasn't one ounce of fat on him. He was eye-candy for sure. He dropped his towel at the end of the bed and Tina's eyes nearly popped out of her head. His tool was massive, like a baby's arm holding an apple; she'd never seen a penis so big in her life. No wonder he was walking around parading it, it was a fine looking thing. Tina lifted her head up slowly and got a better look at his wedding tackle, she was drooling. She wasn't really into sleeping with Asian men but he was different. She would never tell anyone about him. If word got out on the square that she was shagging a Pakistani she would have been slagged off by everyone. If her family got one whiff that she was sleeping with anyone other than a white person she would have been hung drawn and quartered. Her dad hated Asians and he always said they were dirty smelly bastards, he was old school and his view never changed.

Tina wasn't racist; she liked anyone no matter what colour their skin was. She'd kissed a mixed race lad before, so that just goes to show she wasn't racist. She was however amazed by the Asian religion. How they all respected their beliefs and never let their family down. She liked some of the clothes the girls wore too, bright sparkly dresses. Not so much the headscarves though, she could never wear one of them, she would look a right nobhead. Tina listened to Gugz praying in the other room, he was mumbling to himself but she could still make out what he was saying. She was sure he'd said a prayer last night after sex too, she never asked him though as she didn't want to seem as if she was taking the piss out of him. Do Asian men have to say prayers after sex, she'd heard something about this before from one of her friends but wasn't sure if she was lying? Tina smirked, if this was the case she'd have been on her knees praying most of the day, she loved sex. Tina never really knew what love-making was, she'd never had anyone who'd loved her or wanted to please her. She was always just a bang, a sack emptier, a back warmer some might say. It was a shame really because she was a good-looking girl. She had a lot to offer too, she was intelligent and before life on the square began she was set to have a bright future. Tina just got mixed up with the wrong crowd, the party animals that lived every day to the full. They never cared about exam results or what they would be when they were older they just lived every day as it came, no stress, no nothing. Tina's parents were hard to please and every day they pushed her to do well at school. She just couldn't take it, her head was banging all the time and she always felt she had to do more to impress them. They were a well-off family too, she'd never wanted for much in life and they never knew what it was like to live from hand to mouth every day. Tina was a posh kid and when she first landed on the square, a lot of the clan wouldn't accept her. She was different from them; she didn't know what real life was all about. Her parents had jobs, they had a nice home, she'd had it handed to her on a plate, the jammy cow. She'd never struggled.

It was Terry Marland who'd taken her under his wing; he saved her in a way. She was young and vulnerable and there was just something inside her that always wanted to impress people, she needed to fit in. Terry spotted her the moment she landed in his domain. She was different to the other girls on the square, she had class. Even the way she smelt was something he wasn't used too - she smelt of money, the easy life, success. Yet it was Terry who set her on the road to destruction if truth be told. He gave her drugs and he took her virginity. He was falling in love with her too but when he got sent down she was like a bike, everyone was riding her. It was Terry's first love, puppy love everyone called it. He never told anyone he'd fallen for her except his sister Sandy, she was the only person he'd ever opened up to. Tina broke his heart and to this day she never knew what she'd done to him inside, he was scarred. Tina loved Terry at the time she was with him. There was no denying that, they were always together but he wasn't there when she needed him most. Tina needed someone to feed her weed habit, someone to make her feel special like he did when he was on the out. The day he got sent down she went to court with him and when the judge passed sentence her world fell apart. Terry was her rock, the one who kept her sane. He just knew how to make her feel good about herself. When he got slammed in jail she folded in two. Don't get me wrong, even today Terry still slipped her one, when he was bored he'd give her a call and empty his sack. But, there was never love involved, he'd cried enough tears over her in the past and jail had toughened him. He'd never let a women get close to him again, his guard was up.

Tina sat up in the bed and straightened her hair. She licked her lips slowly and watched Gugz enter the bedroom. He smiled at her and sat on the end of the bed. "You're special you are Tina. I could fall in love with somebody like you." Wow, this guy was pressing all the right buttons now and he had her eating out of his hand with the bullshit he was chatting. He knew what made a woman tick and if he was to get her talking he had to up his game and get her to trust him. "Last night was amazing Tina. I'm not just saying it but you're one of the best lovers I've ever had." He crept up to the top of the bed and sank his warm wet lips onto hers. She could feel his warm member pushing deep into her groins.

"You're just saying that Gugz. There's nothing special about me I can tell you. I've got issues, bad issues at the moment and I just need to sort my head out."

Gugz could see her vulnerability and struck while the iron was hot. "How can someone like you have issues? Look at you; you're everything I'm looking for in a woman."

Tina was listening, her ears pinned back and she was caught up in the moment. He kissed her and for the first time in a long time she had butterflies in her stomach, bubbles of love floating around her heart. Cupid had fired the arrow of love. She closed her eyes and melted into his arms. He knew he had her now, he knew she would be singing like a canary as soon as he mentioned Terry's name. The kiss led to sex, not the usual jerk and a squirt she was used too. No, this guy was making love to her, taking his time caressing every inch of her. His body glistened as he held it up over her. Every muscle was ripped and with every movement he made she groaned with pleasure. Usually it was Tina who had to do the work with her men in the bedroom but this guy was the one calling the shots. He knew how to treat a woman and he caressed her softly, teasing her, making her gag for more. He was riding her now and her spine curved as he picked her up from the bed. Last night they'd had a mess about with each other and she couldn't really remember it properly because she was twisted but she knew they didn't have sex. She'd remember this though, this was the best sex she'd had in her life.

Tina moaned as a wave of pleasure circled her, her nails dug deep in his back and he didn't look happy as he pulled her hand away. That was all he needed – his wife accusing him of bedding another white girl. Gugz had been married for over a year. Another arranged marriage that wasn't going to work. Gugz had stepped up to the mark and done what was asked of him and married her anyway just to please his father. He had two lives, just like his father did and he did his best to keep his tracks covered, he was a sly fucker. Tina reached orgasm at the same time he did. Once it was over he lit two cigarettes and passed her one. Tina was still on cloud nine; she was still tingling and feeling frisky. Her hand stroked his chest as he passed her the cigarette. "So, how do you feel about me Tina? Do you think we could have a life together?"

If Gugz would had given her a ring she would have married him there and then. She looked deep into his eyes and replied. "I like you Gugz. You're not the type I usually go for but I'm surprised by you."

"I bet you say that to all the men,"he sniggered. He watched her carefully and he was about to delve deeper. "Have you got a boyfriend or are you single?"

Tina blew the smoke from her mouth and reached over to flick her ash. "No, I'm single."

"Nar, you must have someone in your life. You're gorgeous, no way you're single."

Tina smiled and played with her hair. "There was this one lad I was seeing but we're kind of on and off."

"Who's that then, is he from around here?" Gugz was eager to hear more.

"He's called Terry Marland, a bit of a name around these parts; he's up his own arse if you ask me though. We had something special once, and well," she paused, "that was a long time ago. We're just fuck buddies now so to speak."

Gugz was on it, like a fly buzzing around shit. "I think I know the guy's name, is he from around Harpurhey?"

Tina was opening up, unaware that she was giving this man everything he needed to take Terry down. "Yeah, he's always in the square with his side-kick Skid. They think they own the place because they've got the square on lockdown. Terry had fuck all when I was with him but now he's earning he thinks he's God's gift to women, he's a twat, a self-centred prick who'll come down to earth with bang one of these days."

"How does he earn, does he lick shot?" Tina hadn't heard this saying before and held her head to the side; he could tell she didn't know what he meant. "Licking shot means selling drugs."

Tina giggled and lay flat on the bed with her naked chest showing. "He's into everything; he sells drugs and whatever else he does to keep his head above water. He's had a good graft lately though because Skid always buys new trainers when he's had a good earner."

Gugz loved this, she was telling him everything, he urged her to continue. He tickled her waistline with a single finger just to keep her talking. "Is Terry still living around here? I mean does his family live in Harpurhey?"

Tina looked at him and her face creased at the sides. "Why are we even talking about that nob anyway, he's in my past I told you."

For fucks sake, just when she was about to spill the beans. He needed this information and made sure she couldn't change the subject. "Wow, chill out girl, there's no need to bite my head off. I was only asking you a simple question."

Tina knew he'd spat his dummy out, she noticed he'd stopped tickling her too. She needed him back onside and fluttered her eyelids at him. "I'm sorry I snapped it's just when I talk about Terry it winds me up. Anyway, in answer to your question Terry's family disowned him. Well, not his sister he still keeps in touch with her. I suppose she's the only family he has now. He loves her too, he'd never let a bad word be said about her. His dad was a bastard with him, you know the type, my way or the highway," she ran her finger along his lip and raised her eyebrows as she continued. "Families are funny things aren't they. They say you can pick your friends but you can't pick your family," she was boring him now and he was fidgeting, restless. "His family still live on Collyhurst village near the shop, a big house it is on the corner. They've lived there for years." Tina closed her eyes slowly and she was seeing the image of Terry's house because she started to tell Gugz the colour of the front door and about the large front garden. She was doing his head in, he had to get it out of her, she needed to stop chatting shit and tell him what he wanted to know. "And, does Terry not get his head down at his parent's home or what?" "No, he's got his own pad in new Moston, just off Moston Lane it is number one ,one, six. I've been there a few times too; it's a smart gaff for a single lad living on his own. He's done well for himself." Gugz had what he needed; at last the slut had served a purpose. He was going to keep her close by for sure, even tell her she was his girlfriend. He kissed her again and she was lost in the moment, lost in his conker coloured brown eyes. "I'll take you out tonight Tina. I'll drop you off now back at home and I'll pick you up later on. I've got to go and work now but I look forward to seeing you later." Tina was buzzing, she jumped up out of bed and had a bounce in her step, a twinkle in her eye. She'd not even had any drugs either this morning. Usually by this time she'd have had a little bump just to get her going for the day ahead. She loved cocaine but she looked like she loved this man more. He was just what she needed. So what, he was a Pakistani, but she liked him, and if her family had anything to say they could take a running jump, she didn't care. This was her life and she was going to live it the way she wanted to.

Gugz let Tina out of the car. She'd made him drop her off down the street from her house. If her dad would have seen him he would have kicked off big time. Tina's mother was a fussy cow too. She wouldn't eat curries or any foreign food. "Give us a kiss then," Gugz said as he pulled the handbrake up. Tina kept her eyes open and puckered up. She had to make sure nobody saw her. A quick kiss and she was out of the car. "I'll see you later; you've got my number so ring me when you're ready."

Gugz watched her walk down the street. She had a nice arse and he rubbed at his crotch as he watched it shake with every step she took. He picked up his mobile phone and dialled a number. He pressed the button for loud speaker. "Yo Ali, it's me Gugz. It's all going down here. I've got names and addresses. Meet me later and we'll sort it out yeah." Gugz was laughing his head off and tapping his fingers on the steering wheel. "You know what Ali, the white slut is telling me everything. She loves a bit of black cock inside her too. I'll just keep her a bit longer then cart her. It's a shame because she gives good head too. Proper dirty bitch she is."

Gugz started to drive down the street behind Tina. As he passed her he honked the horn on the car. Tina's dad twisted his head from the garden gate and clocked her waving back at him. As soon as she reached him he was screaming at her. "Who was that Asian cunt? I hope you're not mixing with his sort. You know how we feel about it, don't wind me up Tina." John cracked his knuckles as he watched the back of the car driving down the road. He was such a dickhead and had double standards. To the world he was Mr Perfect but behind closed doors he was sick and twisted in the head, a fruit cake. John worked with Asians too in his job, and other foreigners. Nobody would have known he was a racist, he hid it so well. Tina ran down the garden path and couldn't wait to get inside. She knew what was coming now and prepared herself for the usual lecture that came when she'd stayed out all night. John slammed the front door shut behind him. He marched in the living room behind her and grabbed her by the throat. "I said, I hope that Asian twat is not with you. Tell me now Tina before I lose my rag. You know how I feel about them smelly bastards."

Tina struggled to break free; he was really hurting her, his finger dug deep into her arms. "Dad, I don't even know him. He must have been letting onto someone else. I feel the same way you do about them so just let me go, you're hurting me."

John let out a laboured breath and marched about the front room. "Good fucking job lady, good fucking job."

Tina was doing what she always did best, trying to please, trying to impress, keeping everybody happy. This was her worst trait by far, the root of all her problems. John sat down near the back door and let the gentle breeze from outside tickle his cheeks. Once he lost his temper his blood pressure went sky high and he knew he had to calm down before he gave himself a heart attack. "So, where were you last night? A phone call would have been nice so we would have known you were safe."

Tina raised her eyes. She was always staying out and he'd never bothered before, he was just being an arse. "Where's my mam?" she asked.

"In bleeding bed where she always is." She was sorry she even asked, he was on one now. "Every day she's got a new ailment that woman has. There's something not right in her head I tell you. The minute she walks in from work she's straight up the stairs and asleep within the hour. What kind of life do I have ay, when all she does is work and sleep?" Tina had heard this all her life. Her mother had a demanding job and she worked all the hours God sent, she needed to, for the life she led. Luxury holidays and new cars every year came at a price. John was jealous of his wife and her successful career. He never said it outright but it was there for everyone to see. Tina didn't even know why they were still married because they lived such separate lives. Her mother Marie was working away all the time and he was addicted to playing on his PS3. He played on the game, "Call of Duty," whenever he had any free time. He had the headphones to speak to other players on the net too. I suppose he was a loner, he had no real friends, just his online ones. He loved war and the element of surprise. I think the game got into his head and he fancied himself as some kind of action hero. Tina was edging towards the door before he got onto her life. And, he would you know. Any moment now he would give her the usual lecture about the life she was living. He didn't know the half of it really; he thought she was looking for work when in fact she had no intention of ever working a day in her life. She got by without working. Her mother was always bunging her a few quid and she still provided her with an allowance for clothes each month. Guilt money it was, to make up for all the time they spent apart.

Marie had never really taken to motherhood and Tina had mostly been brought up in nurseries and after school clubs. Any chance Marie got, she would palm her out and carry on with her life as if she never existed. There was no real bond between them, no mother and daughter days out shopping, nothing really. As a child Tina spent most of her youth sat in her bedroom on her own. She was a swot and studied every free minute she got. That all changed though when she found some friends at school. Bad girls they were and it surprised even Tina when she was accepted into their circle. The girls all had attitudes, they shoplifted, did drugs, and sex was there for the taking with them. It's just the way it was; most of the girls were the same. Marie said she was a follower when she found out she'd been going on the square at night, a coward she called her who couldn't speak up for herself. She was right in a way; Tina was bullied into doing a lot of things she never wanted to do, illegal things, sick twisted things. John looked at his watch and dived onto the sofa. He smirked at her and waved his finger about in the air. "Right, piss off if you're going. I'm going online now to take some mother- fuckers down. The lads are logged in so it's all guns blazing. I'm going to blast some brains out." John never even saw her leave, he was lost in the game and the battles taking place on the screen. Loud gunshots were heard, people screaming. He loved this world; he loved that he could kill people. Tina shook her head and left the room.

Tina was different today. She had a lovely warm glow about her, a calmness, a tranquillity. Searching in her pocket she found the last of the cocaine she had to her name. She examined it and for the first time ever she hid it away in the bottom drawer of her bedside cabinet. Gugz was her addiction now and she was going to do everything she could to keep him by her side. This guy could change her life; end the misery she had to face every day. Lying on her bed she grabbed her phone and found his number, she just sat staring at it. She was in love, she'd fallen for him hook line and sinker.

CHAPTER ELEVEN

Terry was raring to go, he kept taking deep breaths and punching his fist into the air. He was in the zone. It was after midnight and he was tooled up ready for action. His favourite weapon, his claw hammer, was never far from his side at times like this. He needed it to take his victim down with one swift blow, no messing about. Skid was driving and he was quiet. He wasn't much of a talker these days and he seemed to have lost his mojo. Terry cracked his knuckles and nodded his head slowly. "We'll sneak in through the back door and Shanghai-surprise the fucker. Once we get the cunt secured we'll torture him. No mercy, we'll make him beg us to stop."

Skid didn't answer him. They'd been watching Darren's house for a few days now and knew his every move. The guy looked like a walking wreck. Every time he stepped foot out of the door he was constantly checking over his shoulder. He was paranoid and he had every right to be. The word was out that he was a nonce and it was only a matter of time before somebody came through his front door and dealt with him. For weeks he'd heard the abuse being shouted at him from outside and never once did he do a single thing about it. How could he, he'd committed the crime. He'd declared his innocence of course to the law but no one believed him. He could never admit what he'd done, ever. He was a kiddy fiddler, end of. His court date was in two months and the police had bailed him to his home address. Darren must have been on tag because he had a black band strapped around his ankle which was visible when he walked. His curfew was seven o'clock each night. The lads knew this because they'd watched him running home when it was nearly time for his curfew to start with his arse flapping. This once main man had fallen to pieces, gone under and disgraced his name. He was thinner than before and he looked gaunt. He looked scruffy too, minging in fact. The only time he went out of his home now was to score some drugs and to get food. His life had been turned upside down since Alice had pointed the finger at him and he would never be the same again.

Even Darren's family had disowned him. The only person who came to see him was his probation officer. He used to go to the office to see her at first but someone had leaked the information that he was paedophile and all the other criminals were ready and waiting for him. The stamp of being labelled a wrong 'un was worse than anything he could ever think of. This once Jack the lad was now a loner leading a solitary life. He couldn't go down to the boozer anymore as even his mates wanted nothing to do with him. Trevor Balding was one of his best mates, too. They went back years and always chilled together. Brother's in arms they'd been. But, once Darren had told him about the allegations he told him straight he wanted fuck all to do with him. A bit harsh some might say but that's how it was, nobody ever tolerated nonces. Trevor had kids too, young girls. There was no way he was chancing their safety. He could never leave him alone with his girls again, he just didn't trust him. Darren was alone in the world and several times he'd tried to take his own life. He used to go and sit outside Janice's house and watch for any sign of Alice. He just wanted to tell her he was sorry, to clear his conscience, to make things right, to make him feel better about himself. Every night when he closed his eyes all he could see was the young girl's face and the pain in her eyes, the hurt he'd caused. It was the drugs that did it, that had made him into the animal he'd become. He'd take that many pills and potions when he was out partying that he never knew what day it was. He was off his face when it happened, not in control of his mind, twisted. Alice was so angelic, so pure, untouched and he wanted her from the first moment he saw her. She was the forbidden fruit he just had to have. Darren lay in his bed and he was chain-smoking. He'd only just finished one fag and he'd spark another one up. Every noise he heard he was out of bed, checking the house for intruders. He'd had threats, oh yes, lots of them to burn his house down, to burn him alive. They said they were going to cut his cock off and hang him too. The list was endless. The community was up in arms when they knew that a paedophile was living in the area and every now and then he'd get a brick launched through his window. This was a warning of things to come. This neighbourhood stuck together and in the past he'd been part of ridding scumbags from the area too. Darren had a gun, a silver pistol. He'd used it a few times in the past. He'd never killed anybody with it but he just had it to make his street cred a bit more powerful. Every night he placed it next to his bed just in case he had to use it. Staring into the night sky he put his ear phones in and listened to some calming music. He needed it if he was ever to get a few hours sleep, he had insomnia.

Terry dug the screwdriver deep into the wooden

frame of the window, scraping and pulling at the frame. He knew how to gain entry into anywhere, he was a sneak thief. In his youth he'd robbed houses too. It wasn't something he was proud of and never told anyone. He'd robbed from the working class, something he had always regretted. It was at a time when he was on his arse and needed money fast. It didn't matter where he got it from, he just needed it to survive. Skid's breathing was heavy; he seemed to be breathing through his nose, grunting. It was cold and puffs of mist shot from his mouth. Everything was ready; they both knew what the other was doing. Terry pulled the pane of glass from the window and placed it on the floor. He'd dug every bit of putty from the frame and made sure he was careful when he pulled it out so it didn't smash. Stretching his hand inside the window he lifted the catch up. "Get your arse in then," he hissed over at Skid.

Skid climbed up through the window and within seconds he was inside. He was fast as lightning and never wasted a second. Terry could see a shadow at the back door as he stood shivering, teeth chattering together. The door unlocked and they were both inside. Skid nodded and patted Terry on the top of his shoulder. "Good job the keys were in the back door isn't it?" Terry never said a single word, his head was in the game now, adrenalin rushing through his veins. He was ready for action. The large vein at the side of his neck was pumping with rage, someone was getting it big time. Skid rolled his neck around in circular movements and his nostrils flared, his breathing was rapid. This shit was going down. Slowly the pair of them started checking the rooms downstairs. Each one was empty and it was time to go upstairs, to face the evil bastard sleeping there. Terry's hands gripped the banister tightly and his face creased as he stood on the first stair, it creaked loudly. "For fucks sake," he whispered. They both stood frozen and made sure nobody had heard them. Terry made his way up the dark staircase first, followed closely by Skid. They were both dressed in black; black hats, black gloves the lot.

Terry held a single finger to his mouth as he opened the first door slowly. They could see Darren facing the window and they knew he was awake because his feet were moving about. Skid tiptoed to the side of the bed, he was quick and light as a feather. Terry pulled the claw hammer from his jacket and swung it high over his head. This was it, the crippling blow that would knock him for six. Darren didn't stand a chance; he was a lamb to the slaughter. Skid had a baseball bat in his hand and they were both smashing fuck out of their victim. There were screams at first but gradually they faded. Darren was covering himself with shaking hands. Skid took over now; this was his shout, time to wipe the nonce from the face of the earth. He had to save his family's name. Darren was blowing bubbles of blood from his mouth, thick red claret dribbling down his chin. Terry grabbed his mouth and held his cheeks together as Skid took over. "You dirty bastard, did you think you could get away with it. You're a fucking dirty pervert who messes about with young girls."

Skid got down to his face and spat right into his eyes. This wasn't just a job to sort some fucker out who owed some money, this was personal. Skid took the hammer from Terry and he swung it back over his shoulder. Bones crunched, blood splurged all over the walls. Darren would never walk again. His kneecap was hanging from his leg, flesh showing all around it. Terry stood back and watched. His eyes clocked the shooter and without any hesitation he reached over and grabbed it. The score was settled now in his eyes. Skid stood hovering over the bed, his eyes filled with madness. He was lost in thought and something in his eyes wasn't right. Was he going to finish him off, kill him? Terry licked his lips slowly. He'd never helped kill someone before and this was all new to him. Of course he'd left people half dead but never had he been the whole way and helped end someone's life. He was game too; if Skid decided this was what he wanted to do, then he'd stand by him. If this was the other way round and his own sister was in the same situation, he would want them dead and never to walk the face of the earth again. Skid walked to the door and turned his head back to Terry. "Leave the cunt to die on his own, he's a rat and deserves everything he gets." Darren wasn't moving, his chest was rising slowly and any breath he had left was struggled, his body was shaking in shock. He didn't look good and death looked like the only option left for him. Terry made sure they left no evidence at the scene of the crime. He checked everywhere and made sure they had everything before they left. Then both of them stormed down the stairs and ran into the night. The deed was done. There wasn't a soul about and the coast was clear. Darren had got his payback and the record was set straight.

Terry sat in the car and popped a cigarette into his mouth. His heart was racing and his adrenalin rush was calming down. Skid was shaking like a leaf and he held his head out of the window gasping mouthfuls of air. "Fucking sick twisted cunt he is. I should have finished him off."

Terry passed him a fag. "Here, get a few blasts of that down you. Come on, it will calm you down."

Skid's hands were covered in blood. He quickly wiped them on his jeans as if they were infected with some contagious disease. All their clothes would have to be burnt now, they would have to destroy anything linking them to this crime. "Take me to our Janice's. She needs to know what's gone on, we have to word her up."

Terry turned the engine over and headed into the night. There was silence - both of them were in a world of their own as the reality of what had just happened was hitting home. Terry felt no guilt whatsoever. It was just all in a day's work to him. But Skid was scared. His own little dark secret was twisting him up inside, pecking at his head. He could have been that man lying on the bed getting beaten to death. He had to get to Alice before she told anyone. He needed to silence her and he was willing to do whatever it took to make sure her lips were sealed.

Janice rushed to open the front door when she heard Skid shouting her name through the letterbox. Her heart was pounding inside her rib cage. She'd not long been in bed and she was just drifting off to sleep. Life without drugs and alcohol was hard for her and it was only the last few weeks where she was seeing any light at the end of the tunnel. She'd gained a bit of weight too, she looked healthier. Her drug's worker was supporting her too and she was confident if she carried on the way she was doing, that she would be able to live a normal life again without being dependant on any illegal substances. Janice had been through cold turkey and she never thought she would see it through. She had been constantly vomiting and at one point she even shit her knickers, she just lost control over all her bodily functions. Life was different now though and she looked at things in a different light. Janice never thought she'd see the day when she was clean and off drugs and if it wasn't for losing her daughter she would never have imagined this day ever happening. It's funny how life throws a spanner into the works and makes people see what's really important to them. These things are sent to try us. Even when you think you have nothing left, people always seem to find the courage to fight until their last dying breath. Janice had a cause now, something to get up for each morning. She wanted her daughter back. She was ready to be the mother she should have been.

Janice knew her name was shit in the area and it was only a matter of time before her neighbour gave her a piece of her mind and put her in her place. Nancy Naylor was a loud-mouthed woman who never held anything back. She called a spade a spade, so to speak. She was feared in the area and was the local battleaxe. Janice was aware Nancy had heard all the violence over the years coming from her house and she'd told her once before, if she carried on she would report her. And, she would have given the chance. At first Janice thought Nancy was the one who'd bubbled her to social services and she was the reason Alice was now in care. She'd told Skid that if she found out this was true she was going to end Nancy's life. Janice had tried everything to see her daughter but she kept hitting a brick wall, nobody was listening to her. And, why the hell would they, she was just as bad as the abusers, she'd let it happen. She was the one responsible for her daughter's safety, nobody else.

Skid barged passed her as she opened the front door. He ran straight to the bathroom. As she walked past the room she could see him washing his hands and throwing cold water over his face. He was trying to wash away his own sin but no matter how many times he scrubbed at his face he would never be clean, he would always be an abuser. Terry followed Janice into the front room and sat down while Janice flicked the lights on. It was freezing in this gaff and Terry was blowing warm breath onto his hands to try and get warm. Janice sparked a cigarette up and sat with her arms folded tightly in front of her. She was aware something had happened and she was eager for Skid to come back into the room. Terry started to roll a joint. He knew that Janice was on the wagon and shot a look over to her. "Am I alright to blaze this joint in here or do you want me to go outside with it?"

Janice was being tested, she was fidgeting about and you could see she was struggling to refuse. Her nerves were shattered right now and just a few blast of the cannabis would have helped her chill out. "Just smoke it there Terry. I'm fine. I'll just smoke my cig."

Terry admired her determination. He'd tried hundreds of times to kick the habit but his lifestyle was just so complicated and it was the only thing he knew that calmed him down. He'd given it up once before but slowly but surely he got back into the habit. There was just too much of it about and as a dealer it was too hard to resist. It was like putting a chocolate addict in a sweet shop.

Skid came into the living room and his face was covered by a hand towel. He was sweating and his cheeks were bright red. "What's gone on Skid? Did you find

Alice or what? Please tell me you've found her."

Janice sat biting on her fingernails; she'd developed a twitch too in her left eye and it kept flicking rapidly. "We've just been and sorted Darren out. We kicked fuck out of him. He'll never mess with any kids again."

Janice stood up and ragged her fingers through her hair. "Fucking hell Skid, did he know it was you? I don't want any comebacks for me, you know what a crazy twat Darren is. He'll do me in if he finds out I've had anything to do with this."

Terry sat back in his chair and chugged hard on his spliff. "That cunt won't be going anywhere for a long time. Skid smashed his legs in and I'm not sure if he's still alive or not. We give it him big time, wasted the fucking scumbag."

Janice was in a panic, Darren was dangerous and his mind was twisted. He'd always told her that he would end her life and now that he had a reason too she was sure her neck was on the line. Skid could see she was worried. He'd witnessed some of beatings he'd given her in the past and knew Darren was more than capable of ending someone's life. "Listen to me Janice. I've just told you that he's going nowhere. He's not the Darren you remember anymore, he's fallen apart. He's about eight stone wet through, he's all skin and bones. He won't dare come anywhere near you, trust me."

Janice went into the kitchen and flicked the kettle on. She was gagging for a drink and ever since she'd been off the vodka her mouth was constantly dry. Terry watched her leave and sat forward in his seat. "So, what's next then? Are we going for Alice or are we leaving her where she is?"

Skid was anxious; he licked his lips and dropped his head low. "We need her back home. Once she's spoken to Janice she'll be alright. Fuck me Terry, what a big mess this all is. What the hell is going on in Alice's head right now? She's pregnant and away from home. Her head must be in bits."

Terry was thinking, he was like that when he was stoned and always pulled things apart, got to the bottom of stuff. "So who's the dad? Has she said who the father is?"

Skid swallowed hard and the colour drained from his cheeks. "Nar, nobody knows. It must be some random lad who she's been seeing or something like that."

Terry was having none of it. He'd met Alice before and knew she was no dirt bag. He could tell a slapper a mile off and there was no way he was having it that she was sexually active. "Alice didn't even have a boyfriend did she? Well, that's what she told me. To me she just looked like a geek, you know a bookworm."

Skid knew he was right but there was no way he was getting into a debate about it. "When did she tell you she never had a boyfriend? I don't remember that." Skid held his head to the side and looked at Terry a bit longer than he should have. "It could have been Darren who tubbed her. I mean, he was around at that time wasn't he?" Terry blew a laboured breath but he wasn't sure. Something just didn't seem right.

Janice came back into the room and the conversation stopped. "So, when are you going to bring my baby home?" Terry raised his eyebrows and couldn't believe what he was hearing. This woman wasn't on this planet. Did she really think it was going to be that easy to get

Alice back? Even if they did bring her back home the authorities would be booming the front door down within the hour searching for her. There was no way they would let her come back here, ever. He kept his mouth shut and listened. He never gave his opinion he kept his trap shut.

"I'm thinking we get her at weekend," Skid said, "but Janice she can't stay here with you. The dibble will be all over here as soon as she's reported missing. No, we have to get her somewhere safe." Skid looked over at Terry. He knew it was a big ask and hoped he could help them out. "I'm hoping Terry, can put her up at his house until we get somewhere proper sorted. It won't be for long mate, honest. Just a few weeks until it's all calmed down. You don't mind do you?"

Terry was on the spot. How could he say no when all eyes were on him and he felt obligated. He'd never had anyone else staying with him at his home and he didn't know if he could cope with someone invading his private space. Jail had made him like that and ever since he'd finished his sentence he was a creature of habit. He liked everything to have its place, to do things in a certain way. Janice was pushing him for an answer. "I could come to your house to see her and even stay a few nights, just until she gets settled. Alice is no trouble you won't even know she's there." Terry couldn't say no. He just nodded his head and the decision was made. Janice was over the moon and she didn't really understand how hard things were going to be. She could go to prison for what she was planning. Kidnapping held a big jail sentence if she was ever found guilty.

Skid started stripping off. "Terry, get your clothes off

and we'll burn the fuckers. We don't want any slip ups that will point the finger to us. We need to be on the ball and make sure our tracks are covered. Janice you're our alibi remember. If it's on top, then we were here with you all night long. We can say we played cards and had a few beers here with you."

Terry knew all the fine details needed to be sorted. If he was getting his collar felt he had to make sure his house was in order. They all needed to be singing from the same hymn sheet. He stood up and waited until Skid passed him some clean clothes. He always had a pile of spare clothing here and tonight was no different. Terry slipped his t-shirt over his head and he could feel Janice's beady eyes watching him. He knew she wanted him and just teased her as he took his pants down. Terry's arse was firm, like two eggs in a handkerchief. He stood tall in his black boxer shorts and made sure all his muscles were tensed. He was a right poser and loved that he never had a scrap of fat on him. He was lean and fit and had a physique to die for.

Skid clocked Janice staring at him and sniggered. "Janice, close your mouth will you? You look like you're catching flies. Bleeding hell, have you never seen a man's body before?"

She was never one to miss an opportunity to flirt and she sat back giggling. "I've seen plenty of men's bodies Skid, but not like that. Do you work out Terry, you're ripped to fuck, proper hench you are."

Skid saw his arse and walked in front of Janice doing a funny walk. "Erm, excuse me. What about me, I'm mint too. Check out my biceps." Skid was flexing his muscles and bending forward. He didn't have anything on Terry.

Yes, he was thin but his muscles weren't defined like Terry's were. He didn't even have a six pack. Janice's cheeks were hot. It had been ages since she'd had a leg over. And, if the truth was known she could have done with a quick shag just to ease her frustration. This was the longest she'd ever gone without having any rumpy-pumpy. Ever since being a teenager she'd always had someone filling her hole, no matter who it was. She was highly sexed.

Terry was dressed now and he was ready to leave. He was on a downer now that he'd said yes to having Alice staying with him. He had nothing against her but it just wasn't his thing. Terry gathered all the clothes together and shoved them inside the black bin liner that Janice had provided. He slung it over his shoulder and headed towards the door. "Right, I'll sort this lot out and make sure they are burnt. I'll go on the back fields and blaze the fuckers."

Skid walked over and shook Terry's hand before he hugged him. "Thanks for tonight pal. You know I'd do the same thing for you don't you?"

Terry smirked and felt proud that he'd been able to help. "No worries mate, see you tomorrow." Terry left and once the front door slammed shut behind him Skid sat down and started to build a spliff. It was time to wind down, time to chill and forget about all his problems.

Janice gulped the last bit of her brew and leant over and kissed his cheek. "You'll never know how much I appreciate what you two have done for me tonight. I will repay you one day when I'm back on my feet. Alice is coming back home where she belongs and I promise you now Skid, I'll never let anyone hurt her again. Cross my heart and hope to die. I'm going to sort my shit out and be there for Alice when she needs me." Skid watched her leave the room. He was alone with his thoughts now, alone with the guilt slicing deep into his heart. Lying down on the sofa with his hands looped over his head a tear trickled down the side of his face. He had so many regrets about the person he'd become.

CHAPTER TWELVE

Gugz sat with his father in the shop and gazed out of the window onto the square while Asif was pottering about filling the shelves with baked beans. "This could be a good little earner here for me dad. Tina said Skid and Terry lick shot from here and they take a right few quid."

Sharif stood tall and nodded his head. "Listen, first we want our money back. Once that's done then we can plan taking over this place but for now keep your head in the game and do what we set out to do."

Gugz stepped away from the window and walked back to his father's side. "I know what needs to be done and Tina is quite helpful. I know where he lives now and what makes him tick. I've found something he cares about, his heart, his jugular and I plan to make him pay for all the grief he's caused our family."

Sharif patted his son's arm as Asif came back to join them. "That's my boy, just make sure you don't leave any traces and clean your path after it's done."

Asif was listening now. He was a right fat fucker and his hand was never far from the sweet jar next to the till, he was constantly munching. He hadn't always been fat. In his day he was a great bit of eye-candy. Back then he had been thin and had a swagger just like his brother did. He had the way with the women too, he could talk any woman's knickers down. He had the gift of the gab. Many a late night after the shop had closed he'd have some woman inside, fucking her brains out. A lot of women had sex with him to keep him sweet. He was great at giving them tick until payday and they knew if they rubbed him up the wrong way he would ban them from having any credit in the shop. Rumour had it that some women actually sucked him off when they couldn't pay their food bills too and somehow I think this could have been true. Asif was a sexual predator and even now he would shag anything with a pulse, any age, any shape or size, a hole was a hole in his eyes and he didn't have any standards. To look at him, Asif was just a pot-bellied guy who looked like he'd given up on life. He ate to comfort the ache in his heart, the ache of the woman he loved but could never have. He hated his wife and he only went home every night to eat her food. His wife was a good cook and that's probably the only thing she had going for her. The family had given them both endless months of counselling trying to sort out the marriage but Asif was never interested, he was only there to keep the elders of his family happy. He loved his children, it was a shame because Asif was a family man and if he had married the right woman he would have been everything a wife was looking for.

Sharif reached over and grabbed a few sweets; he loved toffees too and also had a sweet tooth. Shoving them in his mouth he spoke to his son. "So, what's his weakness, is it his car?" He chuckled and looked at his brother. "That's my weakness you know and if anyone touched it I would go sick. See son, once you do your homework and you find out what you're working with its easy isn't it? I've taught you well son."

Gugz sat down and he was proud that he'd worked

well and impressed his father. "Skid is going to be no problem whatsoever. It's Terry who's the main man, he's the brains behind it all and he's probably the one who set it all up. Tina's told me where he hides his money in his gaff and everything. Honest dad, she's one grassing bitch. I'd never tell her anything, she's dangerous. Imagine if that was your wife telling your business to a complete stranger, because I am a stranger to her aren't I. I hardly know her?" He raised his eyes to the ceiling and gasped his breath. "See with our Asian women we have loyalty. There's no talking out of school, they keep their mouth shut."

Asif screwed his face up. What a load of bullshit they were talking, he was sick to death of hearing it. Asian women were just as bad as the rest of them, they had big gobs and were always gossiping. As soon as he had a problem with his own wife, she couldn't wait to tell her sisters all about it. He only had trouble getting a hard on for a few months and the world and his wife knew about it within seconds. Her sisters were round at their house mixing potions and lotions and setting him a new lifestyle to try and make his penis go hard again. And even to date he could still here them sniggering about it when he left the room. She'd made him a laughing stock. If the truth was known he hated the culture he'd been brought up in, hated it with a passion. His brother did too, if he was being honest but he just dealt with it better than Asif did. Sharif licked arse and always pretended he was one hundred percent committed to the faith. Asif was a great believer in love and thought fate was something that brought a man and woman together. It was written in the stars that his true love was sent to find him, they were destined to meet.

Gugz sat and cracked his knuckles. "Terry has a sister, the apple of his eye she is. And, if we need him talking I need to get her in my grip. Tina said she's all he has in terms of family, the rest have disowned him. I've found out where he lives too and I've checked his gaff out. I'm just sitting back before I go there. I need to get his sister Sandy first, don't I?"

Asif was worried. This was all getting out of hand and he wasn't into violence. The family had lost the money and they should just let sleeping dogs lie, shit happens. Sharif was making sure everything was going to plan. He didn't want any slip-ups, all he wanted was the money back. Gugz however wasn't like his father in that respect. He was from a different generation and knew in his heart that blood was going to be spilled no matter what. It's just the way it was. "I'm going to make them both sorry they ever messed with us. I'm going to take them both down and take the things they love. This square will be our turf soon. Why should we let some little muppets run it when it's right under our noses? This is a little goldmine and I'm going to make sure our lads run the scene around here from now on."

Asif knew this was never going to happen without a fight. He'd seen it over the years; different gangs coming here and trying to take over. Terry Marland was one tough cookie and he would never let this pitch go without a fight. The square was his life, always had been. Without it he would be lost. Asif put his fat fingers in the toffee jar again and sat munching more sweets. Shit was going down and he wanted no part of it.

Sandy Marland sat at the dining table with her mother. She was sixteen and a pretty little thing. She had the same eyes as Terry and they lit all her face up. Sandy was the perfect child, any parent would have been proud of her. She studied hard and had hopes and dreams for the future. Her heart was set on becoming a lawyer and even now she was well ahead in her studies. She knew everything there was to know about law and anytime anyone was in trouble they always came to her for advice. Sandy sat nibbling at her toast; a slight dribble of tangy marmalade was on it. Her mother was washing the pots at the kitchen sink and she was singing along to the radio. It was a shame the family had ended up the way it had and the son she loved so much was banished from her home. Terry had been a mummy's boy when he was younger and all he would have to do was put on his sad puppy dog eyes to his mother and she was putty in his hands. She'd have done anything for him. Her husband though, he was completely the opposite and she knew never to cross him. His word was gospel and if he said jump she would say "How high?"

Sandy grabbed her bag from the kitchen table and walked to her mother's side. "Mam, I'll be late home tonight. I'm going to the library to do a bit of research. I've got an exam soon and I want to make sure I've revised enough."

Her mother smiled as she watched her leave. She was so proud of her and she was a credit to the family. "Take care Sandy and make sure you ring me later and I'll come and pick you up. I don't want you getting the bus when it's dark outside. Just ring me when you're done and I'll nip over for you."

Sandy smiled at her mother she was such a worry wart. "Yes mother I will. See you later."

Sandy was gone and Angela was alone. Her husband was at work and she was sitting down to finish her brew. Angela looked worn out, as if she had a problem constantly on her mind. She put on her reading glasses and lifted the newspaper up to read it. Her eyes studied the date and a tear dribbled down her cheek. Today was her son's birthday. Walking over to the kitchen drawer she dug deep and pulled out several other cards that were all addressed to Terry. She'd never forgotten his birthday or his Christmas card and each year she'd write him one out. Angela held the blue envelope to her beating heart and rested her head on it. Why hadn't her son ever come back to see her? He knew his father was at work and he knew she would never turn him away. They could have met somewhere else; he didn't even have to come home. Words had been said over the years, bad words, hurtful ones and Angela regretted the way she'd acted. But what did Terry expect? She had to stick by her husband, she could never turn her back on him – they had to be united, stand tall together, strength in numbers. Terry had caused so many upsets in this household and at one point his parents were nearly getting a divorce. Proper murders they had and Angela had left to go and stay at her mother's on more than one occasion to get away from the trauma of her troublesome son. The card in her hand was wet with tears. She placed it with the others and dug them deep into the drawer. Nobody knew they were there and that's the way she liked it. Terry's name in the house was never spoken and it was only when she'd had a little tipple that she would discuss him with her daughter. Terry's dad never mentioned him though; he was a heartless bastard who never showed any emotion. To cry was a weakness in his eyes and he never let anyone get the better of him. His poker face was something he liked and nobody could ever read him.

Sandy sat at the bus stop listening to her music; she had one ear piece in. It was cold today and her coat was zipped up tightly. Sandy never wore pants and her thick red woollen tights were all that were keeping her legs warm. She loved colourful clothes and she was never afraid to stand out from the crowd. Sat alone she scanned the area. A car was parked at the other side of the road and she noticed two men sat in it. She never took much notice of them and carried on singing. She had a great voice too, husky and unique. This girl had so many strings to her bow and she was oozing with talent. She could sing, dance and even speak a little French. She was such the opposite to her older brother. Sandy had a close circle of friends and never took to making new friends easily. She was shy sometimes and found it hard to meet new people. Perhaps that's why she spent quite a lot of time on her own studying. There was a boyfriend though; nothing too complicated just good friends really who she snogged every now and then. Sandy didn't believe in sex before marriage and even though quite a lot of her friends had spread their legs already, she was keeping hers firmly shut. She was waiting for "The One." The one who would bowl her over, knock her off her feet, the one who would make her heart beat a thousand times per minute. Sandy was a hopeless romantic and loved the thought of falling in love and having a soul mate. She never had a type either, she never really found anyone who caught her eye and made her heart stop beating. She did like blue eyes though and often thought that when she had children they would hopefully have her eyes. Her father was completely against her having boyfriends anyway. Once she brought her boyfriend home for tea and he kicked up a fuss at the dining table and made sure the lad knew he was not welcome there ever again. Sandy's boyfriend called her family dysfunctional; he said her dad was a couple of butties short of a picnic, a proper head the ball. Sandy was all for a quiet life and she obeyed any order her father gave her. Never once had she defied him and rebelled.

People always asked her about her missing brother and only a few people knew the truth. He was her brother at the end of the day and she would never have anyone bad mouthing him. So what, he was a bad apple. People shouldn't judge him when they knew nothing about his story. Sandy secretly met with her brother whenever she was free. Nobody knew this and that's the way she liked it. He made her smile and their bond was close. They were like chalk and cheese and yet it worked so well. She was so calm and laid back and he was so hyper and stressed. When he spoke with her he tried to make her see the world from his point of view. He needed her to be streetwise and not to be as naive as she was. She knew nothing about the real world and how it ran and he was scared that people would take advantage of her. Every time they met they would go to Costa Coffee and have hot chocolate together. Thick white cream on the top of it and fat fluffy marshmallows floating about. They both loved it and it made them feel like children again. Terry melted when he spent time with his sister. She was the only thing that was pure and untouched in his life and he was so proud of her. He loved that she had dreams and goals to achieve. If Terry would have had his time again he would have loved to have followed in her footsteps. Nothing ever seemed any trouble for her, she saw the good in everyone and never spoke behind people's backs. Everyone deserved a chance in her eyes and she never back-stabbed anyone.

There was a time when he was worried about her though and he'd noticed that she seemed to have lost her happy-go-lucky character. She did confide in him and poured her heart out and together they solved her problems. Sandy's boyfriend had wanted to have sex with her and take it to the next level. Once Terry knew about this he made sure the problem was solved. Unbeknown to his sister he went to find the lad and put the fear of God up him. Oh he told him alright, he held a knife to his throat and told him if he so much as whispered that he'd been to see him he would back for him and the next time he wouldn't be as lucky, he'd slit his throat. Sandy never knew a thing about this and even to this day the lad never breathed a word about Terry's visit. The thought of his sister having sex made his stomach churn. She was too innocent for that and he wanted to keep her like that for as long as possible. Terry always told her everything and the last time she met him a few weeks ago it was his turn to be upset. He'd told her he was in some kind of problem and didn't know how he could get out of it. Sandy thought he was in love with some girl but he denied it and said he would sort his own shit out.

She always wished her brother would settle down with the girl of his dreams and somewhere in her heart she thought he might rekindle his love with Tina. They were good together once, they laughed all the time and it was the happiest she'd ever seen him. Sandy stood to her feet when she saw the bus approaching. She hated travelling by public transport and couldn't wait until she was old enough to drive. Once she paid her fare she sat down and looked out of the window as the other passengers paid their fare too. Her eyes studied the car parked across from the main road. The men were still sat in it and she was sure they were watching her. As the bus pulled off she watched the car merge with the traffic behind the bus.

Sandy turned her head quickly as a man came to sit next to her. He nearly squashed the life out of her as he squeezed his arse into his seat. Sandy was blushing, he was a young Asian man and he wasn't shy at coming forward. "It's bloody cold out there today isn't it princess?" Sandy was taken back and smiled gently. This wasn't her style just to start talking to random guys on the bus and she turned her head away and carried on looking out of the window. Sandy inhaled deeply, this man smelt good enough to eat, like fresh cut cinnamon, spicy and warm. It was a nice fragrance and she found herself inhaling deeper to smell the aroma. "So, are you at college then or what?" The man touched the book he could see sticking out of her bag. He pulled it out and smiled. "Oh, you're studying law. Wow, you must be clever to be into all that legal stuff?"

Sandy knew she would have to reply, she didn't want to come across as ignorant. "Yes, I've nearly finished my course now. I've just got my exams left."

The man nodded slowly. I think he was a bit taken back by her sweetness. "I wish I would have studied harder at school when I was there. I think I would have had a good job if I did."

Sandy was into the conversation now and was ready for a chat. The bus journey was a long one and it would be nice to have a natter with someone for a change. "What do you work as, if you don't mind me asking?"

The Asian man who was in his late twenties flicked the end of his cuff and he held a look of sadness in his eyes. "Erm, let's say I'm self-employed. I kind of make my own money if you know what I mean." He gave her a cheeky wink and hunched his shoulders. Was this a real life criminal she was talking to, had she heard him right? Would she look daft if she asked him to expand on his last sentence? She wasn't thinking straight and just asked anyway. Terry had told her about some grafters he knew and she was excited to hear about a world she knew nothing about. "When you say self-employed, do you mean you do illegal stuff, you know bad things?"

The man got a bit panicky and there was no way he was telling her everything, was she thick or what, he'd more or less just told her what he did for a living. "I make my own money. I'm kind of a buyer and seller." Sandy knew now he was a criminal and wasn't sure if she wanted to continue talking to him but this was going to be her life when her studies had finished. She would be working with criminals every day, it was just something she would have to deal with.

"What's your name anyway, do you live around here?" he asked.

Sandy wasn't sure if she should answer him or not.

She'd only just met him and he was after her life story. Terry had warned her about telling people too much about herself and she remembered that as she answered him. "I don't live far from here and my name is Sandy." Okay she did answer him but she never told him any real stuff about her, did she? She watched the man on his mobile phone from the side of her and she could see he was texting somebody. Once he'd finished, he kind of cut the conversation short. Sandy wondered if she'd hurt his feelings and kept smiling at him in hope he would talk to her again. Just a couple of stops left to go and from nowhere he started to talk to her. He was a funny bleeder and she couldn't work him out.

"I'm going to the college library to pick some information up for my two sisters. They're thinking about enrolling in September next year. Can I walk with you and you can show me where the reception area is?" Sandy looked at him and smiled, he looked harmless enough and what was the worst that could happen. He was only after walking alongside her. She agreed. The bus stopped and they both left together. Sandy turned her head and thanked the bus driver for her safe journey. She was so polite it was untrue. They both started strolling along the main road when the Asian man suggested that they cut through the marsh land at the side of the fence. This would take at least ten minutes off the journey and even though she'd never been this way before she let herself be talked into it. The Asian man was on his phone again texting and Sandy thought it was quite rude that he was more interested in talking to someone else rather than her. This guy was blowing hot and cold and as she started walking faster she started to feel a bit unsure about the choice she'd made. Towards the end of the path was an alleyway and Sandy was looking at the car parked there. Her heart was beating faster and she kept her eyes on the man at the side of her. Sandy was nearly running and she could feel the man's hot breath on her shoulder. With one last look at him she hooked her bag over her shoulder and spoke to him. "Sorry, I'm going to be late. I'll have to leave you here." Sandy was about to carry on running when from behind her she felt the warm hands of the man around her neck. She was trying to scream but his grip on her windpipe was stopping any sound leaving her throat. He had her in a head-lock and was dragging her down the thick brown muddy marshland. Her shoes were dragging along the floor and there was nothing she could do about it. She could hear other men's voices now. She couldn't see anyone as her vision was blurred but she was aware that she was surrounded. She could see feet running about where she stood and she knew other Asians were there as they were speaking in their own language. Sandy felt a warm wet liquid dribbling down the side of her cheek; she was bleeding from the side of her head. She was lifted from the floor and she was flung inside the boot of a car. It was pitch black and she could smell petrol. The boot slammed shut and she could hear lots of commotion from outside. She trembled as the engine started. With her knees up to her chest she knew whatever was going to happen next wasn't going to be good. Digging deep in her pocket she searched for her mobile phone. There was only one person who could help her now; he would never give up until she was found. Sandy had no credit left and texting was her only chance of getting help. With shaking hands she tried her best to text Terry. When the message was done she pressed the send button. This couldn't be happening, the message wasn't sending. Stretching her arm in different positions she tried it again. It was no good there was no reception the text wouldn't send. Her battery was nearly flat too. Sandy was sobbing, this was a nightmare. She's seen stuff like this on TV and the ending was never good. What had she ever done to deserve this, she was a good person. Why did they want her? What were they going to do with her? Sandy lay frozen in the car and she was bumping about as the car travelled faster. All she could hear was the engine roaring. Sharp objects were stuck in her back and whatever it was it was causing her great pain.

At last the engine stopped and there was silence. Sandy's eyes were wide open and she knew her fate was near. Making the sign of the cross over herself, she quickly prayed to the Lord above to help her find the strength she needed right now. The light against her eyes made her squint; she looked like she was blinded. There was more Asian dialect but nothing she could understand. She was dragged from the car and led to a steel grey door. The man she'd been talking to on the bus was by her side and when she saw him she sobbed. "Why have you done this to me, let me go? I haven't done anything wrong."

The man held some compassion in his eyes and he looked at the others for some guidance. "You better tell her what's going on. Go on, tell her why's she's here."

Gugz stepped out from the shadows, he was smoking a cigarette. "Get her inside first. Fucking hell, we don't want anyone to see her do we?" Sandy was ragged about and she was actually putting up a fight. She had Terry's blood flowing through her veins and even though she hated to admit it, she had an evil streak in her. Sandy was flung onto the cold concrete floor. Her head smashed about the big heating pipe on the wall and she was stunned for a few seconds. Once she found her bearings she sat with her knees held up to her chest shaking. She'd heard about the sex trade for young girls and thought it was only a matter of time before she was taken from here and shipped to another country. Gugz stared at her. "She's a pretty little thing isn't she?"

Sandy pleaded with him and her hands were held out in front of her. "Please let me go home. My mother will be missing me now. It will break her heart if I'm not home. I'm a good girl I wouldn't hurt a fly."

Gugz felt her emotion. He had sisters her age and knew he had no other choice than to keep her hostage. "Yes, you are a good girl. But, it's your brother we're after. Once he knows we have you, he'll come running."

Sandy was alert and she was listening now. What the hell did they want with Terry? How long was she going to be kept here? Gugz walked over to her and lifted her head up with his hand. "Just keep your head down girl and you'll be fine. Once you're brother comes and gives us what we want then you can go back home. But, until then you're staying here with me."

Sandy felt a rage coming from the pit of her stomach. She stretched her neck up and spat in his face. "You just leave my brother alone. I swear, he'll come looking for me and when he does, God help the lot of you."

Gugz nodded to his men. "Make sure everything is secure in here and lock the daft fucking bint up. Check everywhere, I don't want her moving. Check her pockets too and make sure she hasn't got a mobile phone." Sandy wiped the side of her mouth and backed herself into a corner as they searched her. The message was still sending and she didn't know if it had reached her brother before they smashed it up into tiny pieces. She studied every man there and knew when the time come she would be able to identify each and every one of them, especially Gugz. He was the ring leader and she knew he was the one calling the shots. The door slammed shut and she was in darkness. Her lips quivered as she heard the car driving away. She was in the middle of nowhere and nobody would ever hear her screams.

"Terry," she sobbed. "Please Terry, come and find me."

CHAPTER THIRTEEN

Skid and Terry sat in the square. Business was booming and everybody seemed to be scoring drugs tonight. Terry was raking the cash in and any money he made was stashed away. He never used banks; he kept his money where he could see it. His money was hidden away at his house. Skid, however, was never careful where money was concerned. He blew it as soon as he had any and never kept any for a rainy day. He lived for today and made sure any cash he had gave him the best of everything for the time he had it. He didn't have a pot to piss in at the moment and Terry was making him wait until the end of the week before giving him any wages. Skid looked as rough as a bear's arse. He'd lost some weight and his jeans were hanging from his arse. His drug intake had trebled in the last few weeks and nothing seemed to be hitting the spot anymore. The buzz he craved never came.

Tina walked onto the square. She was dressed to the nines and couldn't wait to get to Terry's side. Her shoes clipped across the square and once she reached them both she smirked. "Alright lads, it's busy on here tonight isn't it?"

She was making small talk and Terry knew she was up to something. "You want to score some bud then?" Skid asked in hope they could get rid of her as soon as possible. She was a nightmare when she was on the wind-up and he knew any second now she'd have something to say to

Terry.

"Nar, I'm off the weed now. I've not had any for days. I'm sick of feeling like shit when I smoke it so I've given it up. I've got a new boyfriend now and he's my new addiction."

Terry lifted his head up and studied her. Yes, she did look clean and there was something in her eyes that told him she wasn't lying. Skid was a right nosey fucker and instead of leaving it at that he delved deeper. "Since when have you got a new fella. Come on, spill the beans then who is it?"

Tina looked straight into Terry's eyes and smiled. "None of you know him. And, I'd prefer not to say anyway. Just let's say it's the real thing this time. He treats me like a princess and I'm happy."

Terry was having none of it. Although he didn't want her himself he still hated the thought that she wasn't in love with him anymore. "Good news Tina. I'm happy for you. What you doing on the square then if you're not after a bit of bud?"

Tina swallowed hard; he'd caught her off guard. "Erm, I was just popping to the shop to get some fags." Terry could see her crumbling and stood up and walked off to answer his mobile phone. Skid carried on speaking to Tina. "What's up with smacked arse," she asked.

Skid chuckled and made sure Terry couldn't hear him. "I think he always thought you would be around for him I suppose."

Tina flicked her hair over her shoulder and snarled. "Skid, week after week that prick used me for sex and he treated me like a slut. He was so cold towards me and I never knew if I was coming or going with him. I've got a chance now of real happiness and I can't just sit about waiting for Terry to decide if he wants me or not."

Skid blew a laboured breath and rubbed his hands together. "What will be, will be won't it? I'm glad you've moved on Tina and proud that you're getting clean and off the shit. I wish I could leave the weed alone but it just calms me down."

Tina's eyes were all over Terry. She said goodbye to Skid and walked slowly to the shop. Terry came back and he was in a mood. "Come on, shall we go to your Janice's for a bit. If we're going to get Alice in the morning then we need to know all the fine details." This was so unusual for Terry. He hated going to Janice's and once he was there he couldn't wait to leave.

Skid nodded. "Yeah, let's do one then." As they walked across the square Tina came out of the shop. She locked eyes with Terry and for a split second he looked like he was going to say something to her but stopped at the last minute. From the side of the square Gugz was sat waiting for Tina. He's already clocked Terry and he was weighing up the man he was going to bring down when the time was right, he didn't scare him and he was ready for action. Tina jumped into his car and leaned over and kissed him on the cheek. Gugz eyes were still on the game and she was aware he was watching Skid and Terry.

"Where are we going, do you have somewhere special planned?" she asked him.

Gugz started the engine and crept slowly onto the road. As he came to the junction he could see Terry waiting to cross the road to the car park. Tina dipped her head low and didn't want Terry to see her. Too late, he'd clocked her and snarled at the driver. Gugz drove passed them slowly and gripped the steering wheel. He sniggered to himself and Tina looked over at him. Something wasn't right, she could sense it. Skid's jaw dropped as they drove past. "Fucking hell, did you see Tina in that car? Fuck me, the guy looks like he's got a right few quid."

Terry snapped. "He's a fucking prick, the black cunt. What the hell is she doing having a scruffy smelly Asian in her bed. I'll tell you what Skid, I wouldn't touch her with a bargepole from now on. Not after she's had his cock inside her anyway." Wow, Terry was on one. If he still wanted Tina why was he playing all these head games, he should have just told her how it was.

Skid patted the top of his arm. "I know you're gutted mate but come on, you've not been interested in Tina for years. Well, since you went into jail anyway."

Terry hissed back at him aware that he was letting Tina get under his skin. "Listen, if I need any counselling from you I'll ask for it. You need to sort your own shit out before you start having any opinion on my life. Oh," he paused and tried to regain himself, "just for the record, Tina is a skank and any love I had for her has gone a long time ago. So give your head a shake and get with the programme." Skid was sorry he'd spoken. He was only offering a bit of advice, there was no need to bite his bleeding head off.

Janice was smoking like a chimney as they walked into the front room. She was watching the news on the TV, her jaw was swinging. "Fucking hell, it's just been on the news about the attack on Darren. They have no leads and they think it was a gangland attack." Janice twisted her head to Terry. "Did you get rid of all your clothes? Please tell me you did. Fuck me, that's all we need is the rozzers round here sniffing about."

"Wind your neck in Janice. I'm not an amateur you know," Terry snarled.

Janice stood up and her cheeks were bright red. "Say the police come here, say they arrest me in connection with it. I can't go to jail, I just can't." Janice was hysterical, she was going through every case scenario and it was sending Skid under. He had to sort her out, calm her down. He ran at her and grabbed her in his arms squeezing her with force.

"Look at me Janice. I said fucking look at me." She was struggling to break free. Skid brought his hand back and slapped her in one quick swift movement.

Terry was ready to step in as it was getting out of hand. Skid was seeing red and he was about to lay into her. "Whoah," he shouted. "For fucks sake calm down, the both of you. Skid, just leave her alone. And you Janice, just pipe down and get your head into gear."

Skid stood frozen, he was ready to knock her out. Terry guided him to the sofa and sat him down. "Skid, chill ya beans man. What's up with you?"

Janice was up in arms and she was sobbing on the other side of the room. "I can't believe you've just hit me. You know how I've been treated in the past and here you are doing exactly the same as the others have."

Terry sat down he just didn't need this extra pressure. "Listen, everything is taken care of and no police will be knocking at your door Janice. The last thing we need is you falling apart and bringing it on top for us all."

Skid gave his head a shake and realised what had just happened. "Janice, I'm sorry. You were hysterical and I was just trying to quieten you down."

"What with your hands. Don't you think I've had enough of violence to last me a lifetime." Janice was kicking the arse out of it now, she was just after some sympathy.

Skid walked over to where she was sat. "I'm sorry. I would never hurt you for the world. I care about you too much." He leaned over and kissed the top of her head.

Janice snuggled into his waist and the flood gates opened. She was such an emotional wreck these days and the slightest thing got to her. "I'm sorry too. My head is wrecked with everything that's going on. I just want my Alice to come home. I miss her so much."

Terry blew his breath. "Right, let's get things sorted for tomorrow. We need to make sure everything is ready. I don't want any daft mistakes."

Janice dried her eyes and held her arms around herself tightly, she was shivering. "I need to see her the minute you get her home. I just need to set the record straight."

Skid looked over at Terry. Was this the right thing to do so soon? Didn't Alice just need to be on her own for a while? Perhaps Skid could talk to her first and make her see sense. Janice would be lucky if Alice ever spoke to her again. She'd caused her so much pain, would she ever be able to forgive her. Terry paced the room and looked out of the window. In the distance he could see a black Audi parked up with some men sat in it. He'd seen the car before and couldn't put his finger on where he knew the registration plate from. Quickly checking his watch he knew his bedtime had passed. He left Skid consoling Janice and said his goodbyes. Once he was in the car he turned the heater on quickly. Tonight was freezing and his windscreen was nearly frozen. Terry had been driving for around ten minutes when he clocked a car in his rear-view mirror. It was the black Audi, he was sure of it. He jibbed from the main road and sped down the side streets. He knew every jib in this area and he was out of sight as he turned the corner. Terry parked up down an alleyway and turned his lights off. He was alert and his eyes scanned the area. He watched the car go past and held a serious look on his face. Who were these fuckers, what did they want with him? Terry sat thinking for a few minutes. Was he being paranoid or was the car really following him. Perhaps it was the weed playing with his napper again. It did that to people, it made them paranoid. Terry turned the engine over and slowly crept back out onto the street. His lights were still off and his head was spinning trying to see if he could see the car. The coast was clear, they'd gone.

Terry was watching his back as he slid the key into the lock. Just before he went inside his house he gave the area another good look. Once he was inside his eyes dropped to a white envelope on the floor. His heart was in his mouth. There was no postman at this time of the night; he never got any mail anyway, especially not with his name handwritten on the front of it. Terry bent down and picked the letter up. Walking into his front room he slid his car keys onto the table. Peeling his coat off he kicked his shoes to the side of the room and plonked down on the sofa. His eyes were wide open now and he recognised his mother's handwriting. His heart sank low; she must have remembered his birthday. He'd not had a card from her for years and just this little gesture made his eyes cloud over. Looking at the envelope his finger slowly slid inside it. This wasn't a birthday card it was two sheets of paper with writing on both sides of it, his mother's handwriting. Terry swallowed hard and took a few deep breaths before he continued reading. With every word he read his grip got tighter on the letter, something was up and he was ready to blow. His mother had told him that Sandy was missing. She thought she might have been staying with him and asked if he would get in touch with her. Terry ragged his hands through his hair. Sandy would never not let anyone know where she was, she was always on the phone to her mother and even when Terry had met her she was always texting her telling her what time she'd be home. Something was wrong, very wrong.

Terry walked into his bedroom and lay on the bed with his arms looped behind his head. He dropped his head under the bed and dragged out the big furry teddy bear his sister had bought him. He held it tightly to his chest and inhaled the fragrance from it. Reaching for his phone he dialled his sister's number. Nothing, it went straight to voicemail. Terry knew now he would have to go and see his mother. Sandy was his life and if anything was to happen to her he would have held himself responsible. Where the fuck was she? What the hell had happened to her? Terry turned the teddy bear on its front and unzipped the back of it. He dug in his pocket and pulled out a wad of cash. Folding every note slowly he inserted it inside the cuddly toy. There was few grand there too, all squashed neatly inside the bear's arms and legs. Terry stroked the sprinkle of hairs on his chest. Should he just ignore the letter in hope that his sister turned up or should he go and see his mother? The years had passed though; he was used to riding solo. He got used to having no family many years ago and it was a subject he very rarely spoke about. Of course it hurt him that his family weren't there. Especially at Christmas time. Last year he went out and bought himself his own presents. He wrapped every single one and placed them under the Christmas tree. It was so sad that a young man was crying out for love but could never tell anyone how he felt. Sandy had got him a little present of course but she was a student and it was only something small. It was a photograph of them both together. Terry loved the gift and it was at the side of his bed. He kissed his sister's photograph every night before he went to sleep. And, when he had some random dirty in his bed he would always lie the frame face down so she couldn't see what he was doing. Even his Christmas day was spent alone. Skid invited him to Janice's of course but he declined saying he had somewhere else to go. He ate alone on Christmas day. Just a simple microwave meal for one. No trimmings, no turkey, just a basic 'ding' meal. Terry lifted the photograph up from the side. He studied it for a few seconds and placed it back in its place. It had to be straight; it had to be in a certain spot so he could see her. Closing his eyes slowly he knew he had some hard choices to make. He had to go and see his mother.

Tina sneaked through her front door in hope that her father was in bed. It was late and Gugz had just dropped her off. She was pissed off and in a mood. Gugz had said they were spending a romantic night together and it had all gone pear-shaped. He took her to some pub and kept saying he had to nip out. He left her money for the bar of course and told her he wouldn't be long. Two and half hours later he came back for her and he was full of apologises. Tina was no pushover. She knew when something wasn't right. She'd hung about on the square all her life and could smell a rat. This man wasn't all he was made out to be and she had doubts about him, big doubts. She'd tackled him of course when he came back to the pub for her and she proper spat her dummy out. She was nobody's fool and wanted answers. The guy was so hard-faced and she felt so small when he called her a bunny boiler in front of his mates. She wasn't possessive; she just wanted to know where he'd been. What was the harm in that?

The rest of the night with him had been strange. He barely said two words to her and when he did it was just about her past, her ex-boyfriend, just about Terry. Tina opened the living room door and her father was sat there staring at her. He was dressed in military clothes and she could see he'd been playing "Call of Duty" on the play station. Had he lost his marbles or what? He was in cloud cuckoo land for sure. What the hell was he doing dressed like that? Tina's face dropped. "Why are you dressed up in that lot dad?"

He snarled at her and she knew by his expression he was drunk. "I always get into the spirit of things. What else do I have to live for ay? That miserable cow upstairs doesn't bother with me and this is the only pleasure I have."

Tina shrugged her shoulders and sighed. There was no way she was getting into a discussion about her parent's marriage, she had enough problems of her own. The look on her face told her father that she wasn't happy at the way he was dressed. Why the hell couldn't he just watch porn like any other normal man would have done when he wasn't getting any love and attention from his wife? Even buy some fanny magazines to ease his frustration, anything but this. Tina shook her head; this was way too deep for her to get into. Her father had problems, bad psychological problems that she just couldn't face right now. "Good night dad, I'm going to bed." Tina ducked her head down low as a missile just whistled past her head.

"Oh, you don't think I know where you've been do you? I know you've been out with that black twat again because you were seen in the pub with him. What have I told you about shagging Asians, ay?" His eyes were full of madness and she was scared of what he was going to do next. He was a bully and loved the power he held over her. John was the same with his wife he always wanted to be the one in control. Tina knew she'd have to dig deep and confront him. She was scared of him yes, but she knew if he saw one bit of weakness in her he would have broken her in two. "Listen, fucking G. I. Joe, I don't know who's been filling your head with shit but I'm not seeing any Asian."

John was nose to nose with her and liked that she had some balls about her. She was his opponent now, a soldier to take down on the battlefield. "I will find out Tina and when I do I'll cut his black stinking bollocks off and make you some earrings out of them. We don't want them smelly cunts in our country. They bring diseases and all other shit over with them."

Tina was trying to get out of the door but his foot was lodged there stopping her from leaving. "Dad, you're drunk. Just go and finish playing on your game. I'm sure your mates are online."

John's head twisted to the TV screen and he squeezed

his eyes together trying to focus. He couldn't see properly and walked over to get a closer look. Tina was gone, she'd seen her chance and wasted no time. Her feet ran up the stairs and she locked herself in the bathroom. She could hear his loud drilling tones echoing throughout the household. He was a prick, a complete arsehole. No wonder her mother spent most of her time at work. What the hell had happened to him? He was as nutty as a fruitcake! Tina stripped off and found something to wear for bed. She sat on the toilet and looked at her mobile phone. She found Terry's number and just sat staring at it. Did she still love him, what the hell was going on in her head? Tina heard a tap on the door and her heart pounded inside her chest. She couldn't stand another argument with her father and she held her breath hoping he would go away and leave her alone. Tina covered her ears with both her hands. "Just leave me alone will you. Just go to bed." Tina heard her mother's voice now and she felt relief. Rushing to the door she unbolted it and stood shaking as she met the eyes of her mother. "Mam, he's a crank. Have you seen what he's wearing down there? He's sat in there wearing army clothes."

Marie placed her arm around her neck and led her to her bedroom. Once she was inside she bolted the door behind her. "Just try and calm down love. Take deep breaths." Tina sucked in large mouthfuls of air and her mother was right she was calming down. Marie sat her on the side of the bed and stroked her hand softly. This was unusual, her mother never showed any emotion towards her. "It's about time I told you Tina. You're not a kid anymore and I think you need to know why your dad is the way he is." Tina snivelled and wiped her nose on the side of her sleeve. "Come on, get in my bed and get under the covers." Tina climbed inside and she could smell her mother's scent all over the bed sheets. It was a fresh cotton aroma that smelt like washing floating on the line on a midsummer's day.

Marie snuggled down into her bed and just stared into her daughters eyes. She played with her fingers before she began. "I fell in love with a man who was in the army. Tarek was his name and he was Asian. I know I was married to your father but this man just came along and swept me off my feet. I met him when I was working in London. He was on leave from the army and from the moment we met we couldn't keep our hands off each other. Please, don't judge me Tina. I know it was wrong but when your heart is captured by love there is nothing you can do. I loved him and he loved me." Tina was amazed by this story and even though she should have been angry she wasn't. She loved a love story as much as the next girl and was happy that her mother had found some happiness during her life. She just thought she was a workaholic and never really asked her what she did to enjoy herself. Okay, it was her mother and she should have probably known these things but it had never been discussed, never spoken about.

"So what happened next? If you loved each other why aren't you together now?"

Marie closed her eyes and her bottom lip trembled. She was filled with emotion and it was like she was reliving her past. "We were planning a life together. I told your father all about him and I even admitted to him that I was in love with someone else."

Tina dug the blankets deeper under her chin she

was dithering. "So what happened then? Did he let you leave?"

Marie gritted her teeth together and slammed her flat palm against the bed. "Did he bleeding hell. He kicked up a fuss and made it as hard as possible for us to be together. He called Tarek every black bastard name under the sun and told him if he ever came near me again he would end his life." Marie held her hands around her throat and she was hyperventilating. "He would have killed him you know. Oh yes, make no mistake about it, your father is more than capable of ending someone's life. He nearly ended mine when I told him Tarek had come back from the country he was fighting in. Honest, you don't know the half of it. He tied me up and locked me in my bedroom for weeks."

Tina was gobsmacked and couldn't believe what she was hearing. This was a nightmare. No wonder she never spent any time with her father. The man was a lunatic. How can you do that to someone you love? Tina dropped her eyes low and reached over to touch her mother's hand. "I never had a clue mam. I just thought you loved work and nothing else mattered to you."

"I always loved you my dear. It was him who made me how I am. Once you were born he said if I ever left him he would end your life and it would be my fault."

Tina bolted up in her bed and the colour drained from her. "Are you being serious? Why didn't you tell someone, get some help?"

Marie touched her daughter's hair at the side and twisted it around her finger. "I just fell apart love. When I found out Tarek had been killed in action I just crumbled. I loved him so much and my heart was shattered into a million pieces. I had no fight left in me, nothing. I was empty."

Tina was speechless, she could see so much pain in her mother's eyes. "I'm sorry mam. I never once sat down with you and listened to anything you had to say. I just thought I did your head in and tried to block you out of my life."

"Tina, I'm the one to blame for the way things have turned out. Bleeding hell, your dad needs sectioning. He scares the life out of me you know. Every time he looks at me he makes my skin crawl. That's why he hates Asians." Tina felt a chill pass over her, as if somebody had stepped over her grave. "He's been at my bedroom door for nights telling me that you're like me, loving Pakistanis. I had to tell you Tina. You need to make sure he never gets his hand on your boyfriend because he's not a full shilling. He'll do something to him, trust me."

Tina lay down on the pillow and for the first time ever she felt the gentle hand of her mother, stroking the side of her cheek. "I do love you mam," Tina whispered.

"I love you too," she replied. The two of them lay talking in the bed for hours and somehow the past didn't seem to matter anymore. Marie held a single finger to her mouth as she heard a noise outside the bedroom door. It was John listening. He was always outside her room in the late hour. Usually he'd shout abuse through the door and she knew tonight would be different. Tina cuddled closer to her mother. She felt safe knowing she was there to protect her. His voice from outside sent the fear of God into them both, his words were slow and as he spoke he scratched his nail down the back of the door. "Like mother like daughter. You both love black cock.

This won't happen again, not on my watch anyway. Tina your Pakistani boyfriend is going missing in action. Over my dead body will I let my own flesh and blood make the same mistake her mother made."

Tina was ready to shout something back at him but her mother placed her hand over her mouth and stopped her just in time. If they gave him any response this would just add fuel to the fire. He'd have been outside the door all night pecking their heads.

At last there was silence, none of them said a word. Marie flicked the bedroom light off and lay staring into the darkness. They could hear John talking to himself from outside the room. He was off his rocker talking about bombing the Mosque and setting fire to all the takeaways run by Asians. He wasn't of sound mind. Tina rolled on her side and faced the window. Life without drugs was hard. She never felt pain in her heart when she was snorting cocaine. This was all new to her and her emotional baggage was weighing her down. She stared at the moonlight and closed her eyes slowly; she was drifting off to sleep. John turned the volume up on the TV downstairs and all you could hear were gunshots and people screaming. Marie reached for her ear plugs from the side and squashed them inside. This was just a normal night for her and she was used to her husband's antics. She cuddled up to Tina and spooned her. Tonight had been an eye-opener for Tina and she now understood why her mother was the way she was. She understood her father too; he was eaten up with jealousy and could never accept that his wife had loved another man. Love was a funny thing and it changed even the strongest of people. Her mother and father should have split up years ago and then at least they could have had a chance of happiness. Why stay in a loveless marriage when you don't need too? Everybody deserves to be loved, they should just both have called it a day and walked away. What was the point of hurting each other anymore?

CHAPTER FOURTEEN

Alice's morning sickness was worse than ever. The nurse had told her it would settle down further into her pregnancy but it never did. Thick yellow bile splurged from her mouth as she stood over the toilet bowl. She was retching and sank to her knees as her stomach churned. Jenny came in behind her and held her head back. She'd forgiven Alice now for not backing her up and things had settled down in the home. Melanie and May were still there of course but they were living on borrowed time. They knew any wrong moves could land them on their arses. They were still a pair of bitches but they were aware they were being watched and couldn't afford to put one foot out of place. "Come on girl. I don't think you've got anything left in there now. I've heard you spewing your ring up all morning. Why don't you ask them for something to calm it down?"

Alice lifted her head, she was grey, she looked shocking. This wasn't just morning sickness, this was everything that had happened in her life catching up with her; court cases, a child growing inside her and the loneliness she felt in her heart. She missed her mother. We all know what a waste of space she was but Janice was still her mum, she still cared about her and wondered how she was coping without her. Janice never did a tap in the house and she depended on Alice so much for everything, even down to doing the shopping. Each night she would have the same dream over and over again and all she could see was her mother crying. But she had to think about herself didn't she? She couldn't have carried on the way she was going.

Her art work told stories of what she was going through and the portrait she drew of her mother just lay staring into space said it all. The picture had empty cans on the floor and ashtrays piled high with cigarette ends. Alice still kept her talent hidden from most of the girls there, this was her private life. Jenny had seen them though and when she saw the picture of Lizzy's child, she broke down crying. Alice had a talent in capturing the moment. Lizzy had left the home weeks ago with the sketch. It was so sad and they all promised they would keep in touch with her. Promises they would probably never keep. Words meant nothing anymore. Each girl there held the same shame. No matter how you looked at it, they had all made mistakes, some by choice, some by no fault of their own. The home just stank of misery. There were no bright coloured walls or décor, it was all dull and boring. Each bed held a girl who'd committed a sin. Well, that's what Melanie had told them anyway. Each of them holding a bastard child inside them; no father, no marriage, no wedding ring. Even when visitors came to the home they held the shame too. There was never laughter filling the rooms in this place, no atmosphere. It was like a graveyard. There was just an eerie silence where the girls sat thinking all day, dreading the days ahead. The only thing it had going for it was that it was safe. It kept the girls away from the outside world. They could hide away from the public here and never had to see the face of their abusers again.

Alice had given her evidence by video link to the courts. Not once did she see her abusers. It was a good job too, because she would never have recognised them anyway. Darren's face was disfigured and he was now in a wheelchair. The doctors said he would never walk again and they'd moved him from his home to a safe house out of the area. That was all over now anyway and now her evidence had been given it was just a matter of time before the pervert was sentenced. She wasn't sure how she felt about Darren anymore. She should have hated him with a passion and wanted him dead but she didn't, she felt sorry for him. Felt pity for a man who was so fucked up in his own head that he had to abuse young girls to get his kicks. Her other abuser old Dave had dropped down dead. She was told it was a heart attack and he just sank to his knees and took his final breath. I suppose it was for the best really because now his family wouldn't have had to go through a court case and listen to the man they thought they had known all their lives.

Jenny helped Alice back to the bedroom and passed her a cold drink of water. "Here, get a swig of this. And," she sniggered, "see if you've got any mints, your breath is hanging." Alice blew a breath into her cupped hands and pulled a face. Jenny was right, it smelt like a thousand monkeys had shit on her tongue. Alice sat sucking hard on the mint she'd found in her drawer. She kept checking her breath and placing more mints into her mouth. Jenny plonked on the bed and kicked her legs up behind her. "Do you ever wonder if we're doing the right thing? You know, getting these babies adopted?"

Alice lay down next to her and stared into space. "I think I'm doing the right thing Jenny. I don't want anything to remind me of the past."

Jenny had never asked this question before and hoped

they knew each other well enough for her to confide in her. "I know you said you don't want to talk about it but who is the father of your baby, does he know you're pregnant?"

Whoa, this was going too far and Alice was uncomfortable talking about it. She rolled on her side and faced the wall. "I don't want to talk about it Jenny. He doesn't even know I'm pregnant. It was never supposed to have happened but it did."

Jenny pulled a sour face. "What do you mean; he doesn't even know you're pregnant? What if he loves you and wants the baby. Why are you turning down a chance of happiness?"

Was Alice lying or what? Her expression didn't change and she maintained a poker face giving nothing away. She changed the subject quickly. "Are you coming with me today? I've just got to meet Christine my case worker, then I need to go shopping for some bits I need. I mean, my knickers are like bikini bottoms now they're stuck right up my arse cheeks like a cheese grater." They chuckled and it was nice to see this side of Alice. She was quite funny at times and she had a dry sense of humour. "Jenny," she asked in a low voice. "Have your boobs changed in any way because my jugs are massive."

Jenny made sure no one was watching and whipped her breast out. "Look at these if you think you have problems, my nipples are like big giant chocolate biscuits. I only ever had a mouthful before. I swear, these have just appeared overnight."

Alice's eyes were wide open. Wow, Jenny wasn't lying either her tits were huge. Alice had never really seen another girl's body before. She was quite a private person and even in school when they were doing PE she always hid away so nobody could see her. Her scabby underwear was probably a greater reason if she was honest: threadbare briefs and a discoloured bra were nothing to be proud of. Janice never took pride in her daughter's appearance and it was very rare she got any new clobber. Things got so bad that Alice had to shoplift the things she needed to survive, basic things like soap and shampoo and the odd pair of briefs. Alice lifted her top up and revealed her mammoth melons. The pair laughed together and poked at each other's breast.

Christine smiled when she saw Alice. This was more than a job to her and she really got involved with the girls she met. She wanted to guide them, help them make better lives for themselves. Christine had been Alice's rock whilst the trial had been going on. She was the one who dried her tears and kept her safe. The bond between them was real; they really cared about each other. Christine reached over and touched Alice's belly when she sat down. "You're really showing now aren't you?"

Alice smiled and sighed. "Tell me about it. It just seems to have doubled in size overnight. I feel like a beached whale."

Christine smiled. She would have given her right arm to have had that feeling, to look fat, to feel a child moving about inside her. "When the time comes Alice I just know you will be fine. You're stronger than you think."

Alice had been told by the midwife that she could have a birthing partner with her when her child was ready to born and although she liked Jenny she just needed someone who was more sensible at the side of her when the child came along. Biting hard on her fingernails she plucked up the courage to ask her. "Christine, will you be my birthing partner. I'm a right shit bag and I just know I'll just fall apart when it happens."

Christine was taken aback by her request. This wasn't in her job description and if anybody found out, her neck would have been on the line. Her boss was so on the ball about where she should draw the line on relationships between staff and the people they worked with but to see a real child being born, a new life. She would never get a chance like this again. "I'd love to Alice but I'm not sure I would be allowed. I will try my best to be with you when the times comes but don't hold your breath. Our rules are quite strict and there is a fine line between what I can and can't do." Christine sat thinking for a moment and seemed in a world of her own. She coughed and brought the conversation back to the real reason they were there. "Right, sorry about that, I was away with the fairies. Anyway, let's talk about you and how you're feeling. I know your mother is still trying for contact and she's been in touch with us nearly every day."

Alice lowered her head and stared out of the window. "I'm not ready to see her yet Christine. I've got a lot going on inside my head and I need to sort that out first before I can see her." Christine completely understood, she didn't delve deeper she just wrote her notes and carried on asking other question about her well-being. Christine pulled out an envelope with over three hundred pounds inside it. She passed it over to Alice and the corners of her mouth started to rise. "This money is for you. Buy the things you need. I know you left your home with no belongings and this will help you rebuild the personal stuff you left behind." Alice blew a laboured breath. What clothes? What belongings? Was this woman having a laugh or what? Alice owned virtually nothing except the clothes on her back. She had a few books and her art set but apart from that she had nothing. This was more money than Alice had ever seen in her life. To able to walk into a store and buy clothes was certainly a treat for her and she was more than thankful. Jenny popped her head at the window and she was urging Alice to hurry up. The bus into town was due soon and if they missed it they would have to wait another hour before one was due again.

Terry and Skid were ready for action. Terry was still thinking about his sister and as soon as they'd got Alice he was planning to go and see his mother. What would he say to her? How would he act? She was like a stranger to him now. His worst fears were if he saw his father though. If this was to happen he was willing to take him down this time. On their last meeting Terry was left half dead by his father Bob. I suppose the man was at the end of his tether and didn't know what else to do with his son other than give him a good hiding. Bob's own father had done this to him and he couldn't see the harm in giving Terry a good kicking when he deserved it. Times had changed though and the youth of today held no respect for their elders. Terry used to laugh in his father's face and tell him how much of an old man he was. Bob knew this day would come and it seemed inevitable that father and son would come to blows again at some point in their lives. Bob thought Terry was a little bastard. He was into everything. Wherever there was trouble, he was there.

Bob had tried everything with him to try and calm him down but nothing seemed to work. It wasn't through the lack of trying either. Bob took time out to try and rein his son in. He took him swimming; played football with him but Terry was never interested. He was a little fucker. His mind was somewhere else and he couldn't concentrate for long on anything. The first time Terry ever set foot on the square he knew that he'd come home. Even from being a small child he could see the wheeling and dealings going on in the area and he wanted to be a part of it. His father got him a job when he was younger – a paper round to try and keep him on the straight and narrow. Not the best of jobs I suppose but at least he was earning money. Terry had to travel through the square on his paper-round and the kids there tore him to pieces. To have a paper round was kind of a geek job. Only posh kids really worked in this area. Terry lasted two days and he threw his bag back at the newsagent telling him to shove his job up his arse. Terry lied to his father and told him they no longer needed him at the shop but the truth of the matter was he couldn't stand the other kids from the estate taking the piss. Even from an early age Terry always cared what other people thought about him. He wanted to be the best at everything he did and taking the leading role was something that came naturally. His family life suffered after this and even getting him to attend school regularly was a chore for his parents. The truant officer was always knocking at his door and on one occasion his parents were even taken to court regarding his attendance at school. He was a lost cause and no one could stop him from what he was doing. He was rebellious and wouldn't listen to reason.

Skid tapped his finger on the dashboard. He was alert and raring to go. "Terry, this needs to happen. Nothing can go wrong, we need Alice home." Terry scanned the area and made sure they had all exits covered. You could see his eyes in the rear-view mirror checking nobody was watching them. Over an hour they'd been sat here and as yet there wasn't a sign of her. The music was on low and both of them seemed irritated. Skid turned the volume button down. He was sweating and constantly licking his lips. "Where the fuck is she Terry? She must be due out soon." Terry sat with his hands shoved down the front of his pants playing with his nob. You could actually see him pulling at it and squeezing it. Most of the lads had the habit of doing this these days. I'm sure they thought their penises would fall off if they didn't keep checking them regularly. It was a filthy habit and so unhygienic. They had a habit of sniffing their fingers after it too the scruffy fuckers. Suddenly Skid sat bolt upright in his seat. "She's here; quick get your head down before she clocks us." The pair of them slouched down as they watched Alice walk past them with another girl at the other side of the road. The two of them were talking and never really took any notice of the surrounding area. This had to be quick, they didn't have long. They were both ready to pounce.

Jenny walked off to the corner shop and Alice made her way to the bus stop. Jenny was gasping for a cigarette. She knew smoking harmed her baby and was aware of all the dangers it carried but she decided to smoke anyway. She'd cut down, so at least she was trying. Skid was the one waiting to give the call. Terry's hand gripped the passenger door and he was on edge waiting for the go-ahead. Alice sat inside the bus stop and she kicked her legs about in front of her as she sat down. Not a soul was about and she kept stretching her neck looking for Jenny. Skid started the engine and the wheels on the car spun as he drove a few hundred yards up the road. This was it, they were going to rescue Alice. Terry dived out of the passenger side door and he was quick, he just lifted Alice up from her seat and threw her into the back of the car. She was screaming and trying to break free but it was too late she was captured. Skid looked over his shoulder quickly and stepped on the accelerator. Smoke pumped from the exhaust as they made their escape route. "Get the fuck off me. Leave me alone," Alice ranted.

Terry's voice was calm as he lifted her head up to meet his eyes. "Alice, it's me Terry. We're here to bring you home."

Alice was white, she sat back in her seat and could see Skid's eyes watching her every movement in the rear view mirror. "Alice, you're safe. You're mam has been out of her mind. You need to see her, to sort this mess out." Alice looked at Terry, maybe a bit longer than she should have and then she snapped. "Just take me back. I've got nothing to say to her."

Terry shot his eyes to her belly and looked out of the window quickly. "Stop being a nob Alice, your mother loves you. She's not had a drink for ages now and she's off the drugs. You owe her so speak to her at least."

Skid was waiting on an answer. Alice was no longer the girl they both once knew. She was stronger now and not afraid to stand up for herself. "Listen, I owe her nothing. I was abused in her care, and she never gave a flying fuck about me. It was all about her and her nasty addictions. All she was interested in was her life. I needed her and she let me down." Skid was just about to say something when he stopped at the last minute, it was on the tip of his tongue. Alice snarled at him and made sure she held his attention. "She doesn't know the half of what I went through. The people she trusted abused me." Skid was trying to look away from her but she stared at him and made sure he knew what she meant.

"I'm taking you to stay at Terry's" Skid said at last, "You can stay there until we sort things out."

Alice looked over at Terry who seemed to have his own shit going on, he was just staring out of the window. "As soon as I get a chance I'm getting on my toes Skid. You can't make me talk to her. I've got a chance of really sorting my life out and now you've spoiled it. What, do you think she's going to change overnight? The woman is a druggie. She drinks every night and some days she can't even remember her own name."

Skid was pissing in the wind and smashed his head against the window as he drove along. "Arrghh, will you just listen to yourself, Alice. You're mother has been through a lot over the years and she just got a bit lost sometimes that's all. Give her a chance for crying out loud. We all make mistakes."

Alice snarled at him and gripped the back of his seat. Her knuckles turned white and she was ready to deliver the blow. "Have you ever made mistakes Skid? Is there stuff you regret doing?" You could have cut the atmosphere with a knife. Terry was listening now and he was aware something was going on between them. Skid didn't reply.

Terry held Alice by the arm as they got out of the car. They rushed her inside the house and made sure nobody saw her. Alice walked into the flat with a cocky look on her face. She walked straight into the living room and plonked herself down on the couch. Pulling the drawer open she grabbed the remote for the TV. "You can say all you want but as soon as I get the chance I'm going back to the home. And, do yourself a favour, don't let my mother come here to see me because I won't be held responsible for my actions." Alice had changed. Gone were the days when she sat back and took everything that was thrown at her. The time she'd been at the home had taught her that she had to stand up for herself and fight back. No longer would she be the doormat, she had to be ruthless and afraid of nothing.

Terry paced the floor, what a fuck up this was. He didn't have the time to babysit Alice all day. He had his own shit to deal with. Checking the clock on the wall he picked up the car keys from the table. "Skid I've got to get off. I'm going to see my mam to see what's happening with our Sandy. I'll be back later. And, do me a favour ay, don't fucking wreck the joint. You know I like things kept a certain way."

Skid was out of his mind. Never in a million years did he expect Alice to have this kind of attitude. Perhaps it was a mistake bringing her here. He should have left her where she was. The front door slammed shut and there was an eerie silence. Alice was watching the TV and from the corner of her eye she could see Skid texting on his phone. He no longer ruled her life, she was ready for him, to face her demons. "So, whose idea was it to come and get me then?"

Skid swallowed hard and popped a fag in his mouth. "It was your mother's idea, she's in a bad way Alice. On my life, she's suffering. Please, just for me have a word with her then you can make your own mind up, then you'll know if you want to go back or not."

Alice leaned forward in her chair; she looked directly in his eyes and spoke slowly so he understood every word she said. "And, don't think I've forgot what you did to me too, Skid. Oh, I bet you thought you'd got away with it didn't you? You're a filthy fucker. And," she flicked the arm of the sofa. "When I'm ready, I'll pay you back too."

Skid was up in arms he had to defend himself. "What the fuck are you going on about Alice? I've never touched you. You're off your fucking head you are. Don't be saying shit like that."

Alice kept her cool, he didn't scare her, she knew his game and chuckled. "You know as well as I do what happened. If you want to deny it, then go ahead. Remember what they do to nonces in jail Skid. I hope you're prepared to have your arse ripped apart." Wow, this girl had changed so much. Where was all this talk coming from? She continued and held an evil look in her eye. "And, when you're asleep Skid beware, because I'll be watching you now, not the other way around." Skid was shitting himself. He couldn't even leave her in the house either, he had to sit with her until her mother got here. She was playing with his head now, taunting him, making him feel nervous. Skid walked into the kitchen and ragged his fingers through his hair. He punched the wall behind him and stood frozen. His eyes clocked the silver knives on the rack facing him. He walked up and down past them and he was really contemplating doing her in. Alice made him jump when he saw her stood at the kitchen door. She just crept there behind him and he never even heard her. "I need a drink, you don't mind if I make one do you?"

Skid ran from the room and he grabbed his phone and went to sit on the stairs in the hallway. Dialling a number he was panicking as he spoke. "Janice you need to get here as soon as possible. She said she's doing one the moment our backs are turned. I can't stay here with her much longer I've got places to go and all that. How long are you going to be?" Alice sat in the front room and kicked her feet up on the sofa. She made herself at home and searched through the TV channels. Skid could hear her singing from where he was sat. There was no way he was going near her. This girl was dangerous.

Terry pulled up outside his parent's house. It had changed so much in the years that had passed. Looking into the garden he could see the old rope swing he used to play on as a kid. Everything was the same yet different. Terry sat chugging hard on a cigarette. He'd driven around the block twice already trying to get the courage he needed to knock on the door. But this was about his sister and not about him, he needed it sorted. After all, it had been his mother who'd been to his house and contacted him, it wasn't the other way around. Terry flicked his cigarette butt out of the window and filled his lungs with fresh air. This was it, he was ready. Swinging his car keys around his index finger he walked down the garden path. His heart was racing and he was really nervous. Stood back from the door he kicked his foot into the ground still debating his next move, still unsure. He had to do it now though, he'd come so far. His hand reached over and lifted the brass letterbox up. He smiled as he looked closer at it and remembered polishing it when he was younger. He loved the shine it had on it when it had been cleaned and he hated when people touched it leaving their fingerprints all over it. Terry stepped back from the door and held his hands behind his back. He could see a shadow approaching from inside.

The door opened slowly and there she was after all these years, his mother. Terry choked up, his eyes clouded over and he was doing his best not to break down. Angela looked a mess. Her eyes had great big bags underneath them and she looked like she'd not slept for ages. "Terry," she gasped and didn't know which way to look. Angela stood frozen, her hands were twitching and she wanted to hug him, to hold him and tell him how much she'd missed him. She stepped forward and placed her arms around him. Terry looked uncomfortable, this didn't feel right. He pulled away from her and left her standing where she was. Even though he wanted to hug her and tell her how much he'd missed her he just couldn't do it, no way. It was too late for that, too much time had passed.

"So, what's happened to Sandy, has she turned up yet?" he asked. Angela shook her head.

She wiped the tears from her eyes and invited him inside. "Come in, I'll put the kettle on and make us a drink."

Terry was wary, he thought this would be over and done within a few minutes, he could just stand at the doorway and have the conversation. He followed her inside and his heart sank as he walked into the kitchen. This was his childhood home, there so many good memories and so many dark ones. A cold chill passed over him as he rubbed at his arms softly. Angela put the kettle on and placed a plate of biscuits in the middle of the table. Chocolate ones, ones with jam and cream inside, they looked so nice. Terry's face creased. What the hell was going on here? This was no tea party. He was here to see about his sister, nothing else. He needed her to start talking, it didn't feel right and he didn't feel safe here. "So, what's happened? Have you informed the police that she's missing?"

Angela turned around to face him with two cups hooked around her fingers. She placed them both on the table and sat down. She couldn't look directly at him when she spoke, she kept her eyes low. "Yes, they just said they will do a few checks in the area. They said it's quite normal for young girls to go missing."

Terry sucked hard on his gums. "Did you tell them she's not like that and it's out of character for her?"

"Of course I bleeding did but they don't seem to be bothered. I've been out of my mind Terry. She could be lying in a ditch somewhere half dead and nobody seems to care."

Terry reached over and touched his mother's hand. He could feel her warmth, her love for her daughter rising through her. "I'll do a few visits to her friends and see what they're saying. Is she still with her boyfriend?"

Angela shook her head. "No, he dumped her a few weeks ago. Oh Terry, I hope she hasn't done anything silly because if she has I'll kill that fucker stone dead." Terry was finding it hard to breathe. His emotions were rising in the back of his throat and he didn't know if he could hold it together any longer. Angela dropped her head into her hands. "Terry," she paused and looked at him. "I love you, I always have. You're still my son. It's just your dad. You know how he is. We had to respect his wishes."

This was it, the can of worms was open and even though he'd promised himself he wouldn't get involved in the past he couldn't help himself. "Save it mother for someone who gives a fuck. You're about four years too late for declaring your undying love. What kind of mother turns her back on her son just because her prick of a husband says she has to? I thought a mother's love was unconditional? I lay alone in my cell mother. I had nobody, so don't come all the fucking caring shit with me."

Angela sobbed and you could see she was really upset. "I tried to speak with him. I tried to let you come home."

"Well. You didn't try hard enough then did you? If you want something enough mother, you have to fight for it."

Angela was angry now. Did Terry actually remember how things really were? He was a nightmare child who caused them nothing but heartache. "You stole from us Terry, you nicked your dad's car and smashed it up. Do I have to go and name everything you did to us because I don't think there's enough hours in the day to tell you everything."

Terry smashed his fist against the table. Angela was aware her son had a temper and she kept her trap shut. "I'm not here about me. I don't care about what you did to me anymore. I've got my own life now and if the truth was known you did me a favour because I don't want for anything now. I have everything I need."

Angela couldn't hold her tongue. This was bullshit and she knew it. Why couldn't he see things from her point of view? She was fighting back. "Oh, and we all know how you earn your money don't we. Yeah, drugs and crime the same as you always did. I gave up on you Terry yes, because I had nothing left. You sucked every bit of life out of me and you made us both ill."

Terry blew his breath and smirked. "Blah, blah, fucking blah. Just tell me about Sandy and then I'm gone. She's my only concern here."

Angela relayed some of the things she knew about her daughter and Terry was listening. He got so interested in the conversation that he reached over to the biscuits and started munching on one. The front door banged shut and Angela looked horrified. "Hello, who's that," she shouted into the hallway. "It's only me love. I've just been searching the street for Sandy but nothing; nobody has seen sight or sound of her." Angela stood at the kitchen door, she was white. Her husband kissed her on the cheek as he passed her. Then there was silence as he spotted Terry. Heavy breathing, ears pinned back and chest rising. It was like two lions meeting each other for the first time. Bob went beetroot with rage and steam was coming out of his ears. "What the hell is he doing here?"

They ran at each other and blows were struck. The years had passed and Terry's father was old now, fragile. It took Terry only a few moves to put him on his arse. Terry stood over him and spit was hanging from the corner of his mouth. "It's not happening old man. Just stay on your arse before I put you on it again." Bob was struggling to breathe and he hated that he was the underdog. His son was too fast for him and he knew he was fighting a losing battle. "Just get him out of here Angela. We don't need his help. He's nothing but a plastic gangster anyway. He thinks he knows it all, and he knows fuck all."

This was a war zone and just how it was years ago. The only difference now was that Terry was in control. It was his shout and he was the one calling the shots. He snarled at his father but something was holding him back. Usually he would have kicked the living daylights out of his victim and never let them get back on their feet. He stood back from his father and his nostrils flared. "Get up old man. I'm here for our Sandy nothing else."

Bob was bleeding from the side of his mouth and he didn't have the strength to get up from the floor, he was stunned.

Angela was hysterical and she was screaming at the top of her lungs. "Stop it, bleeding stop it. I've had enough. I can't take it anymore. For years I've watched you both at loggerheads and I'm sick to death of it. It's killing me, do you hear me, and you're both putting me in an early grave." Angela fell to her knees and hugged herself tightly in the corner. This was bad, none of them liked to see a woman crying like this. Terry walked over to his father and helped him up from the floor. At first he declined his hand but Terry kept it there until he took it.

Bob wobbled over to the sink and grabbed a dishcloth holding it to his mouth. Once he'd pressed it against his lip he stood over Angela. "Come on love, get up. There will be no more trouble from me."

Terry sat down on his own at the table, he was gutted that he'd just chinned his old man. He dropped his head into his hands and hid away from his parents. He was on the edge and needed a few minutes to pull himself together. He'd not cried for years and thought those days were over. This was getting to him, making him vulnerable. He hated this feeling and had to pull himself together. "I'll go now and try and find Sandy. I'm sorry for all the trouble mam, it just happened." Terry walked over to his father and held his hand out. "I'm sorry for hitting you too." Bob took his time in shaking his son's hand and his lips were moving but no words were coming out.

Angela stood up and pulled the three of them together. "Can we all just put it behind us? Times passed now and we all have regrets. I know I have."

Bob held so much sadness in his eyes, he was one stubborn old fool. He found it hard to forgive and once he made an enemy he would be at war with them until his last breath. It was just the way he was. This was different though, this was his son, his own flesh and blood. If he let him walk away now he would regret it for the rest of his life. Bob had been ill lately and unknown to his wife his chest pains had been getting worse. His lips trembled as his eyes clouded over. "I'm sorry Terry. I know things have been said and we've all hurt each other. I'm willing to leave it in the past if you are?"

Terry was taken back. He never expected this. How would he ever cope with a family again? He'd not had one for years and he never depended on anyone but himself. He liked it like that. Angela was crying tears of happiness. This war was finally over. Her son was back in her life. Terry never said a single word as he left, he was shell-shocked. Angela ran after him and she shouted down the garden path after her son. "Please Terry, help us find her. Come back and see us soon. Please Terry, please." Angela watched her son jump into his car and stayed where she was as she watched him drive off. He had the tunes pumping in the car and he never looked at her once as he drove past. Terry was crying, heartbroken, tears flooding his eyes. This was the first time ever he'd been overwhelmed with emotion. He had to find his sister. That was the only thing on his mind now, he needed her back home.

Skid opened the front door to Janice. She was crying already and her eyes were red raw. "Is she here," she snivelled.

Skid kept his voice low and couldn't wait to get out of the gaff. "Yes, she's in there," he dragged her back and pushed her against the wall. "Listen, I've got to go out. I'll be back in a couple of hours. It will give you chance to talk to her." He was stressed and he looked over his shoulder to make sure Alice wasn't listening. "She's fucked in the head Janice. I swear she's saying some twisted shit. Just be careful with her. I don't trust her, something isn't right."

Janice brushed his comment off and closed the front door behind him. This was her daughter he was speaking about, she knew her more than anyone and thought he was exaggerating. Janice's heart was racing and she'd never been so nervous in all her life. With her hands on the wall she crept to the living room door. She could see the top of Alice's head. "Hello love," she said in a gentle voice.

Alice lifted her head up from the sofa and once she'd seen her mother stood there she plonked back down again. "Oh, I knew it wouldn't take you long. Say what you have to say then piss off back where you came from. I've got nothing left to say to you."

Janice was shocked, Skid was right, she had changed. "Alice, just let me explain to you will you. Just hear me out. For fucks sake what's got into you?"

Alice rolled on her side and watched her mother sit down. She was still watching the TV and didn't give her much attention. Janice looked at her pregnant daughter and her heart sank. It was a mixture of anger and guilt she felt inside. "I'm sorry, okay. I know sorry will never make it right but it's all I have at the moment. If I could turn back the clock I would. I look at you now and I see myself."

Alice shook her head slowly and turned the volume down on the TV. This, she had to hear. "No mother, the difference is you had choices, I never did. You put yourself in the position you were in, nobody else. I was forced into mine mother, are you forgetting that, that's the difference," she snarled at her mother. "So don't you dare come here preaching to me."

Janice had nothing left to give. No words, no magic potion that could make everything alright, nothing. Her hands were tied and she was backed into a corner. "What can I do Alice? I'll do anything to make this up to you. I'm clean now and I'm off the drink and the drugs."

Alice examined her. She did look different, clean even, and sober for a change. "There is nothing you can do to change what's happened. I'm pregnant and in a few months I'll have to give this child away. Just leave me alone."

Janice sat cracking her knuckles, she hated bringing it up but she had to ask. "Is it Darren's baby, is he the one?"

Alice took a deep breath and rubbed the end of her nose with her flat palm. "I don't want to talk about it. I just want to have this baby and move on with my life. I would never put a child through what you have put me through. Come on mam, who's my dad. Come on, let's hear it. Now you're sober tell me the truth." Janice was horrified. This was a question she never wanted to answer ever. She'd kept this secret for years and now even speaking about it made her skin crawl. Janice lit a cigarette up and her hands were shaking. Alice was sat up straight and she was pressing her for an answer. "Yeah, I thought you would be quiet," Alice hissed. Janice was stunned and she just couldn't tell her. "See mother, you have something so simple to tell me and you're still the same old devious cow that you have always been. There is no change in you. You're still the same old fucked up Janice you'll always be. You couldn't manage a fart without shitting yourself. Pathetic you are."

Her daughter's words crucified her, deep stabbing pains in her heart. "I'm not giving up on you Alice. So stop speaking to me as if I'm a dollop of shit on your shoe. I want you back home. I'll never give up on you, ever. Just give me one chance to prove to you that I can be a mother."

Alice dragged at her short cropped hair. "Do you know how I feel inside mother? I feel sick, dirty... abnormal. And, since I've not been living with you I've never felt better. You're evil and never deserved me. You should have had me adopted then your life wouldn't have been so fucked up as it is now."

Janice's temper was boiling and she couldn't hold it any longer. "It wasn't my fault Alice," she screamed. "Stop blaming me for how things turned out. It wasn't my fault either and I know exactly how you are feeling because I was raped too."

Alice's eyes were wide open and now she was listening. Was this just another one of her mother's devious plans or was she telling the truth? Janice sank to her knees and pulled a packet of squashed cigarettes from her jacket pocket. With her hands trembling she flicked her lighter. Well, this was a turn up for the books and Alice was sat hanging her head over the sofa waiting for her to continue. "Why do you lie to me all the time? You said my dad was dead. Do you know how many times I've wondered about him and what he looked like? Every child deserves to know who their father is and you even took that away from me."

"I couldn't tell you I couldn't tell anyone."

"Oh poor old Janice, always the victim, aren't you mother? Go on then, tell me… what's his name?"

Janice sat sucking hard on her fag. Her face was hidden in a thick cloud of grey smoke. "I trusted him too, I thought he cared about me. I was just a child who was in need of help."

Alice blew a laboured breath. She turned her head away and continued watching the TV. This was just another ploy that Janice had put together to get some attention. She couldn't be arsed listening. It was just the same shit, different day. Janice was sat with her head held down. "I wanted to tell you Alice. I know you needed to know and after today I will sort this shit out and you will know who your father is. I just need time to get my head around it all." Alice carried on watching the TV. First chance she could, she was going from this place. Her life with her mother was over and she was never going back.

CHAPTER FIFTEEN

Terry sat on the square waiting for Skid to arrive. He was late and he hadn't even rung him yet to say where he was. Terry kept checking his phone for any missed calls. The square was strangely quiet tonight and only the whistling of the wind kept him company. His head was bursting with thoughts and his sister was lying heavily on his mind. He'd checked everywhere for her, every last friend she had, every nook and cranny, still nothing. Tina was sat talking to some girls on the other side of the square and every time he looked over at her she was watching him. Her new boyfriend seemed to have fizzled out and she wasn't as cocky as before. She was back on the weed too; her attempt to get clean was short-lived and her addiction continued. She was blazing the bud more than ever now. Terry could hear her loud voice shouting his name from the other side of the square. Tina was louder than usual and she was pissed out of her head. He watched her stagger towards him. "For fucks sake," he mumbled under his breath.

"Can you tick me a bit of whiff Terry, just until I get myself sorted out?" Spit hung from the corner of her mouth and she was trying her best to keep her balance. She was already coked up and her jaw was swinging, she was wired.

"Tina, what the hell have you been on? I thought you were clean now and sorted your shit out. Why the hell have you let yourself get into this mess again?" So,

247

he did care about her? You could see it in his eyes that he hated seeing her like this. Had his love for her never really died and did he still have feelings for her? Perhaps him seeing her with another man had made him realise he still wanted her.

Tina sat down on the wall beside him and coughed to clear her throat. "Nothing lasts forever Terry. You know that more than me. Shit happens and there's fuck all you can do about it. I guess, I'm set for disaster aren't I?" Tina was at an all time low and she was definitely on a downer. "Anything good in my life always gets fucked up. I've made some bad mistakes in my life Terry and you were the biggest one. I should never have let you go."

Terry wasn't getting into this now, he'd heard it all before when she was lay in his bed off her trolley on cocaine and anything else she'd popped into her blood stream. "Ssssh Tina, wow, why do you always have to go on about the past? We both know what happened don't we, so why are you going over old ground? It is what it is."

"I loved you Terry but you left me. I had nobody."

There was no way he was listening to this, he snapped. "You loved cock Tina. I went to jail. I didn't emigrate to another fucking country. Do you know how hard it was for me to sit there each night in my cell knowing someone else was banging the life out of you?"

Tina grabbed his arm and made sure he was looking at her. "It wasn't like that Terry. I just got caught up in a world I knew nothing about. I took drugs to get over you. Every day I cried for you. I know you were in prison but I needed you."

Terry chuckled and pushed her away. "Tina, you

needed a free ride and that's all I was to you. You never loved me otherwise you would have waited."

"I still love you Terry. I always have."

There was an awkward silence and Terry had heard enough. He was holding nothing back he was telling her straight. "So, what's happened with that black cunt you've been seeing then? Wow, I didn't think you were into shagging Asians. Tina Patel you'll be called next, dressed in all them pyjama dresses and making them Naan breads all day long."

Tina sniggered, he still made her laugh. "Oh, don't even ask about him Terry. One minute he was all over me and the next he just fucked off. He was a weirdo when I think about it. All he kept going on about was you. He was obsessed by you."

Terry held his head to the side. "Why would he be asking about me?"

"I thought the same thing. I just told him you and me had a thing years ago but he wanted to know the ins and outs of a cat's arse. Spooky really, he was a bit sick in the head."

Terry stood up, and ragged his fingers through his hair. "Why the fuck are you telling people about me. For fucks sake you know what it's like around here for people trying to have us over."

Tina was back at his side. "I just thought he was getting to know me. I didn't think Terry, I'm sorry."

These two were fighting like cat and dog now. "Yeah, that's your trouble Tina, you never think. You never thought about it when you dropped your knickers either did you?" This was a low blow and he was out to hurt her. Tina was crying, she knew she had no chance of getting any drugs now, he was livid. "Go on, fuck off from me. You're just a daft slag. You're like a fart lingering around me. Just do one and stop pecking my head. Go on, jog on you skank."

Terry started to walk off. His mobile started ringing and he stopped dead in his tracks. It was an unknown number. "Yo, who's that?" Terry listened to a voice singing down the phone. It was the track 'Sandy' from the film Grease. "Can't you see. I'm in misery." Terry was confused, was this a wrong number ringing him or just someone fucking about. "Who's this?" he asked again. The voice at the end of the phone changed now and he knew this was serious.

The caller had a deep voice and every word they said hit him in the pit of his stomach. "Have you been looking for your sister Terry? Are you missing her yet?"

Terry switched and he knew now this was no prank call. "Where the fuck is she? I swear to you now if you touch one hair on her head I will find you and I'll kill you." Terry was running about in a circle and he was struggling to breathe. He folded in two and rested his hands on his knees as the adrenalin rushed through him. The vein at the side of his neck looked like it was going to pop. "What do you want, tell me what you want and you can have it. Just let her go?"

Here it was the truth behind his sister's abduction. "We want our money back. We know you did it and I think you should have done your homework before you twatted my uncle over his head. Yeah, do you remember Asif from the shop? Do you and Skid remember how you left him for dead," the caller let out a menacing laugh before he continued. "Ten grand you owe us plus another five grand for being a cheeky twat. You have a week to get it together if not your sister is getting hurt."

Terry fell to his knees and let out a scream like a trapped animal. The call ended and he now knew why his sister was missing. Taking a few minutes to get his thoughts together he looked over at the shop. His fists curled tightly and without thinking he sprinted over to the windows. The shop was closed and he knew somebody was still inside. He hammered on the shutters and he made sure whoever was inside hear every word he had to say. "I swear to you now Asif. If anything happens to my sister I will be back for you and your family. I know where you live you black bastard and I'll blow the fucking lot of you up."

Terry swung back his foot and booted the shutters. Everybody in the square was looking at him and a few of the younger lads came over to see what was going down. "Tez, what's up mate? Do you need some help? We're here if you do, just say the word." Terry walked away from the youths. They were only youngsters and had only recently started chilling on the square. They were no use to him, none whatsoever. He needed men who were ready to fight to the death, he needed Skid. Terry ran from the square and jumped into his car. This was a nightmare; he had to think fast, he had to get his sister back. Tina was stood in the shadows and she heard every word. She was trying to work out what was going on but her mind was puzzled. Whatever it was had really spooked Terry and she knew no matter what, blood would be spilled.

Alice lay on Terry's bed. She'd been there for hours just

staring about the room. Janice was still in the living room and she'd told her point-blank that if she came into the bedroom mithering her she would stick a knife in her. Alice was bored; she was tired but unable to sleep. Dipping her head under the bed she could see a large fluffy teddy bear. Her fingers stretched as she pulled it out to examine it further. Holding the cuddly toy she snuggled her nose deep into it. It smelt like Terry, the aftershave he always covered himself in. Inhaling deeply she had a look of sadness in her eyes. She'd never had anything like this, no comfort at night to keep her safe, no cuddly toys. She squeezed it tightly and lay it under her neck when she stopped suddenly. Something was hurting her chin. Alice pulled the bear away from her and pressed her fingers deep into its fur. There was something inside it. She examined it further and found more lumps and bumps. Just as she was about to have a look at what was inside, her heart jumped into her mouth as the door opened suddenly. She launched the bear on the other side of the bed and shot her eyes to Janice who was standing at the door.

"Go on, go back to the home. You're right I can't give you the life you need," her mother said at last.

Alice wasn't expecting this; she was shocked and took a few minutes to digest what she'd just said. "I'll write and tell you about your father too. It's your right to know who he is and I've been selfish all these years in not revealing his name. Just give me a few days to get myself together and I'll write to you." Whoah, this was not like Janice at all since when had she been so understanding? She looked like she'd given up. All the years of fighting must have taken its toll on her and she had nothing left to give. No killer blow, no last rush of strength, nothing. It was all gone. It was such a shame to see her like this and even Alice looked upset. Her mother had always been strong and she would never give up fighting for what she wanted, she was one hard-faced bitch normally. Does that happen sometimes, do people just change the way they think. Janice was no longer the person she had once been and Alice was finding it hard to come to terms with it. She looked at her and tried to work her out, was she pulling the wool over her eyes or was this the truth?

"Why write it down mother. You can tell me face to face and save yourself the ink." Alice was out to hurt her; she was winding her up just to see if she would fight back but still nothing.

"I can't do it here Alice. I need to try and explain how things were back then, how I was."

"We all know how you were, you were a dirt bag and shagged anyone who would have you." Alice was firing bullets now and each of them hit her mother straight in the heart.

"I'm going now. Just close the door behind you when you leave." Janice turned and made her way out of the door. Alice listened carefully; she could hear her sobbing on her way out. The front door slammed shut and Alice ran to the window. Well, fuck a duck. Janice was telling the truth, she was leaving. She wasn't playing the game after all. Alice ran to the front room and pushed her trainers back on her feet. She had to get out of here she had to go back to the place that made her feel safe. But what about Janice? Alice had never seen her like this before and she was aware she could do something stupid. Janice was like that too, she wouldn't have thought twice about throwing herself under a bus or jumping from a bridge somewhere. Could she ever live with herself if her mother took her own life? Alice sat back down and lowered her head into her hands.

★

Terry walked into the boozer and stretched his neck looking for Skid. He often came here when he had shit going on in his life – he thought drowning his sorrows would help him find the answers he needed to his problems. Terry spotted his wingman and growled. Skid was pissed out of his head and staggering about the boozer. This man was a loose cannon and when he necked a few pints and more often than not he would get jawed for insulting someone. Skid could be a right pain in the arse sometimes and everyone avoided him when he was like this. Terry stood back and watched Skid heading towards two women sat a table near the window. He was wobbling about and nearly crashed into their table. "Alright ladies, do you mind if I sit with you for a while. I'm pissed but I won't cause you any problems."

The women clutched at their handbags and pushed their back against their chairs. He was scaring them and Terry knew it was time to save them from any further distress. He pushed past the crowd and rested his head onto Skid's shoulder. "You need to come with me. Shit's going down and I mean big shit."

Skid twisted his head and tried to focus. "My old mucker Terry! Come and join us. I'm sure these two bints won't mind." Skid was being abusive now and his mouth was filthy when he'd had a skin full. "Look at them Terry. Mutton dressed as lamb, the pair of them. You know what ladies, I wouldn't even take one for the team for you. Terry, wouldn't we have to spin them over and give it them from behind so we couldn't see their faces. Look at that one Terry, she looks like she's smelt a fart."

This was getting out of hand and he was lucky one of the women didn't swing for him. She was fuming and shouting over to the landlord. "Can you get this drunken skunk away from us please? Bleeding hell it's like a night at the Priory in here tonight."

Max the landlord came rushing over. He always looked after his punters and did his best to run a decent alehouse. Skid was ready for a fight. Every time he had a few drinks he was always the same. He thought he could fight the world. Terry dragged him up to his feet and started to guide him to the exit. "Cheers Terry," Max shouted over as he watched him deal with the drunkard. Skid was never one to go quietly and he was wrestling with Terry. "Get the fuck off me man. Are you going to let them two sluts talk about your best friend like that. Come on, let's go back and kick their baggy fannies in." Skid chuckled as he lost his balance. Terry was in no mood for this and used all his strength to swing him over his shoulder into a fireman's lift. He started running with him and made sure there was no way he could get out of his grip. The night air strangled Skid; he was dizzy and had to hold onto the wall. He opened his eyes wide and studied Terry as if he didn't know who he was. When he finally focused on him he giggled as he sank to the floor. "Terry, where the hell did you come from?" Skid was acting like this was the first time he'd seen him all night. He was steaming drunk and Terry had no other choice than to throw him in the back of the car and take him home with him. Skid was spewing his ring up and Terry snapped knowing he'd be the one who'd have to clean it up.

"Skid, just fucking wait will you. I'll pull over. What a dickhead you are. You can pay to get this car cleaned now, you wanker." Skid was oblivious to it all and he was sick all over the back seat. Terry covered his mouth with his jumper. The sick stank like baby's sick and he was gagging himself now, the smell of sour milk curdled his stomach. Ever since being a small child he hated the smell of sick. He had a real fear of throwing up too and whenever he felt like he was going to spew he used to run into his mother's room and slept in there all night long.

The car stopped at the roadside and Terry opened the back door and dragged Skid out by the scruff of his neck. "Skid, we're in deep shit. Someone has taken Sandy because of the graft we did on Asif from the shop. They want fifteen fucking grand from us. We need to do something and quick." Terry was wasting his breath, Skid was drunk as a skunk and there was no way he'd be getting any sense out of him tonight. He stood by the car and watched Skid crawling on his hands and knees across the muddy verge.

Skid was singing now and rolled over on his back looking at the stars. "Yo Terry, get down here and have a look at these stars. They look amazing. Twinkle, twinkle, little star how I wonder what you are." Skid was singing and slowly but surely he was getting ready to go to sleep where he lay. Terry was at the end of his tether and he was debating leaving him. He got back inside his car and started the engine. His eyes shot over to his one and only friend and the only person he could ever trust in the world. He had to bring him home and sober him up.

Terry rolled Skid on his side and threw a duvet over him. He placed a bowl at the side of him and headed to bed. He thought Janice and Alice had made up and he was glad he had his home back to himself again. Gripping his sister's photograph from the side of the bed he cried his heart out, real heartfelt tears. "I'm coming for you Sandy. Don't you worry? I'll have you back home soon." Terry lay on the bed and there was no way he was sleeping tonight. His head was all over the place and he was constantly smoking. One after the other, he was smoking himself to death. With a desperate look in his eyes he scrambled under the bed. He would do anything to make sure his sister was safe and if he had to give them all the money he had then so be it, they could have the lot just so long as Sandy was safe. Terry was throwing everything out from under the bed; he lifted it up from the floor and scanned every bit of area. It was gone, the teddy was gone. Terry was white; he paced the bedroom floor and opened his wardrobe slinging everything out of it. It was no good, his stash was gone. With his fist in his mouth he bit down hard on it until it started bleeding.

"Janice!" he screamed at the top of his lungs. "You dirty robbing low-life slut. I'm going to kill you for this." Terry ran in the front room and his head was all over searching for his car keys. Once he found them he punched the door. "Fucking bitch. Just you watch now. You're going to be in a fucking body bag."

CHAPTER SIXTEEN

Janice hung her head to the side of the phone. Once somebody answered her call she began to speak. "I need to see you," she held the phone away from her ear as the voice on the other end of the line was shrieking. "Listen you daft cunt, I don't need any money. I'm going to tell Alice you're her father. She needs to know." There was silence on the phone. "Hello," Janice stressed as she carried on talking. "Right, I'll come to you now. Leave the back door open and I'll be there soon." The call ended and Janice sat looking at four walls. She thought this was a part of her life she could forget about. To go down this path again was so hard for her, harder than anyone would ever know. She'd kept this secret for years, nobody knew who Alice's father was and she never thought the day would come when she had to reveal his name.

If ever she needed a drink it was now. She sat twiddling her fingers and rocking to and fro. A spliff, that was the answer, it would calm her down. Skid always had some bud in his tin at the side of the chair. She was sitting on her hands and doing her best to resist the temptation but she needed something and fast. What did she have to prove to anyone anymore? She was doing all this for Alice to get her back home. To show her she could be the mother she deserved. It all meant nothing anymore and without Alice she may as well just go back to her old lifestyle. She was happy when she was off her head. The drugs numbed her emotions and any thoughts she had about the past were forgotten. Janice opened the steel tin and focused on the small plastic bag full of weed. Her mind was made up, she had nothing to lose. Janice popped the joint into her mouth and her cheeks sank in at both sides as she felt the first rush from the cannabis. This was what it was all about; melting, relaxing, there was nothing to worry about anymore. This mellow moment was something she'd missed. The tingling from her toes rising up to the top of her head. Sitting back in her chair she blazed every last inch of the spliff. Now she was stoned and ready to tackle anyone or anything that stood in her way. Grabbing a bottle from the side she drained any brandy left inside it. Janice was back; the evil, self-centred woman was raring to go. God help anyone who got in her way tonight, she was ready and ruthless and afraid of nothing. Janice inhaled and her lungs expanded fully. Rushing in the kitchen she searched the drawer for the sharpest knife she had there. Sliding it down the sleeve of her coat she left the house. Tonight blood was going to spill and she didn't care if she lived or died. It was all or nothing in her eyes and she was doing something she should have done years ago. Janice slammed the door behind her and headed into the night. She was walking at speed and on a mission.

A few minutes later Terry was at Janice's door. He knocked – no answer. He was ready to boom the front door in if she didn't answer soon. Lifting the letterbox up, he yelled inside. "Janice you tramp. Open the fucking door. I want my money. I won't go until I've got it. Open the fucking door." There was still no answer and his patience was running out. Running back he turned and faced the door. This was it; he was full of rage and ready to smash the front door down. Terry shoulder-charged the door and nearly took it off its hinges. He fell to the ground and seemed a bit dazed. Taking a few seconds to get back on his feet he ran in every room looking for Janice. The house was empty. He scratched at his head and ran in the bedrooms searching under the bed. "Janice, where the fuck are you? If I find you I'm going to twist you up. You thieving cunt." His voice echoed through the rooms and every second it was getting louder. Terry started searching the gaff now. If she had his money she would have hidden it here. Dragging everything out from the wardrobe he searched every nook and cranny. He searched inside shoes, coats, everything that was there. Still he was pissing in the wind, nothing. He rushed back into the front room and sat down. "Think Terry, think." His eyes were dancing from one direction to the other. His eyes shot to the TV cabinet. This was the one last place he hadn't looked. Crawling over to it on his knees he yanked the cupboard open. His head dug deep and he searched every envelope there, every CD cover but still he found nothing. This was bad, terrible news. He'd seen the state of Janice and knew given the chance she would have gone on a bender. Yes, two days, three days, even weeks she'd gone missing for before. Nobody knew where she went either, she just went vanished from the face of the earth. Terry bolted to his feet. There was no point staying here any longer, it was obvious Janice had the money with her. He had to think fast, he had to get to her before she blew all his money. And, she would blow it, she would have downed any drug and drank anything when she was in this frame of mind. Terry kicked the sofa and ran down the hallway. The door was off its hinges and he didn't give a flying fuck if she was robbed or not. She had fuck all anyway, an old-fashioned TV that wasn't worth a wank in the real world.

Janice sneaked through the night like a Japanese sniper. She was ducking and diving and making sure nobody saw her. The square was just like she remembered it. It had been years since she'd been on here at this time of night. Standing behind the shops she could see a dim yellow light shining. Slowly she edged towards it, cautious with every step she took. Her hands held the side of the door and from nowhere she heard a voice telling her to come inside. The door closed behind her and her heart was in her mouth, beating like a speeding train. There he was stood in front of her, after all these years, Alice's father.

Asif made sure nobody had followed her and opened the door slowly to search the area. There wasn't a soul about. His eyes were wide open as he heard noises near his feet. Asif kicked the boxes piled high near him and a long brown rat ran out from underneath it. He nearly shit a brick and ran back inside. He hated rats and many a night he'd hid away from them in the shop too scared to move because of them. Janice was stood with one foot leaning up on the wall. "You look fatter Asif, a proper porker you are. You've let yourself go. Are you still eating them toffees?" He didn't reply and led her to the small office at the back of the shop. Janice took a deep breath. This was it, the place he always took her when they were alone when she was younger. She thought he cared about her and he told her he loved her, he'd had her over for sure, pulled the wool right over her eyes. Janice clenched her teeth tightly together as if she had a flashback of days gone by. "Asif I need your help. It's Alice," before she could finish he jumped into the conversation.

"What have I told you about coming here? If my family see you, I'll be taken away. You know what they think about you."

Janice walked over and stood right in front of him. "Tell your family to fuck off before I tell them for you. You owe me Asif and you're going to pay every penny you owe me for the child you forced me to have."

Asif looked about the room, he was so nervous. "Janice, I thought things would have turned out differently than they did. I loved you and wanted to leave my wife but it was the family."

"Oh, did the family make you rape me then?" Asif stood still, he was lost for words. Janice sat down and lit a cigarette. "You made an idiot out of me, Asif. You told me you loved me and we were going to get married. Once your family got involved all that went out of the window. You raped me after you told me it was over. You stole my virginity, you evil bastard. All I ever wanted was for us to be together."

Asif's eyes clouded over. He still loved her. He'd never stopped. It was just a love that was never meant to be. After Janice had told him she was pregnant he sealed her silence with cash and quite a lot of it. But as the years passed he'd told her straight that the money was stopping. Oh, yeah she'd threatened to go and see his wife and tell her about his other child but still any cash she got was few and far between after that. Circumstances had torn them apart, two different cultures, there's was a forbidden love. He'd never stopped loving Janice and until his dying breath he would always feel the same about her. But for now he needed her out of here, he had to listen to what she had to say and get her to leave. He put on a show that any actor would have been proud of he was treating her like dirt and wouldn't give her the time of the day. Janice looked at him closer, she looked deep in his eyes. They were just like she remembered them, except they were older. Asif had been the man back in the day and all the young girls fancied him when he was working in his father's shop. He was slightly older than Janice but always had his eye on her from the first moment he saw her. Night after night she came in his shop for beer and fags and gradually they got talking. He'd slip her free beer and lots of other goodies. One night she was twisted out of her head and he found her collapsed outside the shop after an argument with her boyfriend Martin. Asif was a kind, caring person and at first he had done what any other normal person would have done, he helped her. The friendship started there and it was Janice who made the first move.

Asif was a married man and, although he should have turned her away, he just couldn't do it. Janice was like a drug and he was addicted from the first hit. Night after night they secretly met and stayed in the shop until late. It was true love and they were planning a future together. Asif shouldn't have raped her and he told her that he wanted to be her first so she would never forget him. She never did and months later she found out she was pregnant and that's when the shit hit the fan. Asif's family had warned her off, threatened to end her life if she come near him again. Asif was sent back to Pakistan for a few months and after that she never really saw him again. Janice's heart never really recovered from the love she lost and after that her life was set for disaster. Asif studied her and he knew the longer he sat there with her, the more the feelings would come back and he'd want her all over again. He had to get her to leave, she had to go. "Janice, I can't have you here with me. You need to go."

"I said Alice is in trouble you big, fat toffee munching twat. What part of that don't you understand?" Wow, Janice was on one and she was holding nothing back. She was calling the shots now and if he carried on with his attitude she was willing to slice him up into tiny pieces and feed him to the rats. "Alice has been through a lot. I can't do this any more on my own. She's at Terry's at the moment and I've left her in a state. You don't know the half of it?"

Asif was alert, his ears pinned back and he held his head to the side. "Do you mean she's with Terry Marland?"

Janice nodded her head. "Yeah, Terry is my cousin's best mate. Why? Do you know them?"

Asif was running around the office in a panic. "What, she's in Terry's house now. She's not safe; we need to get her out of there. Fucking hell, ring her, tell her to get out as soon as she can."

Janice was confused. What the hell was this dickhead going on about? Terry was a sorted lad and he would never hurt Alice ever. Asif grabbed his coat from the side. "Let's get out of here. We need to go somewhere nobody knows us. Terry and Skid are in big trouble. They robbed me and my family want their blood. They're going to Terry's house tonight they said. Phone Alice, do something before it's too late."

Janice was white, every bit of colour drained from her. She had to move fast, she had to save her daughter. Asif hurried from the shop, he locked all the doors and set the alarm. He cared about nothing but his daughter at this moment. He knew how ruthless Gugz was and he didn't trust him one little bit. He was sick and twisted in the head and he would have tortured anybody who got in his way. Janice and Asif jumped into his car and sped off into the night. Time wasn't on their side and they didn't have a minute to spare. The car was skidding all over the road.

Alice was back at the home. She'd told Jenny a pack of lies about where she'd been that afternoon and it seemed to have worked. She said she just needed some time alone to sort her head out, which wasn't far from the truth if she was honest. Lying on her bed she snuggled the teddy she'd brought from Terry's and kept smelling it. He wouldn't miss it would he? She'd found it under the bed after all. What would he want with a daft brown bear anyway? This soft toy wasn't all that soft, there seemed to be sharp bits inside sticking up. Slowly she unzipped the back of the bear to see what was inside and her jaw dropped. Jumping up from the bed she ran to the bathroom and closed the door behind her. Alice dug her hand deep inside and she started to pull wads of cash out of it. She'd never seen as much cash in her life. Her hands shook as she touched the notes; she smelt them and held a cunning look in her eye. This could be all she ever needed to get her started in life. Sat thinking for a few minutes and slowly started putting all the notes back inside the bear. Alice left the toilet and now she knew what was inside the bear she was holding onto it for dear life.

Lying back on the bed, her mind wouldn't settle. She was thinking about her mother, she was in such a state and she was scared for her safety. If anything happened to her she would never forgive herself. She tossed and turned and there was no way she could rest. Everyone in the room was asleep and she was seriously thinking of waking Jenny up and telling her all about her problems. Alice lifted her head from the pillow, she squeezed her eyes together to try and focus. She was right, everyone was sound asleep. Every time she closed her eyes she could see her mother's face staring back at her. She had to go and find her – she had to make sure she was safe. Slipping her jumper over her pyjamas she bent down and found her shoes. Her feet had swelled slightly and she was finding it hard to get her feet inside them. She had to find another way out of this place too; she didn't want anyone to know she was missing. She'd be there and back before anyone knew she was missing. Sneaking on her tiptoes she shot a look at the bathroom. The window inside there was quite big and she could escape through it with no bother. Alice climbed onto the ledge and flicked the catch on the window. The cold night air hit her and she shuddered as she made her escape. Once she was out into the night she looked in both directions debating which way to go. Her speed quickened and she was on her way to find her mother.

Terry couldn't find Janice anywhere and his only choice was to wait back at her house for her. He wanted what he was owed. He was going to knock her for six as soon as she walked through the door. He was ready to pounce on her. Terry played with his phone, he was bored and cold. Janice had not put any money in the gas meter and it was perishing, especially with the front door hanging off it's hinges. Every noise he heard he was up in position and ready to strike. At one point he had to chase a stray cat out of the house that had wondered in through the open door. He played with the cat at first though; he never carted it straight away. He loved animals and always thought about getting one for himself. But the truth of the matter was he was never at home and the lifestyle he led meant he could land up in jail at any given time. Pets needed love and care. He just didn't have what it took to commit.

Tina sat in her front room watching her father. He was dressed in his army uniform and he looked like he was ready to go out somewhere. As he tied his shoe laces he looked over at her. "So, go on, has he dumped you then because I can tell by your face something has happened. Look at your eyes they're red raw."

Tina was twisted and as she fell back on the sofa she spoke. "Yep dad, he's gone. Who wants to be with a fucked up head case like me anyway? I knew it was to good to last, but ay, what's the point in crying over spilt milk, what's done is done now isn't it?"

Her father snarled and stood looking in the mirror. His hands were behind his back and he looked like he thought he was on an inspection or something. Chest out, shoulders back, legs slightly apart. "I told you what them Pakis are like. Didn't I tell you they were not to be trusted? Who does he think he is ditching you? He's not good enough to kiss your arse. I hope you told him that?" Tina was half asleep on the sofa, she had a pillow in front of her and she never replied. She was too weak to go to bed and she'd slept here many times before and it didn't bother her. Tina's father looked at his sleeping princess. He knew more than anyone that she was damaged goods but he still loved her unconditionally. With the side of his hand touching the side of his head, with a swift movement he saluted himself. "Private is ready and waiting for duty Sir." This guy was totally bonkers and as he turned around he started marching up and down the living room. What a nutcase he was. He opened the living room door and sneaked up the stairs. Crawling on his hands and knees he peeped under his wife's bedroom door. He knew she was awake he could see her bedroom light still on. With his mouth pressed firmly on the gap at the bottom of the door he whispered, "I know you're awake Marie. And I know you can hear me. Do you know your daughter is hurting because her so called boyfriend has fucked her off. She's like her mother isn't she? She loves a bit of curried cock." He tapped the end of his finger against the door slowly. "It all ends here though, I've had enough of it. I'm, going to do what I should have done years ago. I lost you but there's no way I'm losing my daughter too." He rolled over on the floor and crawled on his knees to the bathroom. Standing looking in the mirror he squirted some white toothpaste on his fingers and smeared it under his cheeks. "Its war," he chuckled. This man had some serious issues, he needed sectioning. He was a danger to the public and it was only a matter of time before he went over the edge.

Terry checked his watch. It didn't look like Janice was

coming home any time soon. He curled up in a small ball and snuggled deep into his coat. He would wait here for as long as it took. He wanted his money back.

Alice walked up the garden path. Her mother's house was in complete darkness. She could see the door was off its hinges as she neared the entrance. Sticking her head inside, she stretched her neck to look further. She couldn't see a thing. There was no way she was going inside; there could have been robbers still in there. There was no way she was taking any chances. Alice ran around the back of the house and tried to see if she could see anything. It was obvious there was no one at home and she wasn't waiting around any longer. Janice must have gone back to Terry's. She assumed that Janice had gone and got pissed somewhere and when she'd calmed down she would have gone back to Terry's in hope that she was still there. With her head dipped low she walked down the garden path. She turned her head one last time over her shoulder and headed onto the main road. She just didn't need this extra stress. She only wanted to make sure her mother was alright, nothing else.

Gugz sat in the lockup and he was teasing his victim. "Let's see how much your brother really thinks about you now." He sneered over at her and licked his lips slowly. "You're quite pretty you know, do you have a boyfriend?" Sandy held a look in her eye that told him she was ready for snapping. Her nostrils were flaring and she sat tall with her back against the wall. She wasn't a violent person but she would do all it took to save her life. Gugz stood up and walked over to where she was. He bent down and touched her locks at the side, sliding his fingers up and down. Pressing her hair against his nose he inhaled deeply. "Your hair smells of strawberries." Sandy pulled away from him and her eyes stared back at him, aware that he could strike at any minute. He was right about her hair though, it did smell of strawberries. She'd bought the shampoo from Body Shop in town and everyone always commented on its fragrance. Gugz told the other men to leave. He said he wanted a chat with Sandy. His wingmen asked no questions and just left them alone. He was a right bully and was known for his violent temper. There was an eerie silence. Something was going to happen but she didn't know what. She could hear his breathing at the side of her. Gugz checked they were alone and sat on a chair facing her. He touched his crotch area and smirked at her. "See, we can always work something out me and you. It's not all bad. What do you think to a little arrangement just between us? If you suck me off I'll have a serious think about letting you go home. Your brother will pay the money no matter what. So, it's no skin off my nose. Come on, get yourself over here." Sandy was horrified but knew she couldn't let her fear show. There was no way she was putting his sweaty cock in her mouth and she had to think of something and quick to keep him calm. Gugz was a woman beater, you could tell. He liked control and he liked to be the one calling the shots. His father had taught him how to silence a woman and a few backhanders to his wife in the past was all it took to keep her quiet. Gugz repeated himself but this time his voice wasn't as subtle. "I said, I want you to suck me off. Now get your scrawny little white arse over here and do as I tell you. You white bitches need to learn some manners."

Sandy was a virgin; she was saving herself for Mr Right. She'd imagined her first time having sex over and over in her mind many times before and everything had to be special before she gave her virginity away to any man. She wasn't a slapper and even though a lot of her friends had been sexually active, she never followed suit. She wanted a wedding ring on her finger before she started even thinking about having sex. Gugz walked over to the door and slid the lock across the bottom. Turning his head slowly he tickled his chin with his fingers. "Well, you had your chance. Now I'm going to take it from you." Sandy stood to her feet and she got ready to gouge his eyes out. Her fingernails were sharp and she knew given the chance she could do some damage. Gugz stood facing her, slowly unbuckling his black Armani belt. You could smell the new leather on it as he pulled it through the loops on his jeans. Swinging the belt around in the air he cracked it against the floor and let out a menacing laugh. "Take your knickers off." Sandy was frozen, she was shaking from head to toe and aware that any second now she would have to fight for her life. Terry had warned her over men like this and told her if anyone ever got a grip of her to kick them in the balls. This wasn't as simple as she thought. Her heart was pounding in her chest and she was light-headed. The leather belt whipped across her body, the smell of burning flesh, her skin was on fire. It was now or never, she had to defend herself. Sandy pounced on him like a preying lioness. She sank her fingernails deep into his eyes and she could feel his flesh splitting as she went deeper with her nails.

Gugz cried out in pain and within a few seconds she was on the floor cowering. "You daft slut, you dirty horrible bitch. You're going to pay now. I swear down, you're going to pay." Gugz was like a man possessed he ragged her up from the floor and twisted her over so her face was slammed against the cold concrete floor. She wriggled, fighting for her life but it was no good he had her pinned down so she could no longer move. Gugz ripped her knickers off and slung them behind her. He didn't care which hole he was in now and rammed his cock deep inside her. Sandy howled out in pain but that never stopped him. He lifted her head up and slammed it several times against the floor. She was barely conscious; her eyes were open but no sound was coming from her. Gugz ragged her hair as he penetrated deeper inside her and you could see his penis was covered in dark red blood. Gugz loved anal sex. He never dared to ask his own wife for it and often paid brasses for his guilty pleasure. This was a tight hole and one he would have paid good money for in any other circumstances. The girl must have been a virgin because when he pulled it out of her anal passage and into her vagina he was struggling for quite a few minutes to get inside her. He was one dirty horrible bastard. What a sick, twisted man. His eyes danced with madness as he found pleasure. He held no guilt for his actions and never thought how it would affect this young girl in the future. He was just after his sexual highs, nothing else mattered.

Sandy was still dazed. Her head was swelling by the second and her forehead was sinking low over her eyes. She was in a bad way and barely breathing. Gugz rolled off her and stood up. He searched for his belt and bent down cautiously to pick it up. Swinging his foot back he booted Sandy again in her waist. His eyes were swelled and still bleeding. Deep red gashes appeared under his eyes. How the hell would he explain these to his wife? She was so jealous and made his life a misery if she ever suspected he was fooling around on her. Gita was a strong woman and once her back was up she'd make sure she got what she wanted. Of course he ruled her but every now and then she would stop cooking for him, stop cleaning the house and deny him any sex. He did anything for a quiet life. Gugz kept his eye on Sandy as he opened the door. The other men came inside one by one and knew just by looking at Sandy that he'd raped her.

The man who'd sat with Sandy on the bus shook his head. He wasn't into all this sick shit and voiced his opinion. "Gugz, what the fuck have you done to her, man? She's done nothing wrong; this is bang out of order." His eyes scanned the room and he spotted the girl's knickers on the floor. Covering his mouth with his hand he ran from the room. This was wrong and he wanted no further part of it. The other two men lowered their heads. He was the boss and what he said goes. Who were they to judge him anyway? They'd done similar things themselves when they'd been out partying and off their heads on drugs and whatever new substance was on the market.

Gugz stared at them both and pressed his finger onto his eye, dabbing at it. "She got what she deserved." Not a word was spoken. Not one of the spineless pricks said a word back to him. Cowards they were, nothing but yellow bellies. "Go and bring me Skid. I want that cunt here too before we go to Terry's. If he gives you any shit just fucking shoot him." Gugz passed the silver pistol over to his boys. This was serious and they knew before it all ended blood was going to be spilled. Sandy was waking up and Gugz told the men to do as he ordered. "Bring him back here. Once he's here we'll finish what we started." The door slammed shut and Gugz sat down on the chair. He sparked a cig up and watched Sandy crawling on her hands and knees to the corner of the room. She was moving like a slug. Every movement she made you could see she was in severe pain. Gugz reached for his mobile phone and dialled a number. "Have you got my fucking money yet prick? You're time's up and I told you what I would do if you didn't get what I wanted." Gugz rushed over to Sandy and grabbed her hair back causing her head to fall right back. "Listen Terry; listen to what you have put your sister through." Sandy could hear her brother's voice at the other end of the line and she found whatever strength she had left to talk to him. Gugz pressed the phone against her ear. "Go on; tell him what's been done to you." Sandy swallowed hard; she had to find the strength to talk. Her throat was dry and any talking was a struggle. He dragged at her hair from behind again and screamed down her ear. "Tell him; tell him to get my fucking money here now!"

Sandy gripped the phone in her hands and she was trembling. A wet patch started to appear between her legs, she was bleeding. "Terry, please come and get me. Terry help me please." Gugz dragged the phone from her now knowing she'd said enough to make her brother pay up. "Go home Terry, I'll be there soon. I swear if you haven't got my money I'll fucking kill her." The phone call ended and Gugz threw Sandy back down to the floor. He spotted the blood around her and sniggered. "With any luck I might not have to kill you myself. I hope you bleed to death you dirty skank." Gugz walked to the other side of the room and could see his own eyes in the reflection on his mobile phone. He walked out of the room and she could hear the door locking behind him. Sandy knew if she got out of this alive she would be a lucky person. The odds were against her and the clock was ticking.

CHAPTER SEVENTEEN

Terry had no other option but to go to his parent's house for the money he needed to free his sister. He knew Skid didn't have a pot to piss in and he was pissing in the wind even thinking he could get a single penny off him. It was early morning now and the birds were tweeting. As he parked up near his mother's house he could see her sat in the front room. She'd never been a good sleeper his mother and since she had retired from her cleaning job she still got up at the same time when she was supposed to be going to work. Funny how that happens isn't it? Our body clocks must just know when it is time to get up after years of doing it. This was a nightmare. The shit would hit the fan now, especially when he told his parents that his sister had been taken because of him and the life he led. Perhaps they didn't have any savings left – how did he know if they had any money left at all? They might have spent the money they had and the nest egg no longer existed. It was a risk he had to take as he had no other options. Terry was tired, his head was working overtime and Janice and his money were lying heavily on his mind. If that daft cow hadn't taken his money in the first place, this would have been over by now and his sister would have been back home safe. He'd heard his sister's voice on the phone and even now he could still visualise her crying her eyes out. His heart was ripped out and never in his life had he felt so vulnerable. He was used to working alone with no family involved and no one ever getting hurt that he cared about. Gugz had well and truly found his jugular and he was ripping it from his throat in taking his sister.

Walking from the car he knew what he had to do to make things right. He could never phone the police. No, that wasn't an option. He could never break the code of conduct of the square. He was no grass and knew he'd have to kill a man now for the first time in his life. He would take all his family down if he had to, the fucking lot of them were getting it. If his sister had so much as a scratch on her, then they would pay, he'd make them all pay the ultimate price. Women, children, the lot, he didn't care who he hurt. Taking a deep breath he knocked on the door. He was weak and rested his hands on his knees. He was weak and hardly had any fight left in him. The door opened quickly and his mother was stood there looking at him in a shocked manner. Her hand covered her heart and she knew something was wrong.

"What is it? Have you found her, is she dead?"

Terry walked inside the house and all his emotions gripped him as he sank to the floor. "They've taken her. It's all my fault. They found out she was my sister and they've took her until I get them the money."

Angela started to run about the house in hysterics. "Is she dead? Please tell me she's not dead. My baby girl, please Terry, tell me she's okay?"

Terry lifted his head up and looked his mother straight in the eyes. He'd seen this sadness so many times before and knew he'd caused her pain yet again. "They want fifteen grand."

Angela covered her mouth with her hands and sank to her knees. "I've not got that kind of money, nobody has. How on earth do they expect us to get that?" Her eyes were wide open now and she ran to the phone. She dialled a number and stood waiting for them to answer. "Police please, I need the police."

Terry bolted up from where he was and ran over to her he pressed the receiver down and guarded the phone. "You can't ring the dibble mam, just hold back a minute while I think." Angela pushed him out of the way and gripped the phone in her hands. "I want my daughter home. They're the only people who can help us now. I just knew this was something to do with you. Don't you think you've hurt us enough? I'm phoning the police. I don't care if you get arrested or not. Sandy is innocent and she's been dragged into your criminal world because of you. I swear Terry, if she's not back home soon God help you, because I'll kill you my bleeding self."

Terry couldn't hang around, he heard his mother speaking to the police telling them everything she knew. She'd even told them her son's name and how her daughter was being held for ransom. Terry ran from the house. What did he expect his mother to do? This was her daughter and she was in danger, she had no other option. His mobile phone started ringing again. It was an unknown number and he knew it was Gugz. "Tick tock, tick tock. We'll be coming for you soon Terry. Tick tock." The call ended. Terry punched the steering wheel and banged his head against it. He had to do something and quick.

★

Skid lay on the sofa at Terry's house. He was hungover and his head was still spinning. Licking his dry lips he lifted his leg up and farted. He was in no fit state to do anything. He rolled back onto the sofa and held the pillow over his eyes. "Terry," he shouted. Stretching his neck over the arm of the chair he looked into the hallway. "Terry, where the hell are you? Man down pal. I need help, perhaps a bacon butty or something like that to soak this beer up. Why the hell do I do it to myself? I know I can't take the beer." Skid looked concerned and sat up. He was holding his head in his hands when he heard a door creaking. "Terry, stop fucking about. Just do me a cup of coffee and I'll be fine then. Fuck the bacon butty if you can't be arsed." Still no reply, Skid was edgy and twisted his head around. Gugz's men were stood there and without wasting any time they smashed the silver pistol over his head he was sparked out. Skid came round and they were talking Urdu, it was hard to understand them. One of the men used his phone and he carried on talking in his language. Skid was pulled up from the floor and he was bound and gagged. As he came around his eyes held so much terror that he just sat and pissed himself. Skid was making noises trying to speak but nothing he was saying could be understood. The men just laughed at him and started to search the property. After time had passed they found nothing but a few bags of weed and sniff. The men were making the most of their time there and sat down making themselves comfortable. The boss man would be there soon and that's when the fun would start. Seeing the drugs on the table they all had a line of cocaine each and built a few joints. They needed to calm down too because the way this was going it was touch and go who walked away from here today alive. Skid clocked the silver pistol on the table and shuffled closer. The men were getting stoned and didn't seem to bother about him now he was tied up. It was no good, he couldn't move anymore. He was fucked if the truth was known, well and truly fucked.

Alice had stayed the night at her old friend's house. She lived local and was a regular on the square. Alice had seen her in the late hour and she'd offered her a place to stay for the night. Adele was a little older than Alice and she knew her from school. Adele knew everything and anything and she was always gossiping. As soon as she had seen Alice she wanted to know everything about where she'd been and what was happening next. There was no way Alice was telling her anything though. Once she knew, the world and his wife would know within the hour, she kept schtum. Adele's house was shocking. It stank of misery and depression. It was similar to her own home really. Lifting her head from the sofa she saw Adele asleep on the chair facing her. Sneaking slowly past her she headed to the front door. Alice was holding the side of her waist and she looked in pain. Her stomach was bigger now, much bigger than before and she was waddling like a duck as she plodded to the front door. Opening the door quietly she made sure nobody heard her leave. It was early and the milkman was about doing his rounds. Alice smirked to herself and remembered the early mornings she'd got out of bed at the crack of dawn so she could rob some milk from his float for a brew. Most kids did this in the area and if you got the milkman early enough you'd get some fresh yogurts or cheese too. The milkman smiled at her as she went past. It was nice to see kids up at this time of the morning. Usually they'd be lay in bed until the late afternoon before they stirred. Heading onto the main road Alice knew she needed to get back to the mother and baby unit pretty fast. She didn't want a big scene when she returned she just wanted to sneak back inside and pretend that she'd been there all night long. There was no sight of Janice and she'd given up on her hours ago.

A car honked its horn behind her and her heart nearly stopped beating, who the hell was it? She carried on walking and hoped the car would leave her alone. "Alice," a voice shouted from behind her. "Get in." Alice studied the driver and after a closer look she could see it was Terry. Her cheeks were beetroot and she seemed glued to the spot. The car was next to her now and the door opened. Terry screamed over at her. "Will you fucking get in? Come on, I'm stopping the traffic here." Alice obeyed him and jumped into the car.

"Have you seen your mam? Tell me if you have because the cheeky runt has stolen my money from the flat. I need it back as soon as Alice. Honest, I'm in deep shit without it." Terry started to tell Alice everything that had gone on, he needed to tell someone, his head was going to explode. Alice listened carefully and never said a single word that she had the money. Terry needed a break from driving, he wasn't focusing and he'd already nearly had two crashes. He pulled over and popped a cigarette into his mouth. Alice never took her eyes from him and everything he said, her eyes seemed to be watching his mouth move. Terry locked his eyes on her stomach and turned away quickly.

"It's your baby Terry. You know that don't you?"

Terry sucked in a mouthful of air and he nearly

choked. "What do you mean it's mine?" Alice pushed her chair back slightly and stretched her legs. "It's yours. I conceived the night I met you after I had trouble with them lads off the square. Remember when you asked me to come to your house? I know like I've acted like we never met before but I thought you wanted to keep it like that. Terry, that night I came to your house was one of the best nights I've ever had in my life. You said you cared about me and I think I love you."

Terry couldn't believe what he was hearing. Yes, he'd slipped her one but it meant nothing at the time it was just a jerk and a squirt. He'd thought about her a lot at first but she was too young for him and he knew he had to let her go. That's why he made her keep her mouth shut. Alice was a lovely, sweet girl and she was reading too much into it.

"I'm having the baby adopted Terry. But, if you want us to run off together and have the child then I will. I'll look after it Terry, I just need your support."

Terry reached over and touched her warm, soft hands. "Alice, what happened between us was a mistake. I was wrecked out of my head and I should never have invited you to my home. I'm ruthless when I'm off my head and you should have told me no. Why did you let it happen Alice?" his eyes were wide open and he was panicking. "Please tell me I never raped you. Please tell me it wasn't like that?"

Alice was nearly in tears. She'd kept silent and done everything he asked. She thought he had feelings for her, she thought one day they would run away together and live a normal life. Because that's what he'd told her when they slept together. Terry was so guilty of bullshitting her and should have realised she was taking it all in. "Terry, you never raped me. I wanted to do it. You talked about me and you having a life together, running away, and leaving all the shit behind." He'd really had her over and you could see the sadness in her eyes. In her head she'd painted such a beautiful picture of the future and in her perfect world Terry and her child was with her. She'd even done a portrait of them all together. Alice started blubbering and not just quiet sobs, she was howling with the pain in her heart.

Terry tried to calm her down. He did like the kid but this was all too much. He's had a drunken fling with her and thought in his head it was just one of them things. Yes, he'd told her to act like she'd never met him before when he came to her home but that was just to protect his image. She was underage and he didn't fancy having his collar felt from the old bill. Alice let out a laboured breath and wiped her nose on the end of her sleeve. "I just need to see that my mother is okay and then I'm going back to the home. You'll never see me again. I won't contact you and the baby will be adopted. There, you've got what you wanted."

Terry rubbed at his arms and just sat staring at her. Age was just a number and if he was true to himself he did like her. He loved her innocence and how she looked at the world with a positive attitude. There was no way he could deal with this now though, his head was all over the place. His sister was hanging on for dear life and if he didn't get the money soon Gugz would do her in. He started to head home. His driving was reckless and he was driving like a lunatic.

Janice couldn't feel her feet. The seatbelt was still around her and as she looked over to the driver's side of the car she could see Asif slumped over the steering wheel. The car was on some wasteland and she remembered the moments before they crashed. As far as she recalled they were arguing and she was fighting to take control of the car. All she could remember after that was them skidding into another parked car and rolling down some hill. Blood was hanging from Asif's mouth and his eyes were still wide open staring into space. She reached over and touched his arm. "Asif," she whispered. "Are you alright?" There was no reply. He was cold and she knew he was dead. Pressing the lock for the seatbelt she broke free. The car was on its side and she had to find the strength to drag herself out of the door. There was a deep gash on her leg, blood oozed out of it and she was in severe pain. Janice stumbled onto the muddy marshland and tried to get her bearings. She stood looking at the car for a few seconds and wobbled over to it. She could see Asif's head squashed against the windscreen. Bending herself over, her hand touched the glass and she cried. "Asif, I loved you with all my heart. What you did to me was wrong, but I forgive you. I've done bad things too in my life and before I leave this earth I will put right the wrongs that I've done. Maybe in another life we will have the life we deserve together without judgement from others." Janice was heartbroken. "Asif, I have to leave you now. You'll always be in my heart no matter where this life takes me." Janice kissed her hand and placed it on the windscreen. She had one thing on her mind now and she knew time wasn't on her side. Climbing up the hill she staggered from side to side, she was weak. Janice fell to her knees and you could see her fingers dragging in the thick black mud using every bit of energy she had left to reach the top. The heavens opened and she was slipping back down the hill again, she needed a miracle to ever come out of this alive. She was losing a lot of blood only God could help her now.

Terry pulled up at his home. Gugz had phoned again and Terry had lied and told him his money was ready for him to collect. There was no such thing, not a penny was at the house. All he had was the gun he'd stolen from Darren and he was hoping that was all he needed to get his sister back safely. He dragged Alice by the arm down the garden path. "Ssssh," he snarled as he slipped his key into the front door. He held his finger up over his mouth and stepped with caution inside the house. He could hear laughter, people talking. From where he stood he could see the back door was open fully. The bastards must have got in that way. There was no time to spare. He lifted his eyes to the bedroom window and saw that it was open slightly. "Alice, go and wait in the car. Go on, fuck off out of here before you get hurt." Alice wasn't arguing with him she ran as fast as her feet could carry her. Once inside she pressed the central locking and slipped down into the seat out of sight. Terry was fast, he was like a rat up a drainpipe. He was working like a marine, his teeth gritted together and you could see that failure was not an option. Terry was inside the window now, all you could see were his legs dangling from the window. He crept about his bedroom and went to get the gun from its hideout. Once he'd found it he it loaded. He took his baseball bat too, he was going to whack fuck out of them, club them to death. Sneaking down the stairs one by one his breathing was rapid. The voices were getting louder and he knew they were team handed. He was as quiet as a mouse when he reached the living room door. From the corner of his eye he could see Skid tied up. He had to think fast, how the hell was he going to do this on his own? It was do or die time, all or nothing, winner takes all. Swinging the bat over his head he ran screaming into the room. He was lucky because two of them were sat with their back to him and he was able to whack them both over their head before they knew what day it was. They both fell to the ground like dead weights. The other man shot his eyes to the gun on the table and tried to make a run for it. Skid was rolling about on the floor, he was trying desperately to break free. A single gun shot was fired and the Asian man caught the bullet in his chest. Terry ran over to Skid and freed him. "For fucks sake Skid, there's more of them on their way, this shit is going down. They're bringing Sandy. What the fuck are we going to do when they find out I don't have any money to pay them. Skid wriggled free from the duck tape and quickly ran to get his clothes on.

"Who the fuck are these guys Terry? I mean, can we take them?" Terry was running about the house checking through the window in search of them. They had to think of a plan and quick. Gugz had just phoned again saying he was on his way.

★

Tina walked down the street and sat at the bus stop facing Terry's house. She wasn't giving up this easily and she'd decided she was going to give it one last go to win his heart back. As she sat there chewing on her fingernails she kept standing up and sitting back down again. From the corner of her eye she saw a black Audi pull up. She hid away and kept her head low when she saw it was Gugz who was driving. He had a girl in the back of the car too and there were two other men with him. Her face creased. So that was the reason he'd carted her was it? He'd found another piece of skirt and thought he could mug her off. She'd see about that, she was nobody's fool.

Gugz was vigilant, he was checking the area. He got out of his car and walked up and down the street slowly. Tina could see him speaking on his phone and she was trying to hear what he was saying but she couldn't because of the passing traffic. The other men got out of the car now and the girl was locked inside it on her own. Tina looked closer at her and she could see something was wrong, the girl was crying and distressed and banging her clenched fist on the window. Gugz and his team, headed towards Terry's door. This should be

a quick handover of the money, nothing more. The door was ajar and Gugz sent his men in first. There was no way he was making himself a sitting duck. The door slammed shut behind Gugz and there was Terry with a gun pointing at his head. He grabbed him by the scruff of the neck and told the others to back off. "Where the fuck is my sister? You'd better tell me now you black cunt before I blow your fucking head off."

Gugz was so cool and he wasn't even trying to break free. "You've made such a bad mistake Terry. Take your hands off me now before I give the order for my boys to blow her fucking brains out. If I don't go back out of the house now and give them the sign, then she's a goner." Gugz was bluffing of course there was no such plan and he just thought this was going to be plain sailing. Nobody had tackled him before now and this was the first time in his life he'd ever been in any real danger. Terry swallowed hard. He'd not thought this through. He couldn't risk his sister's life. He was in a panic. Skid was facing him and he shrugged his shoulders. "Fuck, fuck," Terry snarled as he let him go. Skid had the two men covered and Terry watched as Gugz opened the door slowly. He turned back and looked over his shoulder and sniggered. "Dickheads, you've had your chance, now she's getting it. Nobody fucks with me." Gugz stood at the gate and from nowhere a bullet struck in the top of his forehead. He sank to the floor and he wriggled for a few seconds more.

Tina was watching everything and from the corner of her eye she could see movement in the bushes near the bus stop. Somebody had shot Gugz from there. Terry ran out of the house and clocked Tina near the car. He sprinted over and he could see Sandy for the first time. Some pepper spray had come in handy and once he'd blinded the two men he chased them onto the street and they both left like rats leaving a sinking ship. A blood trail followed them. Terry picked up a brick from the roadside and smashed the window on the car. He was with Sandy now; holding his sister in his arms. Tina was gobsmacked and speechless. She could see Terry crying his eyes out. She knew Sandy from years ago and couldn't believe the state of her face. Tina ran with speed to the bushes and stuck her head through the gap. Who the hell had shot

Gugz down? Stood looking at the wasteland she could see a man running off. He was dressed as a soldier and her mouth dropped when she looked at him in more detail. "Dad," she whispered under her breath.

Alice sneaked from Terry's car and ran down the street. There was nothing left here for her anymore. She hated this life and promised herself that as long as she lived she would never come back in this area again. The square was cursed and everybody who'd ever set foot on there had destroyed their lives in some shape or form. Her feet pounded the pavements and she never looked back once. Terry was heartbroken as he sat with his sister in the car. His mother had phoned the police and now sirens could be heard in the distance. Skid sat inside Terry's house, he had no intention of getting recognised, he was keeping his head down and getting ready to leave. He jumped out of his skin when he heard a noise from behind him. "Fucking hell Janice you shit me up then. Have you seen all the dibble outside or what?"

Janice just stood with her back against the wall and she was struggling to speak. Skid turned his back on her and carried on looking out of the window. He didn't even notice she was injured. Blood surged from him as Janice plunged the knife deep into his flesh. "You dirty bastard. I trusted you Skid. I let you stay at my house. And you abused my daughter. I've seen you in her room and put two and two together. I should have killed you then. You are my family, I trusted you." Janice held a menacing look in her eyes as she plunged the knife for the last time. He fell to the ground and his eyes were fixed on her. She sniffed up hard and spat into his face. "Bastard, rot in hell." For the last time, she held the knife over his head an plunged it deep into his heart. His body shook for the last time and she knew he was dead. Janice staggered out of the backdoor and headed into the entry at the side of the house. Her deed was done, her daughter's abuser had been paid back in full.

Terry watched his sister leave in an ambulance. His parents were there now and not once did they look at him. Gugz's body had a white tent around it. The neighbourhood was out in force. This was the crime of the century, the biggest gangland fight they'd ever witnessed. Tina grabbed Terry by his hand and pulled him out of sight. It was only a matter of time before the police would be looking for him and she knew she didn't have long. "Quick, come with me. The dibble will be all over here soon. Come on, we need to get away." Tina took him on a shortcut she knew and never once did she stop running. There was an old shed at the bottom of the field where she was heading and she knew they'd be safe there for a while. The hut was called "The love shack" by all who knew it. And over the years Tina had spent many an hour with Terry. It was nothing much but it just gave people a bit of privacy when they needed time alone. Terry wasn't on this planet. It had all happened so fast and he didn't know if he was coming or going. He stopped running and started spewing his guts up. "I need to get away Tina. They'll be coming for me soon and I can't go back to jail. I just can't."

Tina took him in her arms and held him close. She could feel him shaking and hated to see him like this. "Just come in here and sit down for a bit. You need to calm down, here, get a fag." Tina passed him a cigarette and watched him light it. He sucked so hard on it that she never thought he was going to stop.

Terry held his head in his hands. His shoulders were low and he was ashamed of where his life had taken him. Ashamed that he'd let his family down yet again. There was no way his mother wouldn't tell the police everything. He was a dead man walking, a wanted man.

"Terry, can we start again. I promise no matter what, I'll stand by you. You're the only man I've ever loved and I'll never stop loving you until my dying breath." Terry looked at the wall and sank his head low. Of course he still felt something for her but the feeling of what she'd done to him would never leave him. You can forgive but you can't forget or so the saying goes. "Tina, I'm leaving Manchester. Me and you would never have worked out and the police will be on my trail. It won't be a life for you. I've got to start again and build my empire from scratch. I need time alone away from the people I care about. I can never put them through this again."

Tina gripped him by the arm, she was desperate. "Terry, will you come back for me one day? I'll wait however long it takes. I swear to you, I'll wait forever."

Terry walked to the front door. He scanned the area and looked at Tina for one last time. "Enjoy your life Tina. I hope you find happiness." Terry was gone and all she could see was the back of him running like the wind. Tina sat crying, she'd never get over him, she'd wait forever.

CHAPTER EIGHTEEN

Janice sat at the train station. Her head was dipped low and with her she had a small bag containing her belongings. Before she came here she'd been to her parents' house and told them she was leaving for good. There were a few tears but in all fairness they were glad to see the back of her. Pat couldn't even look at her when she turned up and it was only because of her father that she was allowed to set foot in the house one last time. Janice had an old friend in Liverpool and she'd been in contact with her already to arrange for a place to live. The police thought Skid died during the fight and as it stood now there was no evidence linking Janice to the crime. Things were different for Terry though. There was a worldwide search going on for him. His face was on every newspaper and he was constantly on the news. Nobody had seen sight or sound of him and when the police went on the square at night hoping to find him, he was never there. The kids on the square were missing a leader now and things had quietened down. The police were managing the area after the public outrage and their presence there each night stopped most of the crime that usually went on. Of course you could still get drugs, or whatever else you needed, but not from the square. There was a new place now in the park, all the youths had relocated there and the residents were already signing petitions to get rid of them. Tavistock Square in Harpurhey was never the same after Terry and Skid left. It's like a ghost town there now and very little goes on. Of course, the stories are still told throughout the generations and the square will always have a place in a lot of people's hearts.

Asif's family took the deaths of their family members badly. Sharif was out for blood and every night he was searching the streets for Terry. He wanted him dead, to suffer a slow, painful death. Sharif had been watching Terry's parent's house every night and never once did he see sight or sound of him. He looked old and tired now and the past few months had been hard on him. Gugz was his eldest son and without him his life seemed to be over.

Alice screamed as she pushed her baby into the world. She was howling at the top of her lungs, she wasn't coping at all. The doctors were at her side and Christine had kept to her promise, she was there as her birthing partner. Alice wriggled about on the bed and screamed from deep within her. This baby was big and its head was stuck in the birth canal. The midwife was stressed and each time Alice moved she shouted at her. This baby had to come out now if it had any chance of surviving. Alice had told the authorities that she was keeping her baby and adoption was no longer an option. This was strange; she had seemed all set for adoption not that long ago. Girls her age had babies and they did alright for themselves so why couldn't she have a chance too? Alice gave once last almighty push, her chin dug deep into her chest and the baby was out. She was blue and needed urgent medical help. Christine was nearly collapsing and she had to sit down on a chair with a drink of water, she waved a piece of paper in front of her face to try and cool down, she was bright red. Doctors were running about and shouting over to each other. It was touch and go if the baby made it. It was a baby girl. There were pipes being shoved into its small mouth and an oxygen mask being placed onto her face.

Alice sat up in her bed and watched everything that was going on. She tried to get out of the bed but the nurse made sure she stayed where she was. The last thing they needed was a hysterical mother making things worse than they already were. At last the panic was over, the baby girl was alright. After five minutes of trying to clear her lungs she finally let out a loud scream and everyone knew she would be okay. The midwife wrapped up the baby and walked over to Alice's bedside. She passed the infant over to her mother. Alice choked up, her baby was so fragile and perfect in every way. She had jet black hair and her skin had a slight yellow cast on it. Christine stood up and looked at the baby too. "I'm so proud of you Alice, you were amazing. I'll never forget this moment as long as I live. Thank you for the opportunity." Christine touched the top of Alice's forehead and stroked her softly. A tear fell from her eye and the pain of a woman craving a baby was there for everyone to see.

The weeks ahead were so hard for Alice and everything that had gone on in her life came to a head. There she was one day just drawing and the next she was in floods of tears unable to stop crying. The doctor said it was post-natal depression but Alice knew he didn't know the half of what had happened in her life, she wasn't depressed, she was just dealing with her past. Of course her nana Pat had been to see her and she was all she had left in terms of family, without her grandparents she would have been completely alone. Pat told Alice about her mother's visit and how she'd regretted everything she'd done over the years, but it was all too late now. Time had passed and no bridges were ever going to be built.

Christine made sure Alice got some counselling and each day that passed she was actually starting to believe in herself again, realising she could be so much more. Her art work was displayed all around the home and everyone admired her talent. She was even drawing portraits for all the young mothers who were giving their babies away. It was something they could always keep and remember their child by. So many girls had come through the home's doors in the last few months. Jenny had helped a lot of them settle in too. She was a lovely girl and when her had come for her to give birth Alice stayed by her side all the way. These girls had nobody but each other in the home and somehow they all pulled together to get by when times got hard. Jenny kept to her word and her baby went up for adoption. This was so heart wrenching to watch and she never thought Jenny would smile again after it. Alice could remember the day like yesterday. Jenny was sat with her baby boy feeding him. He was a lovely little thing too, cute, innocent. She'd had him for six weeks now and every day she would bath and feed him and make sure he was well looked after. She knew the day was dawning when she would have to let him go but nothing prepared her for what lay ahead. She didn't think the bond with her child would have been that strong and when his new parents came along she would just hand him over. She was in for such a shock. Jenny sat feeding her blue-eyed boy and Melanie came to the door with Christine by her side. Alice was sat there and even without anyone speaking she knew it was time for Jenny to say goodbye to her baby. She had called him Frankie after her late grandfather. She knew his name would be changed but for the time being she knew as Frankie. Alice stood up when she saw Christine and Melanie at the door. The look they exchanged, the girls knew only too well. It was the look that told them it was time to say goodbye to their child. Jenny gripped her baby and sank her head low into his neck. She was smelling him, taking in every last detail of the child. Christine stepped over towards her and Jenny stood up. Her eyes clouded over and she growled at the two women. "Just leave me for a few minutes while I say goodbye." Hats off to them both Christine and Melanie backed off and left the room. They were stood outside and you could hear them whispering. Alice just sat frozen. Jenny had no words to say, nothing that would ever make her pain go away. Jenny started to sing to her baby, she held him on her lap and rocked him slowly. When she'd finished she started to put his coat on. She never once looked at Alice, she seemed in a trance and unaware of her surroundings.

Jenny sobbed and her words were something that Alice would never forget. "Son, I know you will be happy and you'll be with people who love you. Our time will come one day when we will meet again. Circumstances and life have torn us apart and I hope one day you'll be able to forgive me for my choices. There will always be a space in my heart for you and no matter where you are in life you will always be close to my thoughts. When I wake each morning I will think about you and every night before I close my eyes you will be with me too." Alice snivelled and she couldn't stay seated any longer.

Jenny needed some support and she was right there with her trying to ease her pain. As Melanie came back in the room to collect the baby Jenny just stood up and passed him over. No more words were spoken and once the door closed behind them Jenny sank to her knees and cried her eyes out. Standing at the window they both watched Frankie leaving with his new parents. So much pain was in that room that day. The walls of the home had seen this time and time again and even the girls said the damp patches at the top of the walls were the walls crying every time a child left. It could have true because as Alice looked at them they were pouring with water, slow drops of moisture trickling down the wall. All Jenny had left was the portrait Alice had done of them both together. It was special and something she would never part with. Jenny knew her life would somehow go on and perhaps in time she would have more children but at this moment she was inconsolable. Jenny cried for days after Frankie left. Every hour of every day she sobbed her heart out. And, when the time finally came for her to leave the home she pledged to Alice that they would always be friends. The girls had a bond and a secret they shared. The home had taught them some hard lessons in life and ones they would find useful in the future.

The day Jenny left, Alice felt so alone and scared. Night after night she lay awake planning the fate of her child .The home did try and talk her out of keeping her child of course, telling her she could never look after a child and how hard it would be but nevertheless Alice stuck to her guns and told them her mind was made up. Alice named her baby Hope. She'd thought long and hard about naming her child and after many hours she came up with her name. Hope was such meaningful word and all that had kept her going during her darkest hours. Hope that her life would change, hope that her mother would change her life too. Yes, this child would certainly have hope.

Alice was due to leave the home today and she'd planned a bright future. The home was sad to see her go and when she walked down the path she could see the faces of her friends old and new all waving behind her. Alice had planned to go to London and study art. Everything was set up for her but she just had one last thing to do before she left. Sitting in the back of the taxi she held her baby's hands and kissed every single finger. Alice had asked to meet Christine alone before she left for London. She was special to her and wanted to give her some gifts she'd brought her before she left. Without Christine's support Alice would have never got back on her feet. In her darkest hour she was there for her and she always found a solution to any problem she had. Alice paid the taxi and made her way to Christine's house. She'd been here before and even though the worker should have never given out her home address she just felt she had to as the bond between them was so close.

Christine smiled as she opened the front door. "Bloody Hell, look at the stuff you're carrying. You look like you're moving home." Christine was aware that Alice was leaving today and the pain in her heart was visible to see. She really cared about Alice and she'd done up and beyond her job role to help this girl. She'd helped her find accommodation in London and also made sure she got into the right college too. "Well, sit down then. I've got us a cake to celebrate your new life." Alice sat down and took Hope out from her pram. She was curled up in a small ball and still fast asleep. Alice pulled a card out of her bag and a box of chocolates and placed them on the table. Christine came back into the room and she was holding the cake in her hands. "Just let me get our cups of tea and we can enjoy this cake together." Christine left the room again and Alice could see she'd been crying. Goodbye's were so hard to say sometimes and today was no different. Christine was back and she had a white tissue in her hand that she kept dabbing it in the corner of her eyes. She was an emotional wreck "I don't know what's wrong with me today I just can't stop crying. I think it's my hormones playing up."

Alice raised a gentle smile and played with the cuff of her jacket. She shot a look over to her baby who was resting at the side of her and swallowed hard. "Christine, did you ever wonder why I stopped the adoption at the last minute?"

Christine raised her eyes to the ceiling and held her head to the side. "I did at first but every woman has the right to choose don't they and after all this is your baby and nobody else's."

Alice reached over and sipped her drink. "I did it for a reason Christine." Alice played with her baby's foot and turned to face her again. "I didn't have my baby adopted because I wanted you to have her. Why shouldn't you have a baby? You'd make the best mother ever and Hope is my gift to you."

Christine choked up and her face was bright red. "Alice, you can't just do that. Things have to be done properly. Oh no, you can't just give her to me."

Alice sat forward and smiled at Christine. "Then, we

will do it properly. I will leave a letter signing complete custody over to you. You don't have to adopt her straight away, just foster her for now." Christine started to cry, a baby, a real baby to love and care for. This couldn't be true. It was a dream come true. "I'm leaving her with you Christine. You've got the biggest heart I've ever known and I know you will love Hope with all your heart. She'll have the life I never did. I know it's not going to be straight forward but we can make sure somehow, someway that you get to keep her."

Christine stood up and walked about the room. She knew this was going to be hard work, she needed to get her head round it all. She knew the law inside and out and was sure there was a loop hole somewhere allowing her to keep this baby. Alice was right; she could foster Hope and later adopt her when everything was sorted out. Alice stood up and checked her wristwatch. "I've got to go now. My train leaves soon. Keep in touch and if you need anything for her let me know. This is our secret and I'll never tell anyone what has happened here. You've been like a mother to me and without you my head would have been in bits. I've never said this to anyone before but, I love you Christine." Alice leaned over and kissed Hope on the top of her head. She had no worries leaving her child behind and knew she was doing the right thing. In time, her heart would stop aching for Hope and her life would go on. She would never forget her no way; she would always be in her heart.

Christine hugged Alice so hard that she nearly squeezed the life out of her. She was shaking and her head was spinning. "I've never been this happy in my whole life Alice. This child will be so loved and I'll never let anything happen to her. You've given me a life again Alice, a life of love and happiness. I'll never forget this. I will ring the social services now and start the ball rolling." They both shared a moment and Alice headed towards the door. As she walked down the garden path she smiled back at Christine. She knew she'd made the right choice and warmth flooded her heart.

Alice sat on the train and looked out of the window. She opened the top of her bag and there it was, the teddy she'd stolen from Terry. She had enough money to set her up for life. She'd never want for anything again. The train stopped at Euston station and once she left the platform all she could see were a flock of people walking about, rushing, pushing and eager to get to their destinations. Alice looked at the large clock hung in the middle of the station and placed her belongings on the floor. The train journey had taken it out of her and she was still bog-eyed. This was her first time in London and she aware of the crimes that took place here. Closing her eyes slowly she held her bags near her legs with a tight grip.

Alice felt her head being touched and slowly she opened her eyes. Her face lit up and she sprang to her feet. "Terry," she sobbed. "I knew you would come. I just knew it." The couple walked off together and held hands. This was their new life together and fate had brought them back together. For months they'd been planning their lives together and they were so in love. Terry knew from the moment he met her that he loved her and even though she was younger than him he couldn't help his feelings for her. The money they had helped rent them a new home, a loving home where they could give each other the love they were both denied when they were younger. Terry knew the day would come when he would go back to jail but for now he was living for the moment. He pulled Alice next to him and whispered down her ear. "My life, my world, my everlasting love." Terry yanked his hat down further over his head and kept his head dipped low. He was a wanted man and knew given the chance someone would grass him up. As they left the train station his arms were around her.

From the corner of the station a plain clothes police man stretched his neck long, he wasn't sure at first and he held a puzzled look on his face. He knew this man, he knew he was wanted. Running outside he searched the busy streets for them both but they were gone with the wind. With a look of frustration the officer sighed and went back inside. The clock was ticking again for Terry Marland and it was only a matter of time before the police were on his trail. The officer got on the phone and spoke in a frustrated tone. "Hi Donald mate, tell the department that Terry Marland is in London. I've just seen him with my own two eyes, but I've lost him. He was too quick for me. Let the boys know down at the station too. We'll have this bastard once and for all. His days are numbered."

THE END

Other books by this author

Broken Youth
Black Tears
Northern Girls Love Gravy
Bagheads
Teabags & Tears
The Visitors
Sleepless in Manchester
Covering Up
Riding Solo
The Pudding Club
Grow Wars

An extract from Karen's next novel '*Team Handed*'

Behind them there was rustling and the sound of crunching gravel, somebody was watching them in the alley. They could hear their heavy, struggled breathing. Dipping her head Michelle Buckley covered her mouth with her hand as she watched. "Well, you dirty bastard," she whispered under her breath. "Oh, you just wait now Larry you slimy cunt." Michelle hid away out of view. She stood gawping at the lovers, her mouth was wide open. You could see the whites of her eyes. She wished it was her Larry was fucking, she wanted him so much, she always had. "Oh, let´s see you talk your way out of this one Larry Watson," she sniggered as she moved closer to get a better look. Larry could sell sand to the Arabs, he was quick witted and could always think on his feet, he was good like that. He always had an answer to everything. A smart-arse he was. The corners of her mouth started to rise. Michelle Buckley licked her lips slowly as she twiddled the piece of hair dangling near her cheeks. She was turned on by what she saw and her nostrils flared as she watched Larry Watson have sex with his brother's wife-to-be Dawn. Cracking her knuckles slowly she carried on watching the lovers with eager eyes. This was hot gossip and something she would keep it close to her chest. For now anyway...

When Larry had finished, Dawn yanked her knickers up and straightened her red mini- skirt. She loved this skirt and always thought she looked like a model when she was wearing it. It was cheap and tacky though, just like she was. "Do I look okay or what?" She demanded as she grabbed Larry by his arm as he walked away trying to catch his breath. "Oi," she snapped. "Will you look at me? Is my hair alright? Do I look respectable?" she flicked her fingers across her blouse removing the grit and dust from her. "If I go back in there with my hair all over the show people will start being suspicious. Bleeding hell, do I look alright or what?" Dawn's bobbed hairstyle was backcombed beyond belief and full of hairspray; there was no way it was moving about, not even after Larry had just banged her brains out.

Larry sighed and pulled his strides up. He lifted his eyes up and gave her a quick once over. If the truth was known he wasn't arsed how she looked anymore, he'd got what he wanted, he had no further use for her. He'd emptied his sack and that was all that he cared about.

"Yeah, yeah, stop flapping, you're fine. You're sorted. Just check me out for any lipstick marks on my neck. You know what you're like for biting me." She gave him a quick once over and carried on straightening her hair. Scouting about the alleyway Dawn found her missing red shoe near an old sofa someone had flung out. She shoved it back on her slender foot with haste and flicked a moth from her blouse that had settled there.

Larry inhaled deeply and rubbed at his crotch. His eyes met hers and he knew he'd satisfied her. "That was the dog's bollocks that was. You can't beat a good old knee trembler can you?"

Dawn shook her head; she loved this guy's sense of humour and couldn't help herself when he was about, she was butter in his hands. It's just the way it was, he excited her. Larry sniggered and tucked his crisp white shirt down the front of his pants. He grabbed his grey suit jacket from a nearby refuse bin and dusted it down before he casually slung it over his shoulder. This was his favourite coat and he always thought he looked the main man in it. He thought he looked like Jud. Larry walked to Dawn's side with a smirk on his face. He was playing with her now, full of himself as per usual. "How can you say you don't want any more sex like that? You're tapped in the head if you ask me. My body's much sort after you know? Top of the range it is." He opened his eyes wide and he pushed his pigeon chest out in front of him as he continued. "Ask anyone if you don't believe me. Larry Watson is sex on legs."

Dawn walked towards him and stroked her long fingernail over his plump lips, sliding it slowly. There was no way she was listening to his bullshit any longer. Yes, it was true what he was saying but there was no way she was admitting that to him. His ego was big enough. "Larry, I said I'm done. It's over. Call that," she jerked her head back and paused.

"One, for old time's sake. I love Jud and I'm going to be his wife. You have to back off now and forget about us and what we've been doing behind his back." Dawn was as bad as him, they were both playing a dangerous game. A game where people got hurt, lost their lives. In her heart Dawn did love Jud and she still wanted to be his wife. But it was in her blood, she was a dirt bag, she just couldn't help herself. Who was she kidding? She could never be faithful, she was a tart and always would be. She loved the chase, she loved having secrets, dark secrets that kept her awake most nights. A leopard never changes its spots....

TEAM HANDED

LIVE BY THE SWORD, DIE BY THE SWORD

Due July 2015.